MARK de CASTRIQUE

DANGEROUS UNDERTAKING

DANGEROUS UNDERTAKING

MARK de CASTRIQUE

ibooks
new york
www.ibooks.net

DISTRIBUTED BY SIMON & SCHUSTER, INC.

A Publication of ibooks, inc.

Copyright © 2003 by Mark de Castrique

An ibooks, inc. Book

ibooks, inc.
24 West 25th Street
New York, NY 10010

The ibooks World Wide Web Site Address is:
http://www.ibooks.net

The Poisoned Pen Press World Wide Web Site Address is:
http://www.poisonedpenpress.com

ISBN 0-7434-8702-8
First ibooks, inc. printing July 2004
10 9 8 7 6 5 4 3 2 1

Printed in the U.S.A.

For Linda and our daughters Melissa and Lindsay

Acknowledgments

Thanks to the many friends whose encouragement and support made this book possible. Thanks to Robert and Barbara, their nurturing staff at Poisoned Pen Press, and my agent Linda Allen, and a special thank you to Steve Greene, whose fingerprints are on every page...admissible evidence of his conscientious service to the reader. And my father, Arch, whose years as a funeral director in the mountains helped bring the characters to life.

MARK de CASTRIQUE

DANGEROUS UNDERTAKING

Chapter 1

Crab Apple Valley Baptist Church sat high on a grassy knoll overseeing the sinners scattered along the valley floor. A gravel road curved up to a parking lot adjacent to the simple, white-framed structure. Our hearse was already backed up close to the front door.

On the other side of the church, the cemetery sprawled down the hillside. A green canvas awning rose over a freshly dug grave and advertised the services of Clayton and Clayton Funeral Directors. We had been able to set up close to the sanctuary because Martha Willard's family had been one of the valley's first settlers and enjoyed a family plot of choice proximity.

Wayne Thompson, my uncle, waved to me as I pulled into the far corner of the gravel lot and left closer parking for the family and mourners. For such a small funeral, he had brought only one other man. There would be no family limousine or procession.

Wayne smiled from underneath the oversized black umbrella as he came over to offer me its temporary shelter while I pulled my own from the back seat.

"Everything's under control, Barry. Freddy and I have already positioned the casket in front of the altar." He stepped back as I pressed the release button and my umbrella launched into shape.

"Good. Any problem with the vault?" I asked.

"No. Rain is flowing away from the grave. The immediate family can fit under the tent and the rest of us will be under umbrellas. I threw an extra ten in the hearse."

"How's the family doing?"

"Pretty good, I guess," said Wayne. "Preacher Stinnett's been dealing with them. I gather there's a little family tension."

We began walking toward the front of the church. I kept glancing down to avoid the puddles. Wayne glided along in the precise gait bred by years of escorting the bereaved, as he watched the main road for any sign of early mourners. Uncle Wayne and my father had been burying the people of Laurel County for over forty years.

"Norma Jean's taken charge of things," he continued. "She's the one who prearranged the funeral."

That had been unusual, even if the service was for someone like Martha Willard who got so out of it toward the end. Most of the mountain people I knew were too superstitious to finalize a funeral unless death was imminent—as in before sunset.

"And the others?" I asked. "Lee and Dallas? They doing all right?"

"Lee is doing what Norma Jean and Preacher Stinnett tell him. Dallas? Well, I ain't seen him yet. Nobody's seen him. Leastwise, that's what Preacher Stinnett said earlier this morning. Norma Jean told him when Grandma Martha died, Dallas walked out of the room without saying a word. At first they were mad, then after two days passed, they got worried. I think they're afraid he might have hurt himself. Lee and the preacher stopped by his cabin at seven this morning, but he wasn't there."

"I was afraid he'd take her death awfully hard."

"Yeah," said Uncle Wayne. "Well, Dallas is a strange one, that's for sure."

We spent the next forty-five minutes arranging flowers, placing folding chairs at the graveside, and setting up the

"Those Who Called" book in the vestibule for attendees to sign. About quarter to ten, people began to arrive. I worked in the parking lot, passing out umbrellas and directing traffic.

At ten o'clock, Wayne joined me. He scanned the valley, and the irritation broke through his voice. "I got the family all settled in the front pew, but no one has seen hide nor hair of Dallas." He checked his watch. "I hate a third of the family ain't here, but I'm giving Preacher Stinnett the signal in ten minutes whether Dallas has the decency to show up or not. You may as well go on in."

Inside the narrow sanctuary, mourners sat in scattered clumps along the hand-hewn pews. Necks twisted around as my footsteps echoed on the wide-plank pine floor. I felt like a bride at the wrong wedding, and I made a hasty retreat off to the side. People continued to look toward the rear of the church, making me realize they were awaiting the arrival of Dallas Willard. Many faces were familiar enough to have names attached. Others belonged to the nameless folks you cross paths with in a small community, seeing each other at the post office or farmer's market.

Across the aisle sat a man who seemed out of place with the simpler mountain folk. The tailored cut of his dark suit spoke of power, and the perfectly trimmed steel-gray hair and robust tan reeked money. I couldn't place him though he looked at me and nodded a silent greeting. Then he glanced behind me to the door. I turned and saw Wayne give a single distinct nod to Preacher Stinnett.

The scripture was read in predictable order: a few passages of Psalms followed by New Testament assurances of Everlasting Life. Preacher Stinnett kept his eulogy brief, emphasizing Martha Willard's good works and her love for her family. I suspected he wanted to get everyone out to the grave and back before the heavens opened up. He walked to the closed casket in front of the altar and gave a prayer for Martha's soul with a plea that all would know Jesus like Martha now did.

At the "Amen," our assistant, Freddy Mott, motioned for the pallbearers to stand. Then the congregation rose as Martha left the church for the final time.

We led the procession down the steps and around to the cemetery. The weather had thickened. Umbrellas sprang up in the dampness like mushrooms. A British novel of forgotten title came to mind because it was the first time I had read the word *mizzle*—to rain so fine that the droplets hung in the air without falling to earth. Mist and drizzle merged to mizzle. The effect was "mizzlerable."

Norma Jean and Lee joined Preacher Stinnett and the casket under the tent. The rest of us encircled them, the men giving way for the women and a few children to stand under the protection of the canvas. I wound up just behind the family, positioned beside a frail, thin tombstone, trying to keep the water on my umbrella from draining down the necks of my neighbors.

Preacher Stinnett cleared his throat, and then stopped short of speaking. Through the silence came the steady crunch of gravel from the footsteps of a latecomer. All heads turned toward the approaching sound.

Dallas Willard, lips drawn tight across his expressionless face, strode stiff-legged out of the mist, his head uncovered, his body shrouded in a long gray coat that brushed the ground, and his hands buried in his pockets. He materialized like some Civil War soldier snatched from a Mathew Brady photograph. I wouldn't have been surprised if a ghostly cavalry horse had trailed him.

People parted to let him get to the casket. Dallas walked through them like they didn't exist. He stopped at the foot, not crossing over to stand beside his brother and sister. He looked neither at them nor at Preacher Stinnett. Instead, his gaze fell upon only one person. His gaze fell upon me.

I nodded but said nothing. His hair looked like wet straw. Rivulets ran down his cheeks, but I couldn't tell whether they were tears or simply condensed moisture. Then his thin lips broke into a smile of some shared secret that set my neck tingling.

"And now that we are all finally gathered here," lectured Preacher Stinnett, "let us bow our heads, close our eyes, and pray together the prayer our Lord taught us."

Reluctantly, I looked down, sensing that Dallas still stared at me.

"Thy Kingdom come" was followed by the ear-splitting blast of a shotgun. I snapped my eyes open to see Lee Willard hurled back against a tombstone. Dallas stood with the great coat open and the twelve-gauge level at his waist. Before anyone could take a breath, he pumped the action and kicked the spent shell onto Martha's casket. Norma Jean tried to turn away, but the second blast caught her in the side, and I heard the sickening gasp as the life-breath was wrenched from her lungs. Again, Dallas reloaded, but this time he swung the gun at me. Steam boiled off the hot barrel.

"They're goin' to Hell," he shouted. "And so am I. Tell Grandma I'll save the land. Tell her I love her."

Even before he began speaking, somehow the muddled gray cells of my brain realized Dallas Willard meant to kill me. In that split-second, I reacted. I threw the open umbrella at him as I flung myself toward the protection of the tombstone.

The buckshot blasted through the flying umbrella as if it were tissue paper. The pellets hit my left shoulder with such force that the impact twisted my mid-air flight and sent me crashing on my face lengthwise behind the grave marker. Pain seared down my arm and I couldn't move.

Dallas fired again and the century-old tombstone disintegrated above my head. Dust and granite chips rained down on me. Somewhere, a woman screamed. I rolled over on my back and clutched my shoulder. The warm, sticky dampness spread between my fingers. I opened my eyes and saw only the thick gray sky.

Time passed in a blur of detached images. Preacher Stinnett's face obliterated the sky as he knelt over me, trying to save my soul. I heard myself shout for Uncle Wayne which must have been alarming—a wounded, bleeding man calling for an undertaker. Wayne was the only person I knew skilled in first aid. Others rushed around me amid a continuous chorus of screams and moans. Hysteria predominated.

Suddenly, he was there, pulling my hand away from the wound. "Winged you," Uncle Wayne said, and smiled with reassurance. "No artery damage, but your Sunday-go-to-meeting suit is a goner."

I squeezed his arm and let him know I was okay. "The others?" I asked.

"Norma Jean and Lee are dead. Dallas got away in his pickup. It's a miracle none of the bystanders were hit. I guess the buckshot never spread out enough." Wayne looked up and yelled, "Freddy, get the hearse up here. Make sure someone phones the sheriff. And tell the hospital we're coming in." He turned back to me. "You don't mind going by hearse, do you?"

"As long as it doesn't become a habit."

A few minutes later, I was lifted into the back of the long black vehicle. The floor was not padded, but then the regular passengers rarely complained. Several of the men shed their raincoats and tucked them under me. I felt a weariness wash over me, and my arm and shoulder began to throb. I closed my eyes. Sounds collapsed into a muffled roar as I tumbled down a long well into darkness.

Chapter 2

I opened my eyes to a small, dim, private hospital room. The institutional clock by the wall-mounted television read six P.M. My stay in the recovery room must have been textbook timing.

I tried to move and felt the bandages crossing my chest. My right arm was free, but the left was bound tightly to my side. A mound of dressing covered my shoulder and arm down to the elbow. My left hand rested on my stomach, and with cautious concentration, I wiggled each finger. Everything seemed to be in working order.

My mouth was so dry I thought my tongue was welded to the roof. Post-anesthetized cotton mouth makes swallowing a Herculean effort and chips of ice more precious than diamonds. I wanted a few slivers to melt down my throat and would have sold everything I owned to get them.

A service cart was adjacent to the right side of the bed, and on it sat a white Styrofoam water pitcher. The Holy Grail could not have been more desirable. I searched for a cup, but the nurse's aide had forgotten to leave one. She had also forgotten to put the call button by my good arm, and no amount of stretching could bring it within reach.

Where there is a will, there is a way; and I figured water straight from the pitcher was better than no water at all. As I lifted it to me, the weight didn't feel like water. Sure enough, only ice was inside. The aide must have left it just moments before I awoke. No melting had occurred.

I tipped the pitcher against my lips, thrusting my tongue out to snare this frozen manna from heaven. Nothing. The ice remained fused in the bottom half. I banged the rim against my teeth, hoping to shake loose a few crystals. Instead, the confined snowstorm broke loose, and the entire contents crashed into my face and tumbled down my neck and under the flimsy hospital gown. My "god-dammit" was followed by the sound of unrestrained laughter. I brushed the ice from my eyes and saw the blurry silhouette of a woman standing in the doorway.

"Well, if you nurses had any brains, you would have put the damn button within reach."

The laughter abruptly halted.

Her voice took on the tone of one used to being obeyed. "And how many times do I have to tell you the nurses in this understaffed and underfunded hospital work their tails off? As for me, I didn't have the brains to be a nurse. I had to settle for being a surgeon who carves up undertakers that are so foolish they let their clients shoot them."

She marched over, bent down, and kissed me on the lips. Without another word, she began picking up the clumps of ice now melting through the sheets and gown. The chill had cleared my head enough to appreciate her delicate hands. I shifted my attention to her long neck and mahogany-colored hair. Dark brown eyes and pursed full lips gave evidence of the concentration and concern she brought to her work.

"Okay, Susan, you already know I'm a jerk. I had just hoped to keep you from discovering how big a jerk I am. I can only plead that I don't get shot every day."

She smiled. "I don't often see my patients try to freeze themselves, and I don't operate on my boyfriend every day."

"I thought it was policy not to operate on loved ones?"

"Then next time I'll just let you bleed till Dr. O'Malley drives back from Myrtle Beach. I suppose now you're going to weasel out of our Friday night date."

"Of course not. How big is this bed?"

She didn't laugh at my joke. "Not nearly as big as your male ego. You're going to be out of action for a while, Barry. That was a close call. You almost wound up in your own funeral home."

Her words sobered me. "Tell me how it went. What's the prognosis for patient Barry Clayton?"

"Good," she said. "Mostly because of luck, not my skills. The mass of pellets missed you. The anesthesiologist shoots ducks and figures from the size of the pellets they were number one buck with about twenty in the shell. Only six struck your shoulder and upper arm. They hit head on and lodged in the joint space. We had to extract them and re-tie some of the muscles in the most traumatized area."

"Movement restricted?" I asked.

"You'll have reduced latitude. Sort of like you had a chronic dislocation problem only the damage wasn't done by the bone popping out. It was the pellets tearing their way in. You'll need six weeks for healing along with simple physical therapy to stretch the muscles we had to shorten. The shoulder will be sore and stiff for a while, but you can return to work in a week or two."

"Oh, yes, work. Have you talked with my mom?"

"She and your uncle were here when you came out of surgery. A neighbor came over to stay with your dad. They went back about an hour ago. Your mom said to tell you Wayne has help coming from Wilson Funeral Home in Asheville. They're handling the arrangements for the Willard burials."

"What a way to get business. I'm sure Mom's upset."

"She's just glad you're alive. I sent her and Wayne out the back entrance to avoid the reporters."

"Reporters," I said, emphasizing the plural. "Has the *Gainesboro VISTA* assigned two? That must be half their staff. I can see the headline—'Undertaker Nearly Conducts Own Funeral!'"

"Network reporters, Barry. CNN and at least one other. They've been calling the hospital switchboard trying to reach you."

I stared at Dr. Susan Miller like she had just announced her Martian ancestry.

"I told the switchboard no calls," she said, "and the floor nurses no visitors, except for family. Everyone understands I'll be keeping an eye on you." She gave me another, and this time, lingering kiss.

The telephone rang, breaking the moment.

"So much for doctor's orders," she said. She lifted the receiver and spoke curtly, "Room 237, who's calling please?"

Her face flushed with the slightest hint of red. She cupped her hand over the mouthpiece and offered me the phone. "She says she's your wife. I think I'd better excuse myself."

She left me alone to confront the voice of the woman who still managed to disrupt my life, even by long distance.

"Hello, Rachel."

"My God, Barry. What happened? I heard your name on the news. The news here in Washington. Are you all right?" She sounded so genuinely concerned, I suppressed the sarcastic tone I usually used as defense against her constant criticism of my small-town life.

"Yes. Just got in the way of a little buckshot. I'm sure the press has exaggerated my involvement."

"Don't deny you could have been killed." She sighed. "And people say the cities are dangerous."

After a few seconds of long-distance hum, she went on, "I'm glad you're all right, Barry."

"I know you are, Rachel." There was a knock at the door, and the face of a pirate leered at me. "Sorry, someone's here," I told her. "I've got to hang up. Thanks for the call. I'll give your best to Mom."

"And your dad too," she added. "Even if he doesn't understand."

"Thank you, Rachel," I said, and I meant it. She and I couldn't live together, but there was still a basic bond of caring. In some ways, she had been the victim of my father's Alzheimer's as much as any of us. I had been forced to quit my job with the Charlotte police department and leave my graduate studies in criminal justice at the University of North Carolina at Charlotte in order to help Mom and her brother Wayne care for Dad and run the funeral home. Even Charlotte had been too small for Rachel, and there was no way she would survive in a mountain town the size of Gainesboro. The divorce had been sad but polite, and she had carried her life away to Washington.

The pirate bent over my bed. The upper edge of his black eye-patch cut diagonally across a bushy brown eyebrow, and from underneath it, a thin, pale scar sliced over the sharp cheekbone to the corner of a wide, tooth-filled grin. He fixed his one eye on my bandaged shoulder.

"Well, now, Barry," said Sheriff Tommy Lee Wadkins in a gravelly voice. "Mighty thoughtful of you to get shot in a cemetery. Inconvenient as hell not to die. You feel like telling me why Dallas Willard wanted to take you out along with the rest of his family?"

"No," I croaked.

"Hmm," he grunted. "Sounds like you need a drink." He looked in the empty Styrofoam pitcher, and then brought a glass of water from the bathroom. "Want to sit up?"

I nodded an "okay" and the sheriff pressed a control button that set motors whirring. The top half of the bed rose to a forty-five-degree angle and jerked to a stop.

"Here, sip on this."

I took the glass and let the cool water seep between my cracked lips. I was acutely aware of the ache in my shoulder and just as acutely aware that Tommy Lee Wadkins would not be sympathetic if he thought I had any information he needed. Pulling a chair beside the bed, the sheriff straddled it backwards, took a notepad and pencil from the chest pocket of his desert tan uniform, and stared at me.

"What happened?" I asked, beating him to the question.

He smiled. "Not much. Just the bloodiest mess I've seen since 'Nam."

Everybody in Gainesboro, or the whole of Laurel County for that matter, knew Lieutenant Tommy Lee Wadkins was a bona fide war hero. He had brought his ambushed platoon through a hellfire, refusing to leave anyone behind. Even though shrapnel to the face had taken an eye and slashed through his cheekbone, the young officer had dragged a dying comrade through the jungle and provided cover while the choppers evacuated his men. Hanging from the skid, he had emptied his magazine as the last chopper lifted him above the smoke and fire to carry him to safety and unwanted glory.

Sheriff Tommy Lee Wadkins never spoke of the war. In all the years I had known him, the word Vietnam never passed his lips until today.

"You're one lucky son of a bitch," he said. "So, we've both been shot, but at least I knew why 'Charlie' wanted to kill me. You got any ideas?"

"Not a clue. You get him?"

Tommy Lee shook his head. "As soon as I got the word, we issued a BOLO."

Since I'd served three years as a patrolman in Charlotte, Tommy Lee freely used cop lingo with me. BOLO. Be on the lookout for.

"Dallas and his truck have disappeared," he said. "A manhunt is underway in four counties and the state has lent a chopper for aerial surveillance. There is no sign he returned to his cabin. He could have gone to earth anywhere within a twenty-mile radius. I figure that's the travel time he had before we got organized."

"He knows these hills," I said.

"As well as anybody. For all we know, he may have an arsenal stored somewhere. I'm hoping this is just some family feud taken to the extreme and he's not a danger to anyone else."

I saw Dallas Willard smiling at me from across the casket. "But I'm not family. I suggest you learn what happened to Dallas Willard during these few days since his grandmother died."

"I've already started. Did you know that last night Dallas filled up an answering machine tape at the mental health clinic?"

"No. Was he trying to reach Dr. Soles?" Dr. Alexander Soles was the psychologist who led a support group for families who were coping with Alzheimer's. Mom and I attended, and Dallas, Norma Jean, and Lee had been a part of it until two weeks ago when Martha Willard's condition took a sharp turn for the worse.

"No, not Dr. Soles," said Tommy Lee. "Dallas Willard was asking for you."

"Me? At the clinic?"

"Yeah, he said he had to reach you and that all he got at the funeral home was an answering service. He said he needed you to tell his grandmother something." Tommy Lee scooted his chair forward as if closer proximity would somehow inspire me to find a sane answer to an absurd question. "Barry, why would Dallas Willard think you could talk to his dead grandmother?"

I shifted on the bed, trying for a more comfortable position that would clear my head. "I don't know. The only times I ever spoke with Dallas were when he came to the Alzheimer's meetings with Lee and Norma Jean."

"You must have said something," Tommy Lee said.

I took another sip of water as I tried to remember the few conversations I had with Dallas. "I first started talking to him a couple of months ago. During one of the sessions, Norma Jean told everyone how Grandma Martha had started calling him Francis."

"Francis?"

"Yeah, for Saint Francis. Martha Willard thought he could talk to the animals. Dallas became very upset. He said that was private. Between him and his grandma. He stormed out of the room. I went after him to try and calm him down. I guess I felt sorry for him."

Tommy Lee looked at his notes. "Alex Soles told me he suspects Dallas is a borderline paranoid/schizophrenic and believes his grandmother's death may have triggered a full-blown psychotic episode."

"Triggered is right." I moved again and felt the pain in my shoulder. "I'd always sensed something odd about him. He had difficulty expressing himself in our sessions. The night he got so upset I found him leaning against the hood of his pickup, crying like a baby."

"Did you say anything to him?"

"I told him not to let what other people said bother him. That it was obvious he had a special relationship with his grandmother just like I did with my father. He said he didn't care about what other people thought. He just didn't like to think of living without Grandma Martha. We talked for a while, and then I asked him to come back inside with me because I didn't want to leave my mother alone. He followed me in as docile as a lamb. At the next meeting, he sat beside me. He would say hello and goodbye only to me and hardly anything else in between."

"He's always been a quiet one," said Tommy Lee, "but then a lot of these mountaineers are. Since he was never in trouble, I never gave him much thought."

"Then he stopped coming altogether. Must have missed three sessions in a row. I asked Norma Jean where he was and she said my guess was as good as hers. She said Dallas spent more and more time alone, wandering off in the woods. Two weeks ago, he came to the last meeting before Martha's general health failed. He sat next to me, and as we were leaving, he caught my arm and asked to speak to me alone. 'Mr. Clayton,' he said, although he was only a couple years younger. 'How do you think a person gets to Heaven?'"

"Where'd that come from?" asked Tommy Lee.

"Out of the blue. We'd never talked about an afterlife in the group sessions."

"What did you tell him?"

"I said I believed each of us has to find God for himself, and that as for me, I tried to be a good person, treated others like I wanted to be treated, and tried not to harm anyone. If I did that, then I felt sure God would take care of me when I died."

Tommy Lee chuckled. "Billy Graham can give thanks you won't be taking over his ministry. What did Dallas say then?"

I paused, remembering the scene in the hallway of the mental health clinic. Dallas had backed away from me and smiled the same strange smile I had seen right before he shot me.

"Well?" prompted Tommy Lee.

"The last words Dallas said to me at the clinic were, 'You're a good man, Mr. Clayton.'"

Tommy Lee jotted something in his notepad and asked, "Do you remember the last words he said to you in the cemetery?"

"Remember them? I'll never forget them. He'd just shot Lee and Norma Jean, and he shouted, 'They're goin' to Hell, and so am I. You tell Grandma I'll save the land. Tell her I love her.'"

Tommy Lee gave a low whistle as we both reached the bizarre conclusion.

"Dallas meant to send me to Heaven as a personal emissary to talk to his grandmother. He was sending me because he thought he was going to Hell for killing his brother and sister."

"I know it sounds crazy, my friend, but it looks like being a good man nearly got your head blown off." His pencil scribbled across the page. "'I'll save the land.' He'd never said anything about the land before?"

"Never."

"I'll look into it, but the first thing I've got to do is find Dallas," he said, flipping the pad shut.

"And do me a favor," I said as he headed for the door. "Keep me posted."

Tommy Lee and I enjoyed a special kinship. At fifty, he was twenty years my senior, a bridge between the generation of my father and my own. He had led countless funeral processions for Dad in the eighteen years since he was first elected sheriff, and during the past two years, he and I had forged our own friendship. He knew I had given up my own law enforcement aspirations in order to help Mom cope with one of the most painful, heart-wrenching situations a family can face. Alzheimer's is a cruel and malicious disease, stealing the person and leaving the shell as an ever-present reminder of the loss. Tommy Lee understood sacrifice, and for all his teasing, I knew I had his admiration. He didn't have to tell me he was upset that Dallas Willard had nearly gunned me down. I felt confident that when Tommy Lee said "I'll look into it," his one eye would see more than any other two in the county.

The nurse came in so quickly that she must have been waiting outside the door. She carried a tray with a hypodermic syringe and a menu for tomorrow's meal selection. I checked off an assortment of bland options and let her assist me in rolling over on my good side.

"Now, Mr. Clayton," she said, "that ought to take the edge off and let you sleep."

She came around to help me lie on my back. "Nurse…" I left the word hanging as I struggled to see her ID badge.

"Carswell, but I go by Millie."

"Millie, would you hand me the phone?"

"I'll be glad to dial for you."

"Just the hospital switchboard."

She punched zero and gave me the receiver.

"Thank you," I said. "I'll be all right."

Millie left as the operator came on the line.

"Is it possible to order flowers out of the hospital?" I asked.

"You have flowers in your room you don't want, sir?" The woman was clearly surprised a patient would make such a request.

"No, I want to order flowers to be delivered elsewhere."

She connected me to the hospital floral shop where the elderly proprietor complimented me on my thoughtfulness. I had him repeat the message for the card. "For Dr. Susan

Miller, at the O'Malley Clinic—Patient Barry Clayton is grateful for her loving care."

I hung up the phone and rewarded myself with sleep.

I awoke to a Saturday morning much like the day before. Low clouds coated what little scenery was visible from my hospital window with a scrim of white. The shoulder still hurt, but the pain had leveled out to an even plateau. There was a creak in the shadowed corner of my room, and Dr. Alex Soles stood up from the visitor's chair. A big bag of Snickers dangled from one hand and a magazine was curled in the other.

"Brought you something to eat and read." He laid his gifts on a table under the window, then pulled the chair closer to the bed but didn't sit down. He grabbed my wrist and gave a gentle squeeze.

"Glad you're in the hospital and not your own funeral home," he said.

"Thanks."

Alex stood for a few seconds, not saying anything. He and I did not know each other well. Outside of the sessions on dealing with Alzheimer's, I had only crossed paths with him a few times at social functions. I pegged him in his late forties. Cordial, professional, and dedicated were adjectives that best described him. Especially dedicated. He had the reputation for being a therapist who calmly and confidently steered others through their own trials.

"Any word on Dallas?" I asked.

He shook his head. "Why in the hell did he do it, Barry?" Alex's eyes locked on mine, and I knew he had submerged his personal feelings for the moment and was professionally struggling for an answer. "You must have some idea. My secretary played the answering machine tape yesterday when I came in at ten. Of all days to have a damn Rotary breakfast meeting."

"What did he say?"

"Dallas just rambled on about how you had to talk to his grandmother. Tell her he'd been cheated. Cheated by his family. I phoned Sheriff Wadkins immediately, but it was too late. The call had just come in from the cemetery."

Again he reached out and squeezed my wrist. "I'm so sorry. I wish I could have gotten to him. He sounded so agitated. Extremely paranoid. So much so that I'd have to say his actions were in keeping with his mental state."

"Can I hear the tape?"

"I turned it over to Sheriff Wadkins. But you're in no condition to worry about it right now."

"I'm in no condition to forget it. The man tried to kill me, Alex."

Alex smiled and sat down in the chair. "We're alike, Barry. You know that?"

"In what way?" I asked.

"We've got to know why people act as they do. That's why you were studying criminal justice before your father's illness, isn't it? Curiosity as to why people behave as they do, and how anti-social, illegal behavior can be modified. Psychology and criminal justice are linked because when psychology fails, the criminal justice system usually inherits the problem. And you and I both feel guilty that we didn't do enough for Dallas Willard in time."

"Nobody could find him, Alex."

"I mean earlier, before Martha died. Linda Trine mentioned Dallas to me several weeks ago. She handles the social services for a lot of the migrant workers. Seems Dallas kept coming down into the camp accusing them of taking his land. Like they were some foreign invaders. The migrants have been picking for forty years or more. Nothing new about them being here, and Dallas doesn't even have any cleared land in production. Linda thought Dallas needed some help because he'd never acted that way before. That last Alzheimer's session wasn't the appropriate time, and I was swamped with other cases and didn't follow up with him."

"I know other members of the staff must also have people they can't get to, Alex."

"But how many shoot three people?"

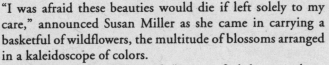

"I was afraid these beauties would die if left solely to my care," announced Susan Miller as she came in carrying a basketful of wildflowers, the multitude of blossoms arranged in a kaleidoscope of colors.

"That's comforting," I said. "Do you feel that way about your human patients?"

She ignored the question and cleared a spot on the table by the bag of Snickers and the magazine. "Who thought you needed *Psychology Today*?" she asked.

"Alex Soles was by earlier. Must be from his waiting room. Probably from the last century."

She laughed. "No, for a doctor's office, it's current. Last April." Susan set down the basket of flowers and turned the arrangement to catch what little light came through the window.

"Good. This way I can take care of both of you at the same time," she said. "And thank you. Saturday deliveries aren't cheap."

"I'm billing that portion to my ex-wife."

She came over to the bedside and gave me a kiss. "I know she means well. I stopped by the funeral home and gave your mom an update. She hopes to drop by after lunch. Now let me take a look at my handiwork." She laid her hand on the bandage, testing the security of the wrapping. "O'Malley been in yet this morning?"

"Yes. About an hour ago. He said you had the morning off and I may have to go home today."

"And that's bad?"

"Room service here is better than my cabin. I had to let the butler go. And I don't know where the chauffeur parked my limo. Actually, Mom will insist I come to the funeral home. You know she already spends most of the day waiting on Dad, and I'd just as soon stay here until I can fend for myself."

"Okay, I'll let you rest up one more night, but I'm afraid tomorrow your insurance company throws you out on the street." She winked. "Maybe I'll leave my condo door unlocked."

Chapter 3

Standing in my kitchen, I watched the pure spring water turn the color of dark molasses as it flowed out the coffee filter and splattered against the glass bottom of the Pyrex pot. Steam swirled off the trickling stream and carried the invigorating aroma of freshly ground beans. I took a deep breath and stretched, one hand nearly touching the rough hewn rafters overhead, the other wriggling helplessly against my stomach because that arm was securely taped to my body.

I filled a mug of coffee and took it out on the back deck of the cabin where I could watch the sunrise boil the mist out of the valley below. The morning light seemed touchable, a golden shroud resurrecting life with its soft glow. A pair of gray squirrels chased each other through the branches of a nearby hickory tree, their chatter blending in with the caws of unseen crows who sounded hell-bent on driving some intruder from their territory. I felt just as possessive of my mountain retreat. Growing up, I had taken these ancient hills for granted. It's when you lose something that it becomes more precious. A part of me had always remained here. Even when I rejected my father's funeral business and moved away, I couldn't reject the Appalachian heritage fused to my soul.

I had purchased the cabin and the five-acre tract of land from a psychiatrist in Charleston, S.C., whose own health kept him from making use of what he had planned to be his summer home. Logs had been culled from at least four original cabins scattered across western North Carolina and eastern Tennessee. Their century-plus heritage created a rustic atmosphere that I found rejuvenating after a day of toil at the funeral home. To think that a hundred and fifty years ago a living, breathing man felled the trees and hewed the logs that now gave me shelter put my problems in perspective. These reassembled walls with modern mortar chinked between the timbers enclosed conveniences my woodsmen forefathers could never have imagined.

As I sat in the cool, gentle breeze, I thought about Dallas Willard's final words to me—"I'll save the land." So far, nothing had come to light. A week had passed since the slaughter in the cemetery. Dallas had not been captured, and the reasons for his murderous rampage were no clearer than when I lay bleeding under the shattered gravestone. Speculation grew that he might have committed suicide, except no one had seen his truck and a truck is harder to overlook than a dead body.

It was nearly nine when I went back inside for the last cup in the pot. I had just finished refilling the filter with fresh grounds, no easy task with one hand coming out of your belly button, when I heard footsteps on the gravel outside. My first thought was of Dallas Willard and the sound he made walking across the gravel to his grandmother's casket. With my heart in my throat, I turned to the open front door as the footsteps trod heavily across the porch. Sheriff Tommy Lee Wadkins' familiar face peered through the screen, his one good eye scanning the room. He was in full uniform with the holstered .38 Smith & Wesson revolver prominent on his hip and a smile forced across his lips.

"Good morning, Barry. Sorry to drop in unannounced. How you feeling?"

"I'm okay," I said, hoping I didn't look petrified. "Though I itch like crazy under this tape."

"Anybody else here?" he asked in a whisper.

"Just spit it out. You mean is Susan shacked up with me?"

At least my question drew a laugh. "Hey," said Tommy Lee with a shrug, "you know I turn a blind eye to you and Susan cavorting in sin."

"She had hospital rounds, and for your information, she does not cavort. I just have an occasional night-time medical appointment. I am injured you know."

"If you've found a doctor who still makes house calls, then more power to you. So, you're doing okay?"

"Yes and no. Yes, I'm doing okay because I'm healing like I'm supposed to and Uncle Wayne told me not to worry about the funeral home. No, because I'm going nuts cooped up here while Dallas is out there somewhere. What's happening, Tommy Lee?"

"Well, the department is too small to keep working the hours we've been putting in. Yesterday, I decided to return to normal schedules with Dallas being a top priority yet not consuming all our resources. At least, that was yesterday's plan."

"Something changed?"

"Of course. Always happens when you set your mind in one direction. You get it yanked in another. Dallas Willard's truck showed up."

"Where?"

"Dirt road about five miles from here. Hikers found it and must have remembered it from the description on the news. My deputy Reece Hutchins got their cell call this morning."

"Any sign of Dallas?"

"That's what I'm going to see. Reece is at the scene. Thought maybe you'd like to ride along, if you don't mind missing Oprah."

"Don't worry," I joked. "I set the VCR first thing every morning. So, how come y'all missed the truck?"

"That's the interesting part. We'd already checked and re-checked that road. As recently as yesterday afternoon. Seems like our boy Dallas went for a little drive last night."

I wedged my knee against the dashboard as the patrol car took another sharp jolt from an exposed boulder. The dull ache in my shoulder was beginning to sharpen.

"Dirt road?" I grumbled. "This ain't much more than a two-rut footpath."

"Shouldn't be much farther. Dead ends at the railroad bed. That's how the hikers found the truck. They were walking the tracks."

Another rough and tumble quarter mile passed, then the road curved and we emerged from the forest shadows into the brighter light of a clearing. In the sunshine stood Dallas' rusted red pickup. Beside it was parked another patrol car. Deputy Hutchins stood beside a young man and woman who wore small backpacks and looked rather bewildered. Their fall foliage hike had turned into quite a different outing.

We got out and Reece introduced us to Shane and Liz Colbert. They had started walking the rails from a more accessible crossing a couple miles to the south.

"Glad you folks recognized the truck and phoned us," said Tommy Lee.

"We heard the description on the TV, and we didn't see anybody around," said Shane Colbert. He looked at his wife sheepishly. "We kinda hid in the bushes in case that crazy man came back."

His young wife nodded in agreement and reached out to take his hand.

"You were good to stay. And you were smart to be cautious," said Tommy Lee. He turned to Reece. "What have we got?"

His deputy shook his head. "I walked the tracks a hundred yards in each direction, Sheriff. There ain't no sign of him. It's like he vanished into thin air again."

"I work for a god-damned power company and have no electricity. Otherwise I could offer you some coffee."

The man who introduced himself as Fred Pryor stood outside the door of the construction trailer and made the apology.

"Who backed into it?" asked Tommy Lee.

"I don't know. Happened overnight. I discovered it this morning when I arrived. Just one more thing to deal with." He glared at the nearby utility pole lying askew with its black snaking cable dangling in the dust. Then he looked at my hand dangling from the front of my shirt.

"You were shot up at the Willard funeral, weren't you? Saw it on the news. Damndest thing I've ever heard of."

I studied him more closely. Fred Pryor didn't look like a power company senior executive. He wore a green wind-breaker with an "R P & E" insignia, jeans, and black cowboy boots.

"What the hell got into that boy?" he asked.

"We don't know," said Tommy Lee. "Still looking for him. Something about their land. Borders this project, doesn't it? You had any dealings with the family?"

Pryor's face flushed. I didn't know whether he was insulted or embarrassed that Tommy Lee thought he might associate with the Willards. "Not me. Our real estate division might have talked to them. Their property is part of the watershed, and it could be affected should we decide to raise the lake level."

I looked at Tommy Lee and saw his eye squint. Fred Pryor had gotten his attention.

Tommy Lee and I had driven to the construction project when a search around Dallas' truck proved fruitless. The site was within a few miles of the main rail line and would be a logical destination if Dallas were on the run. I looked beyond our powerless host and down the bulldozed valley to the mammoth wall of gravel and stone rising up at the narrow point between the steep ridges.

Just yesterday, I had read an article in the newspaper about the Broad Creek excavation. The first phase of the hydro-electric project had progressed on schedule and under budget. Soon Broad Creek would be dammed, and as the new lake began to form, Ridgemont Power and Electric would focus on the construction of the facilities, turbines, generators, and network of transmission lines necessary to convert nature's aquatic energy into electricity for the power-hungry consumer.

The article announced Senior Executive Vice President Fred Pryor was personally overseeing the project. It was a challenge that skipped all the political headaches of a nuclear facility, but there were still the environmentalists and EPA inspectors to deal with. "Keeping the project on time and on budget is the company's top priority because Broad Creek is good for the public and good for the shareholders." So said Fred Pryor in the newspaper.

"Ridgemont Power and Electric was buying the land?" Tommy Lee asked.

"Not that I know of. Not my area. I think I saw a memo at the home office that the family didn't want to discuss it while the grandmother was alive. That's understandable. Ol' timers get so attached to their memories."

Except Martha Willard didn't have any memories. Not at the end. But Dallas had so strong an attachment that he murdered his brother and sister. Was that the reason Ridgemont Power and Electric had only gotten as far as inquiries? Had Dallas refused to sell?

"Any leads on where Willard might be?" Pryor asked, changing the subject. "You think he came on our property?"

"We don't know that," said Tommy Lee. "It's just that we found his truck on an old logging road a few miles away. It dead-ends next to the main rail line. You've got a spur running in here. We thought he might have taken it."

The engine whistle broke through the sheriff's comments. We looked up the valley to the track running along the water. The power company's own yard engine rolled along hauling out several carloads of debris to the truck loading zone at the main highway. From there it would bring back more gravel or other construction supplies directly to the dam site.

"That's the old Pisgah Paper Mill's abandoned spur," said Pryor. "Activating it was my idea. It's proven to be a real asset for transporting materials in and out of the valley. We never go all the way out to the main line, and we chain a gate across the track each night. I'll alert the crew to keep their eyes open. Good luck, Sheriff. Nice to have met you, Mr. Clayton. Hope you're on the mend." Tommy Lee and I had been dismissed.

As we walked back to the patrol car, Tommy Lee said, "I don't like him."

"Pryor? Why not?"

"See that blue Mercury parked by the trailer?"

I turned around and stared at the car, one of several parked by the edge of the mobile office. When I noticed the "Cain for Sheriff" bumper stickers plastered all over the rear, I thought I understood why Tommy Lee disliked the man. Cain was challenging him in next month's election. "Maybe it's one of his employees," I said.

"No, it's not," said Tommy Lee. "And it's not Pryor's either. That's my esteemed opponent's car. Bob Cain himself. He does security consulting. Explains why Fred Pryor hustled outside to meet us." Tommy Lee smiled. "The son of a bitch is aiding and abetting the enemy."

"What now?" I asked. "We don't even know which direction Dallas may have headed."

The sheriff leaned in the open car door and yanked the mike from its cradle. "I'll have the deputies organize search teams. We should walk the tracks."

I looked up at the hills surrounding the excavated valley. Dallas Willard was out there somewhere, mentally unstable, exposed to the elements and dangerous. He had reached out to me for help by phone, and then tried to kill me with his gun. I couldn't stand the idea of being out of the action. A part of me still was and always would be a law officer.

"Count me in," I told Tommy Lee.

He looked at my useless arm.

"Hey. There is nothing wrong with my legs."

He smiled. "No, I guess not. Too bad I can't say the same thing about your head."

Chapter 4

The next day was a cool and breezy Saturday. Reverend Lester Pace and I were hiking along a five-mile rail spur that ran to an abandoned quarry. Friday afternoon's search had netted no sign of Dallas in the immediate area. The truck yielded no clues, and there were no missing person or stolen vehicle reports to indicate Dallas had hijacked someone on departing the scene. Tommy Lee had checked with the Norfolk-Southern and the CSX rail lines. Neither reported trouble with any of their freights running along that stretch. It was as if, as Deputy Hutchins had said, Dallas had vanished into thin air. The search was being conducted regardless, and Tommy Lee had coordinated groups of officers from other counties with his own team, pairing the searchers so no one worked alone or without someone familiar with the area. A few civilian volunteers were included who knew the coves and hollows, but each was instructed to adhere to any orders or commands issued by the accompanying law officer. Tommy Lee's goal was to comb the rail lines within a thirty-mile radius of Dallas' truck.

Pace and I were the exceptions. Tommy Lee had reluctantly given in to my request to be a part of the search because he respected the training I had received on the Charlotte force. He teamed me with Reverend Pace because Pace knew the area as well as anyone, and he too wouldn't take no for an answer. We were given a dead-end stretch of track and told to stay on it. Tommy Lee insisted we be armed for our own protection. I carried my five-shot .38 Smith & Wesson Special high on my hip. Tommy Lee also insisted that if we saw any sign that Dallas might be or had been in the vicinity, we were to summon up the proper authorities to take further action.

Of all the preachers I dealt with in the funeral business, Pace was my favorite. He had been a Methodist circuit-rider for over forty years. Time might have lessened his step but not his stamina. He carried a twisted rhododendron trunk as a walking stick, which he brandished like a drum major marshaling the band. Although the temperature couldn't have been above forty-five, I worked up a sweat matching stride with him. As we walked along the rusted steel rails, the preacher searched the right side of the gravel bed and I took the left.

"Haven't seen your dad in about a month, Barry. How's he doing?" Pace asked the question after we'd covered a couple miles and thoroughly talked out the shooting at Crab Apple Valley Baptist Church and the possible reasons for Dallas Willard's actions. It was not lost on Pace that the missing man was mentally disturbed and needed compassion along with capture. Pace's compassion was genuine; so was the .32 Colt tucked in his belt.

"Dad is more frightened," I said. "Stays upstairs most of the time. A few steps out in the hall and he forgets where he is going. Forgets where he is. And there are times he looks at me and can't quite place my face."

The old preacher shook his head. "Alzheimer's is a hell of a thing. Hardest on the ones closest. God give you strength."

I didn't say anything. I didn't want God's strength. I wanted Him to take this curse off my father, the gentlest man who ever lived. Pace read my thoughts.

"Your father is quite courageous. You know that?"

"Yes," I replied tersely.

"A few years ago, he told me he had only one fear. That fear wasn't for himself. He knows his death will come through a painless oblivion. His fear is for you."

"Me?" I stammered before I could stop myself.

"He's afraid you will become bitter. Bitter that your love for him and your mother disrupted your own life. Brought you back to the small town and the job you had no interest in having. He has accepted you wanted more than Gainesboro could give and that he would not pass the funeral business on to you like your grandfather had handed it to him. But then, it happened." Pace took a deep breath and seemed to stare back five years to that dreadful day when the whole town realized something was wrong with my father.

Mother had called in tears. Dad had been driving the limousine behind the hearse en route to Good Shepherd Cemetery when, to the shock of the grieving family, he pulled out of the procession and passed both the hearse and Tommy Lee's escorting deputy. Dad had forgotten where he was and what he was doing. A host of doctors and tests yielded a diagnosis that was more of a slow death sentence: Alzheimer's at age fifty-five, an age struck by fewer than three percent of the cases and a statistic of brutal consequences. For three years, he and Mom struggled to keep the business going while seeking someone to take it over. Uncle Wayne, Mom's brother and a man older than my father, had neither the ambition nor the finances to buy it. No other individual came forward with an offer, and none of the big chains were interested. The burden fell to me.

Pace spoke again. "You have my respect, Barry, for what you did. But, if it turns you against yourself and against your God, then you should make every effort to sell and go back to the life that made you happy."

"What life," I said. "My wife wouldn't follow me here. So much for 'for better or for worse.' What do I have to look forward to? Going back to working nights on the Charlotte police force? Re-enrolling at the university in a foolish quest for a master's? Chasing some half-baked notion of working for the FBI? No one should feel sorry for me or worry about me, Preacher. I'm not the one whose personality is being erased each day. I'm not the one whose body will be a living shell of the man who won't remember being husband or father." I felt the words choke me up, and I stopped walking and looked away.

"And you've no one to lash out at but God," he said. "I understand and God understands. He's there for you and He can lift the anger off of you. Take comfort."

"Here's my comfort," I said, sweeping my good arm in an arc wide enough to encircle the ridges surrounding us. The fall colors—orange, red, and yellow—blazed across their backs and the ice-blue sky arched over them like an infinitely deep canopy. "I take comfort in this. No offense, but they speak louder than any sermon I've ever heard."

Pace looked at the panorama surrounding us. "They latch onto you, don't they? These mountains."

"Yes," I agreed. "Yes, they do. Despite my efforts to escape them."

"But it's the people hidden in the coves and hollows who keep me here. The people your father has served all his life." He started walking again, slower, and he spoke in a cadence matching his stride.

"Whenever I get discouraged or think that God has abandoned me, the people hold me. First time it happened, I'd been here only six months. One Sunday morning in a little shack of a church near Hickory Nut Falls—chicken coop churches folks used to call them—I finished my last service for the day. Back then, I'd preach over in Yellow Mountain community at eight in the morning, hop in my forty-eight Plymouth coupe and high-tail it like a bat off the devil's doorstep to Eagle Creek for nine-thirty worship, and then be in Hickory Nut Falls at eleven. There were only ten to fifteen families in each congregation."

"Chicken coops?"

Pace laughed. "When I say 'chicken coop,' I'm not straying from the God's truth. The church was a combination of old plank boards, tar paper, and tin roofing that a couple of the families had pulled together from their own houses.

"No cross, no white steeple, no sign out front with my name and this week's sermon topic. Just a shelter from Life's storm where these folks could escape their poverty and hardship for an hour and praise God for the simple joys money can't buy. Inside, the pews were only wooden benches, the pulpit was a post with a board nailed to it, and the music was whoever happened to bring a dulcimer or guitar. I wanted to build a real church and fill the pews, but it wasn't happening. I was down on myself and down on the calling. I'd petitioned the bishop for a new assignment."

"Bet he didn't want to hear it," I said.

"I wasn't the first young pup old Bishop Wallace had to train. He said he'd pray about it, which meant I couldn't complain while a divine response was in the making.

"Several weeks later, after Sunday service, I boxed up my Bible and the hymnbooks I carried from church to church, though most of the congregation couldn't read. A few folks came up to talk with me, mostly some of the ladies and their young-uns as the men tended to hold back or even sit outside during the preaching and singing. Like I said, I'd only been here a little while, so people were a little gun-shy.

"When I thought everyone had left, I lifted up the box with the Bible and hymnals and walked down the narrow aisle to the front door. Just before I reached it, a man stepped in the doorway, blocking my path. He was about six foot tall, lean as a twig, wearing a beat-up pair of overalls and a gray, sweat-stained work shirt. Pushed back atop his head was an old, floppy-brimmed, brown felt hat. A squirrel rifle lay across his folded arms. I especially noticed the squirrel rifle."

"Guess he didn't like the sermon," I interrupted.

Reverend Pace smiled. "That's what I thought, Barry. I took some comfort that the hammer wasn't cocked. Yet.

"'Preacher, you in a hurry?' he asked.

"I had never seen him before. Didn't know if he was one of the men who sat outside, but I did know that in my six months experience, no one brought a gun to church.

"'No, not particularly,' I said. 'Can I help you?'"

Pace stopped walking and leaned on his stick. His eyes held mine and his smile disappeared. "What I at first thought was meanness in his face melted with my offer. I realized the old man was tensed up over something. Evidently, I could help. I felt the pastoral call to feed the flock.

"'I'd be obliged if you'd come back to the house with me. I got a burial needs tendin' to.' He looked at the box in my arms. 'Bring the Good Book.'

Pace laughed and started walking again. "Well, now there's nothing more confounded than a speechless preacher. I must a looked like every bit of sense had been snatched from my head. At last I stammered, 'But has the body been prepared? Paperwork filled out and everything?'

"'All ready,' he said. He looked down at his feet, ashamed to meet me eye to eye. 'I ain't learnt enough to say the words. Ain't no church goer.'

"Having made his confession, he made his demand. 'So, you goin' to help?'

"Now I'd done a few burials, and even interred one on family property with your dad, but never an impromptu funeral. I didn't know what to say, but I sure didn't say no. Just nodded my head and followed that mountaineer outside."

A flash caught my eye along the edge of the rail bed. I jumped back toward Pace. "Wait," I said. "I see something." In my mind, it was a glint off Dallas Willard's shotgun.

We stood silently for several seconds. The only sounds came from a chorus of blue jays. Then somewhere down the track a squirrel chattered.

Pace and I ventured back to the edge of the crossties. Instinctively, he stepped away from me so that one shotgun blast could not take both of us. I carefully stepped down the gravel rail bed. While Pace covered me, I grabbed a handful of green mountain laurel leaves and lifted the branch.

"Beer cans," I said with relief. "Can you believe it? We're two miles from nowhere and here are the relics of a party."

"I'm surprised the astronauts didn't find beer cans when they landed on the moon," said Pace. "You got good eyes, Barry."

He extended his walking stick so that I could grab the tip and steady my climb up to the track.

"Yeah, good eyes but bad nerves," I said. "Sorry. I left you facing a real gun in church."

"Like I said, nothing like this had ever happened before. A command performance at a funeral. So, this old man and I stepped out of the church and all I saw was my Plymouth and the cornfield down to the creek. I knew he had walked out of the hills.

"'Can we drive to your place?' I asked.

"'Partly,' he answered.

"We got in the Plymouth and drove off. Me and the old mountain man, the Bible and hymnals bouncing between us. He never spoke. Just pointed the turn at each crossroads. The pavement became gravel, the gravel became dirt, until finally two ruts were all that marked what had been an old wagon trail. I stopped the car, afraid to push my luck any farther.

"'Don't forgit the Good Book,' he reminded me.

"We walked up the ridge on an overgrown footpath till we came to a little clearing of a couple acres of pasture. In the middle was his cabin. Shack, I should say. Front porch roof propped up with small tree trunks, bark still on them. Side planking had been covered in black tar paper for weathering. It was torn through in places and I saw cracks in the slats through to the inside. In front, a few chickens and guinea hens scratched for grubs. No other sign of life.

"We walked around the side by a pile of cordwood. A couple wedges and an axe lay up under some of the logs. In the back, a well-traveled path led from the rear of the cabin to the outhouse, its door half off makeshift hinges. Over at the edge of the clearing, about thirty yards away, was a freshly dug hole. Maybe three foot by four foot. The dirt was heaped up beside it with a shovel lying atop the pile. At the far edge of the hole, I saw an old tattered tarp stretched out over something and weighed down with stones.

"A chill rippled down my spine, and I shuddered in horror at the size of the tarp.

"'My God,' I thought. 'It's a child. This man has lost a child.'

"Calling up every ounce of courage, I followed him over to the grave site. I braced as he bent down and pulled back the tarp. There before me lay the mangiest ol' coon dog I've ever seen. His eyes glassed over and body stiff as a board. His legs were so straight and rigid, I swear to God, if you'd set him up, he could have been a footstool.

"All the fear, the dread that had built up inside me since the stranger blocked my doorway busted loose and I did one of the meanest things I've ever done in my life. I laughed. Laughed till I thought my insides would pop loose.

"I heard the squirrel gun cock. The sound snapped me out of my hysteria.

"The man stood up from bending over the dead animal. He glared at me with a look of hurt and hate. The gun barrel pointed straight at my belly.

"'That's Roddey,' he said. 'The finest friend I ever had.' He held the rifle in one hand and removed his hat with the other. Tears ran along the creases in his weathered cheeks. 'Am I goin' to have to dig this hole bigger?'

"My heart stopped. I must have gone white as a sheet. I don't know what kept me from passing out and falling into the hole. I felt my knees start to give on me and my hands were shaking so much I could hardly get the Bible open." Pace smiled at the memory.

Looking at the white-haired preacher with a staff in his hand and pistol in his belt, I found it hard to imagine him as once being terrified.

"But I found passages of Scripture I didn't know I could find. We went through the birds of the air, beasts of the field, lions laying down with lambs, anything that had an animal, I read.

"Then I prayed for Ol' Roddey—the finest dog that ever lived. It was somewhere in the prayer—two prayers actually, the vocal one for Roddey, the silent one for me—that I heard him uncock the gun. I said a few more 'Thank you, Lords' from the bottom of my heart and we committed Roddey's carcass back to the mountain."

Reverend Pace shook his head, then started walking again, carefully placing his rhododendron stick on the crossties. "Yeah, we covered Roddey up and the old man asked me into the cabin. He and I shared some corn—liquor that is," he added with a chuckle. "As a Methodist, I considered it medicine to calm my nerves. Only then did he tell me his name. Jake McGraw.

"You see, Barry, I'd performed a spiritual function for Jake no one in my seminary class could have imagined. I was an outsider, but Jake McGraw needed me. Praying over Roddey was doing the Lord's work. I understand that now. After that, Ol' Jake came down every Sunday and sat on the back corner of the back bench. He was still a strange old hermit, but in his own way, he gave me a stamp of approval. Believe me, it didn't go unnoticed by the other mountain folk. In a year, Hickory Nut Falls was my largest congregation. Today, there is a church there instead of a chicken coop. And a parking lot too.

"Ten years later, your dad and I buried Jake beside Ol' Roddey. And I swear at the final 'Amen,' a coon dog howled from the mountain top."

"Yeah, right," I laughed. "You're doing a number on me."

"It's true," said Pace. "You can ask Charlie. He was a friend of Jake's."

The preacher pointed to a break in the bordering pines. I saw a field sloping away from us. Halfway down the hillside, a massive workhorse plodded along. Behind him, with both hands guiding the wooden plow, a skinny man in blue bib-overalls stepped over the clods of freshly turned earth. The old guy was eighty if a day.

"That's Charlie Hartley," said Pace.

"Don't believe I know him."

"Well, you're about to." He swung the walking stick in the air and caught the farmer's attention. The man pulled back on the reins and hollered "whoa-up." The gentle beast lumbered to a halt and snorted his displeasure. He shook his head, twisting his neck around the sweat-stained collar to roll an eye toward the barn at the far end of the field.

"Charlie's never had a tractor touch his soil. Got no use for them. His horses are his children." The preacher left the railroad tracks and started across the field. "Come on," he said. "Rude not to talk a spell."

"Hello, Reverend," said Charlie. He wiped the sweat from his hands with a red bandanna and grasped Pace's right one with both of his own. "Good to see you." He looked me over. "They finally get you some help?" he asked Pace.

The Reverend laughed. "Yeah, but he ain't it. This is Barry Clayton. He's Jack Clayton's boy. Barry got shot up at the Willard funeral last week."

"Heard something about that," he said with a nod. "You work with your pa?"

"They don't call me Buryin' Barry for nothing."

The old man didn't crack a smile at the joke I'd been saddled with since junior high. He turned to his horse like Pace had turned to me.

"This is Ned. He's paying for his pleasure. Told him last February he shouldn't have jumped Nell. With her foaling just a couple months off, it's just him and me to ready the winter field." He turned and lectured the animal. "Remember that next spring 'fore you go mountin' your plowmate."

The horse flipped his tail as if to say "lay off." Charlie chuckled at the big stallion's rebuttal. "Course you are giving me a grandchild of sorts. Guess I should be grateful." He reached into his shirt pocket for a sugar cube, and, as the horse took the treat, Charlie scratched the coarse hair between his dapple ears.

"What are you fellows doing walking in on the Hope Quarry spur?"

"Guess you didn't know Dallas Willard's still missing," said Pace.

"Nope. Ain't been to town since Monday."

"He hasn't been seen since the shooting. Then his truck shows up yesterday by the railroad about two miles south of where the quarry spur splits off. Search parties spent today combing half the county."

"Anything I can do?"

"We could use your phone to check in. After we walk down to the quarry."

"How much farther is it?" I asked.

"Couple hundred yards," said the preacher.

"I'll do it," I said. "You call the sheriff's office."

"I'll take Ned to the stall," said Charlie. "Come get me when you're ready."

On my return, I walked into the shadows of the old barn. The sound of my footsteps died in the carpet of brown hay strewn over the dry, packed earth. The rich pungent odor of manure, sweat, and feed rose up like a barricade. I stopped for a moment while my eyes adjusted to the dim light.

Against the golden backdrop of the barn's open rear door, I saw the motionless silhouettes of Reverend Pace and Charlie. They sat on barrels and watched the mare drink from her water trough. The barn odor mellowed into an aroma of age. With reluctance, I intruded upon their silent pleasure.

"I didn't find anything," I said. "You talk to Tommy Lee?"

"Yeah, patched through the two-way radio. Nothing."

"Great day in the morning," muttered Charlie. "What's the sheriff planning?"

"To keep looking at least through the weekend," said Pace. "It's about all he can do. National Park Rangers have agreed to scout park land at Montgomery Rock and Black Bear Bluff. Sheriff's got a couple of the mountain families to do the same on their own land. He hopes somebody will find some sign. Maybe a campfire. Dallas could be lost if he wandered too far into the gorges."

Charlie Hartley kicked the dirt with his work boot. "Tarnation. He's a local boy who knows these hills as well as anybody. He's been up and down them since he could crawl. He ain't lost. If he ain't dead, he's bad hurt. Dogs. Ought to bring in dogs."

"Tried that," I said. "Tommy Lee got the SBI to bring them to the truck. No use. Nothing for the dogs to follow. Scent ended at the tracks. Said Dallas may as well have caught a train."

"Maybe he hopped a freight," said Charlie.

"Railroad told Tommy Lee that would be impossible," I said. "It's not a crossing, and they're usually going thirty-five to forty miles an hour. SBI ran aerial surveillance over the tracks, but it's not as effective as walking the ground, which is what I guess we'd better get back to doing."

Pace stood and clasped a hand on Charlie's shoulder. "Take care of Nell, you hear."

"You come up and see her colt."

"Sure. I kiss all the new babies."

Pace picked up his walking stick and followed me out of the barn, leaving Charlie to lean against the stall and admire his mare.

I knew something was wrong as soon as Pace and I got to the funeral home. From the high corner eaves, the spotlights blazed even though the sky still held the last purple rays of twilight. They were the sign of official business, the illumination for visitors and mourners going to and from the circle of grief.

"Uncle Wayne told me nothing was scheduled for this Saturday night," I said. "That's why we invited you to stay over."

Pace glanced at me as he slowed my Jeep to a crawl.

"Maybe you've got company," he said.

We saw the old blue pickup with dented aluminum camper-top parked at the edge of the pavement. Next to it was a rusted Chevy Nova. "No, not the social kind," I answered. "And I don't see Uncle Wayne's car. I'd better not leave until we know what's going on."

We walked through the side yard to the back porch off the kitchen. My mother bustled out of the door, waving her arms in frantic ellipses, her plump body bobbing up and down as she exhorted us into the house.

"Oh, Barry," she whispered. "It's awful. Just awful. And Wayne's not back from looking for Dallas Willard."

Pace gently held her by the shoulders to calm her. "It's all right, Connie. Tell us what happened."

Her voice quivered and she blinked back tears. "They brought him in the back of a truck. Wouldn't even call for the ambulance."

"Who, Connie?"

"The mother and father. And a neighbor too. He was just a boy. An eight-year-old boy."

"You'd better go on in, Barry," said Pace. "We'll be there in a moment."

As I entered the foyer, I heard whispered voices coming from the viewing room on the left, the one more comfortably called the Slumber Room. I was surprised that Mom had not left the family across the hall in the living room where the homey, informal atmosphere could put the relatives more at ease as they discussed funeral arrangements. The Slumber Room was reserved for visitation when the family greeted friends and neighbors coming to extend sympathy.

A young woman sat hunched in a straight-backed chair, her face buried in her hands. She wore a threadbare cotton dress and should have added at least a sweater or a jacket for the autumn chill. At her side stood a slender man whose face still bore the marks of adolescent acne. His jeans hung on his hipless body like rags on an understuffed scarecrow. His brown eyes were puffed with red circles, and though the tears no longer flowed, he had to clear his throat before he could speak.

"You Mr. Clayton?" he asked, skeptical of my youthful appearance. "We were told to ask for Jack Clayton." What little weight he had he shifted from foot to foot in nervous agitation. The woman looked up and stared through me, revealing a thin face with translucent skin. Her features could be taken as childlike from a distance, but the sunken eyes and flat cheekbones told of age beyond her years.

"No, I'm his son, Barry."

"Then would you find him," ordered a voice from the back of the room.

Out of the shadows where the dark green drapes hung behind the casket viewing area stepped a man. Light first caught his brown hair, scraggly and dirty, dropping over his shoulders like twisted strands of Spanish moss. The face had a gray pallor, created by unshaven stubble. His pale blue eyes looked out of place beneath heavy dark-brown eyebrows that merged together over his sharp, hooked nose. He raised an oversized black Bible in one hand, letting the scuffed leather cover fall open as if he expected the words themselves to leap from the page.

"The Lord has need of him," he proclaimed. He swept the Bible in a wide arc toward the couple. "There is nothing more we can do but praise His Holy Name."

The woman shook with silent sobs.

"My father is ill," I said. "I'll take care of things."

Beyond the path of the Bible, I saw the child lying on the low oak pedestal where a casket would rest. The small body was stretched out, hands across the chest, face slightly canted toward the wall as if a mischievous boy mocked the solemnity of the grown-ups. I pushed past the Bible-toting neighbor and stood over the child. Dull quarters rested on his eyes, opaque monocles closing out a world filled with new wonder. With my good arm, I lifted them from his face one at a time. There was no need for such nonsense. The child's eyes were shut forever.

"Those are mine," said the belligerent man.

The coins slipped from my fingers and scattered across the hardwood floor. The Bible slammed shut as the man chased after his money. Other footsteps sounded from the hall, and I heard Reverend Pace's gentle voice introducing himself. The father responded "Luke and Harriet Coleman" and the other man said "Leroy Jackson." Then the murmur of conversation blended into a background hum as I focused all my attention on the boy. The sneakers a size too big, yet worn enough to have belonged to someone before him. Jeans rolled up in double cuffs, patches at the knees. A brown belt with scratched silver buckle shaped like a cowboy's six-shooter. A sweatshirt decorated with a montage of Saturday morning super-heroes, animals or aliens, I didn't know which, but a new cast of characters that had become the coveted property of eight-year-olds.

The boy's face carried a layer of summer tan beneath the dirt. A shock of coarse brown hair spread over his forehead while an untamed cowlick sent strands in a rooster tail against the polished wood of the pedestal. The twist of the mouth and the colorless lips drawn back over his teeth were chilling signs of the child's final moments of pain and fear. I reached out and turned his face toward me. Two puncture wounds marred the taut skin just below the right ear. The purple swollen neck rose up like a demon's brand, claiming the child in sadistic triumph.

"What happened?" I spoke to the room, cutting through the voices and sobs, demanding an answer. "What happened to this child?"

My eyes darted to each of them. Reverend Pace stepped closer to see for himself. The neighbor looked from me to the boy's mother and father. He gave a slight nod.

"Snakebite," replied the father. He steadied himself by resting his hand on his wife's shoulder. She stared at the floor. "Rattlesnake. Jimmy was playing on some rocks near the house. Musta crawled up under a ledge. We heard him screaming." The man's voice faltered. He looked at Leroy Jackson.

"I was just driving up to their house when it happened," said Jackson. "The boy was gone in a matter of minutes. I was the one killed the snake. It's out in the truck."

"Did you call a doctor?" I asked. "There should have been more time."

"No phone. And I couldn't put no tourniquet round the kid's neck, now could I."

"Call Ezra Clark," I told my mother. "It's required procedure," I explained to the others. "He'll need to sign a coroner's statement."

"I don't want him cuttin' on my Jimmy," said Luke Coleman. His wife started sobbing again.

Mother started for the telephone, then hesitated. "Barry, we should get Travis McCauley."

"Who's that?" asked Leroy Jackson. "We don't need a lot of people in here gawkin'."

"Mr. McCauley runs a furniture store," I said. "He also makes a few caskets. We don't have one appropriate for this child."

The father cleared his throat again. "I'm afraid we're kinda short on cash money."

"That can wait, Mr. Coleman. I'll make the calls to the coroner and Mr. McCauley. This boy deserves a decent burial."

"My wife and I'll be carrying him back to Kentucky," said Luke Coleman. "It's where my wife's people are buried."

"Certainly," I said. "But first there are necessary things we have to do regardless of where he's going to be interred. I suggest you and your wife follow my mother back to the kitchen for a cup of tea. We can talk about those arrangements there."

Then my mother said something that made me want to hug her. "And Mr. Jackson, I suggest you either be of comfort to these good people or you be quiet."

"Sorry, I've done it again." I made the apology as soon as Susan opened her front door. "I really couldn't say much on the telephone. I was standing in Mom's kitchen."

She nodded. "I hope you didn't look as pitiful as you do now. Well, our dinner reservations are beyond salvaging, and I expect you're in no mood for a night on the town. You may as well stay awhile."

I went to my customary spot, an overstuffed armchair across from the sofa.

Fifteen minutes later, I still sat in the armchair, but my clothes sloshed in the washing machine, and a beer sloshed down my throat. Susan convinced me of the wisdom in spending the night in Gainesboro and then going straight to the sheriff's office at dawn to rejoin the search for Dallas. I pulled the terry-cloth bathrobe tighter around my waist so that I could rest the ice-cold beer bottle on my lap without singing soprano.

"I just couldn't leave those people," I began.

Susan stretched out on the sofa opposite me. She had changed into a silk dressing gown and wrapped her delicate surgeon's hands around a long-stemmed glass of white wine. Her dark brown eyes stared at me over the rim of the glass. I would willingly lie on any operating table if that angelic face were looking down at me.

"Of course, you couldn't," she said.

"Uncle Wayne came in a few minutes after I called you. He'd been walking track in the northern part of the county. He's no spring chicken, and he and his partner tried to cover too much ground. He was exhausted, but he still came back to the mess at the funeral home as soon as he got word."

"The Colemans. Does anybody know them?"

"No. They've been down from Kentucky about a year. Luke Coleman is on the crew clearing the Broad Creek dam site. Ten or so families migrated here to work on the project. Evidently, the power company has let them build a shanty commune on some of their land. They keep to themselves. And Jimmy, the little boy"—I paused as I saw the child's face in my mind—"the family's adamant about no autopsy."

"Well," said Susan, "that's understandable. I've witnessed enough to know the procedure is pretty dehumanizing. If it were a child of mine, I don't know how I'd react. No question about the snakebite? Ol' Ezra Clark is not the sharpest coroner in the world."

"We saw the rattler. It was huge, over six feet, and the venom must have gone directly into the jugular. This Leroy Jackson, their neighbor, smashed its head with a stone. Snake blood was all over the front seat of his truck from where he tossed it in. Still writhing according to him. He quoted the old wives' tale about snakes not truly dying until sundown. If there were any question about the cause of the boy's death, an autopsy would be mandatory. Ezra said it's pointless to put the mother and father through that ordeal."

"What happens now?" asked Susan.

"Wayne put a call into a funeral home in Harlan, Kentucky. He's making arrangements for transportation of the body and he's coming in tomorrow for the embalming. We agreed I'd do more good looking for Dallas. Tomorrow night at seven-thirty there will be a short visitation. You'll be gone by then."

"Me?" Susan's eyebrows arched into question marks.

"Mom's invited you for dinner. At six. It would really cheer her up."

"And you knew I just couldn't say no," Susan said, stealing the words from my lips.

"Wayne will be there, getting ready for the Colemans. And Reverend Pace. He's staying in town for some meeting with his Bishop. I'll be back from the search by then. With luck, tomorrow we'll find Dallas and this will become just an unwanted souvenir." I patted my wounded shoulder. The beer did wonders for the itch.

Chapter 5

Reverend Pace blessed more than the food. Starting with the Creator, in five terse sentences he moved from the cosmos through the plant and animal kingdoms, across the fields of the farmers, to the God-given culinary talents of my mother.

"Amens" echoed around the table. I opened my eyes to see Pace looking at Fats McCauley. Pace must have been watching him while the rest of us sat with heads bowed and eyes closed. "Soul-tending," my grandmother would have called it: the ability to see a troubled spirit.

The serving dishes heaped with Sunday fixings began their clockwise loop around the dining room table. Mom could have fed three times as many as the six of us. Dad had eaten earlier up in his room. More than a few people around him made him nervous.

By the time I had gotten home from the search party, showered, put on a coat and tie, and picked up Susan, we had been nearly fifteen minutes late. Again, the hunt for Dallas had yielded nothing. Since Reverend Pace had had to preach at his churches and meet with his Methodist bishop, Tommy Lee had paired me with Deputy Hutchins. We scoured more than ten miles of the main line track between Gainesboro and Asheville.

The trek had been exhausting. Not that the physical effort was that great. It was the tension. Any bend in the track, any depression in the roadbed could have concealed the man who tried to kill me. I had felt both frustration and relief when, mid-afternoon, the bottom of the gray heavens opened, and a cold, brittle rain drenched us. Neither Reece nor I could have gone any farther. We had walked back a half mile to my Jeep, and I had driven the deputy to his patrol car parked at Allied Concrete's rail yard, the spot where we had begun our search. The two-vehicle shuttle had saved the time and effort of hiking all the way back to the start.

The rain still beat against the dining room window, but I was no longer wet and cold. I was starving. Fortunately, I stared at a table laden with Thanksgiving proportions.

Mother had included Fats McCauley at the Sunday evening feast. He and my Uncle Wayne had brought the Coleman boy's casket over by hearse, and it had been easy to convince Fats to stay for dinner. All of us called him Travis to his face, but at three-hundred-plus pounds, "Fats" was the nickname most commonly heard around town.

When the dinner plates had been smothered in fried chicken, coleslaw, crisp cornbread muffins, and mounds of mashed potatoes coated with brown gravy, the flow of conversation trickled to limited exchanges of observations on the weather and compliments on the food. My mother, satisfied that each had been well-served, joined in the discussion.

"Was your meeting this afternoon important?" she asked Pace.

The preacher looked up from a drumstick and laughed. His face cracked into hundreds of weathered crevices, and he pushed back the strands of gray hair that dangled from his high forehead. "Are you saying some Methodist meetings are unimportant, Connie?"

Mom blushed. She knew he was teasing, but his question embarrassed her. "Oh, no," she rallied. "I'm sure it was very important if the bishop himself came."

"Yeah, that old coot," said Pace. "If Gabriel sounded his trumpet tonight for Judgment Day, Bishop Richards would organize a committee for how the Methodists should respond. We'd be the last in line at the Pearly Gates."

"No," said Fats. "If it were bingo night, the Catholics would be behind the Methodists. Especially if they held double cards."

"At least a bingo game ends," said Pace. "Well, I'm not being very Christian now, am I? The bishop is all right. Somebody has to make the tough decisions and weigh their theological implications. He leaves me free to wander the mountains serving my three little churches." The Reverend took a second bite from the drumstick.

"And the meeting?" asked Susan.

Pace smiled as he swallowed. "Should have known I couldn't duck the question. The bishop is assigning a young seminary graduate to assist me. Just for a couple months. You know, ride the circuit, get out of the classroom and into the flock."

"Who is he?" Susan asked.

Reverend Pace winked at me. "Quite a sexist assumption. It's 'Who is she?'"

"A woman? A woman preacher?" Fats McCauley's eyes widened at the astonishing prospect.

"I haven't actually seen her," replied Pace, "but the name Sarah Hollifield implies we won't be sharing the same tailor." The preacher rubbed the lapel of his worn tweed sport coat. "She's driving over from Asheville with the bishop tomorrow. I'm not sure he is so keen on the idea of a woman ministering to the mountain folk, but she applied and it would reflect poorly on modern Methodism if she were denied the assignment."

"What do you think?" asked Susan.

"If the mountaineers accepted me, a wet-behind-the-ears Duke graduate, forty years ago, anything is possible. Sarah Hollifield will get my full support. God's work is done by a multitude of hands, male and female."

"God moves in mysterious ways, doesn't She," said Susan.

"Humph," grunted Pace. "I'll leave that question for the bishop and a committee."

The business telephone rang as Mother served coffee and apple cobbler. Wayne excused himself, slid back from the table, and glided into the adjoining room. His lanky, thin frame was what the locals described as "a tall drink of water" or "high pockets."

Uncle Wayne and my parents were a disappearing breed. They personally cared for the funeral needs of their community in much the same way Reverend Pace cared for the spiritual needs of his flock. They were not employees of a large chain of funeral homes. Mom and Dad literally lived where they worked. Their antebellum, white-columned house, set off the street on a gently sloping lawn, was a beautiful home in the tradition of family residences and town funeral businesses. I had rejected both the home and the business when I moved to Charlotte. Clayton and Clayton Funeral Directors was a dying entity in more ways than one.

In a few minutes, Wayne returned, his normally pale complexion flushed. "That was Freddy Mott. He was coming in to help us tonight, but he thinks his distributor cap has got moisture in it. Must be the rain. He can't get his car started." Wayne glanced at his wristwatch. "The Colemans will be here in less than thirty minutes."

"I'm planning to stay," I said.

"We can all help," offered Pace. He stood up and tossed his white linen napkin on the table. "Make us earn our supper."

Mom barred everyone from the kitchen. Even Fats McCauley offered to help with the dishes, but she would hear nothing of it. "The rest of you get things ready for the Colemans," she ordered. "I'll work faster alone."

Susan arranged silk flowers in the Slumber Room and set out a "Those Who Called" book. Wayne and I wheeled in the casket on a rolling cart and Reverend Pace helped at my end to transfer it to the pedestal. We removed the lid and stopped for a moment to look at the boy. Pace said a spontaneous prayer.

The child appeared to be sleeping. Last night my mother had washed and mended his clothes. Gone was the swelling and discoloration from the snakebite. He looked as if a call from his Mom or Dad, or the bark of his dog, would set him in motion, sneakers skimming across the ground in pursuit of a new day.

Fats had had the child's coffin in his inventory. It had been meticulously crafted as a final cradle, a work of art to ease a family's pain that could never go away. The size was right. I hated the thought of a little boy lost in the wide span of satin and ruffles that adults required.

Fats ran a soft cloth over the brass corner trim, wiping clean the dull haze of polish residue. The stillness of the moment was broken by his muffled sob. He turned away, his eyes brimming with tears.

"Y'all leave now," a voice called from the doorway. Leroy Jackson stood with his Bible under his arm and swept his gaze across the room. No one moved. "I said you should leave. You ain't needed. I'm here on behalf of the Lord."

Reverend Pace stepped from behind the casket. He laid his hand on my arm as he passed, signaling me to keep my temper in check. I felt Pace quiver and feared if anyone lost his temper, it would be he.

"The Lord is already here," said Pace. "He has been working through these good people to bring dignity and honor to this child."

"You preach words of damnation, old man." He lifted the Bible above his head. "The Spirit has forsaken you and all the heathen who refuse to heed the commands of the Almighty."

Before Pace could reply, Fats McCauley spoke in a low rumble, the words erupting from deep inside his corpulent body. "Judge not lest ye yourself be judged. For the Lord knoweth the way of the righteous, but the way of the ungodly shall perish." With the last syllable, his face froze. His eyes never wavered from Leroy Jackson as he silently challenged the man to dispute him.

"Amen," said Pace.

Leroy Jackson looked away, unable to tolerate the weight of Fats McCauley's soul-piercing scrutiny. Through the doorway came Luke Coleman. He moved past his neighbor and self-proclaimed preacher as he led his wife Harriet by the arm. The young mother had draped a remnant of black lace across her head. The brown hair was pulled into a bun, and her dark eyes darted beneath the drooping veil, painfully searching each face for reassurance that her son was not lost to her.

She caught sight of the casket at the far end of the room. The profile of the child rose above the padded rim as if he lay suspended over a sea of white satin. Harriet Coleman drew back. Her legs crumpled. Luke tried to catch her, but she sank to the hardwood floor.

"My boy," she sobbed. "Why would God let him die? He didn't need to die." Her husband struggled to raise her to her feet. Pace took her other arm and together they managed to carry her to a folding chair that Wayne set up against the wall. The woman shut out all attempts to comfort her, only staring at the casket, her grief grown too deep for any physical expression.

"Are you expecting others?" I asked Luke Coleman.

"Some friends and neighbors. Leroy will say a few words before we all leave for Kentucky."

I nodded and patted the man on the arm. "I'll be close by to be of assistance." I gave a slight wave of my hand indicating we should withdraw. Fats McCauley was not watching for the signal. He was fascinated by the young mother and studied her as if she were the only person in the room.

"Travis," I whispered, then repeated more distinctly. There was no response.

"Travis, let's go," said Pace.

The big man nodded, but instead of following the Reverend, he crossed the room and knelt in front of Harriet Coleman, putting his bulk between her and the casket.

"You have a beautiful little boy. Nobody will take that memory away from you. Believe me."

Harriet Coleman reached out and touched Fats McCauley on the cheek. She rubbed her fingers across his tears.

"He is with Jesus, isn't he?"

"Yes. Yes, he is. And my Brenda is with Jesus too. Happy and whole in the shelter of His arms." He took a deep breath, then whispered so low that the rest of us strained to catch the words. "Too cold. It was too cold."

Fats McCauley got to his feet, looked back at the boy and walked out of the room without another word.

"I'm going to sit with Fats for a few minutes in the kitchen," said Pace.

I turned to Susan. "Would you mind helping me at the front door? Folks can put their coats in the hall closet."

About fifteen or twenty people came. Most were like the Colemans, poor, ill-clad, and terribly distraught by the tragedy. Like the Colemans and Leroy Jackson, they had migrated over from Kentucky. As the colony's spiritual leader, Jackson dealt with the mourners more as tribe members than as a congregation.

I was surprised at the one exception to this group of backwoods mountaineers. Fred Pryor, the Ridgemont Power and Electric executive, walked into the foyer wearing a tan cashmere overcoat.

Accompanying him was a lean man with oily black hair and the dark stubble of a well-past-five-o'clock shadow. He wore a wrinkled gray suit and would have been almost presentable if not for the scuffed brown shoes. I figured him for late forties. He helped Pryor out of his coat while never taking his eyes off me. There was no chance I could mistake his expression as friendly. He was wary, like a dog protecting his turf.

"Mr. Clayton," said Pryor. "Sorry to meet again under such sad circumstances. And I gather there is still no word on Dallas Willard?"

I shook my head. Pryor turned to his companion.

"This is Odell Taylor. He is one of our foremen. I asked him to have the crew check the security gate at the head of the rail spur and walk the track."

I reached out to shake the man's hand, but instead Taylor laid Pryor's heavy coat across my forearm.

"Nothin'," he said. "We found nothin' because that Willard knows better than to set foot on our property."

Pryor quickly touched the man's wrist and interrupted him. "I know, Odell, but Mr. Clayton and the sheriff are just doing their best to pursue every possibility. All of us hope the poor demented man is found alive. The loss of the…the…"

He faltered for a second, and Odell Taylor said, "Colemans' son."

"Yes, the loss of the Colemans' son is enough tragedy to deal with. We'd better go pay our respects."

Pryor eyed the visitation room as if studying the fairway before a golf shot. Then he and his "caddie" walked into the crowd. Susan took Pryor's coat from me and whispered, "Who's Mr. Personality and the Big Shot?"

"The Big Shot is Fred Pryor, the guy Tommy Lee and I met at Broad Creek. Mr. Personality is his foreman. He's helping his boss keep faces and names together. I'd just as soon he forget mine."

Susan and I stood at the doorway where we could be of assistance in case someone needed a restroom. Uncle Wayne stayed close to the young mother. She sat in her chair blankly staring ahead. People made short statements of condolence and then moved on to small circles of conversation.

Fred Pryor spent about ten minutes making small talk with folks he recognized from the construction site, but whose jobs kept them nameless. As I expected, Taylor positioned himself beside Pryor and cued each first name so that the boss could say hello and agree how terrible a tragedy it was and what good friends they were to come.

Then I saw Pryor look around the room and decide it was time for him to get to the purpose of his visit. He cleared his throat just loud enough to halt conversation around him. The silence rippled through the room as he walked over to the Colemans. He pulled a brown envelope from his inside pocket and handed it to Luke.

"We hope this can help in your hour of need."

Everyone watched intently, recognizing the standard pay envelope of Ridgemont Power and Electric. Luke opened the unsealed flap. He studied the enclosure without removing it, and then passed it to his wife. "Thank you, Mr. Pryor," he muttered, never lifting his eyes.

Harriet removed the check and held it between her splintered fingernails. She looked over its edge to the body of her son. Tears flushed her eyes and the check shook uncontrollably.

"A hundred dollars. A hundred dollars for the life of my Jimmy." Her face twisted, and the check fluttered to the floor.

The color rose in Fred Pryor's cheeks. Those were not the words of gratitude he expected. The woman had humiliated him. I knew he wanted to snatch up the check and storm out.

"It's an hour of need. Need and understanding," said Wayne. "We thank you for your thoughtfulness, Mr. Pryor." My uncle stood behind the sobbing woman and turned his gentle smile on the whole room, diffusing the tension. Wayne's sensitivity, like that of my father, was something you don't learn in embalming school. It was something I found difficult to express.

Fred Pryor pushed the bile back in his throat and managed to nod an acceptance of the compliment. Leroy Jackson knelt and picked up the check. As he raised it past Harriet Coleman, she reached out with the swiftness of a serpent, snared it from his hand and clutched it to her breast.

I felt a body bump against me, and I slid aside as Fats McCauley squeezed between me and the doorjamb. He made no apology as he stood staring into the room, his heavy face moving side to side as he searched for someone.

"Brenda," he said. "I want to tell the mother about my Brenda."

Only the rustle of clothing broke the silence as people turned to see who had spoken. Odell Taylor stepped forward as if challenging Fats to intrude farther.

A hand grabbed Fats firmly by the shoulder and pulled him back into the foyer. With strength beyond his physical appearance, Reverend Pace spun the obese man around.

"Not tonight, Travis." Pace put his face only inches away from the other man. "This is not the time. Right now we have to take care of the living." Pace looked at Susan and me. "Would you take him home?"

We got Fats' raincoat from the closet. He draped it over his shoulders like a cape and followed us out the rear of the funeral home and into the steady drizzle. We drove to his furniture store in the old section of Main Street. Gainesboro's small downtown had not yet been totally cannibalized by the shopping malls, but on this rainy Sunday night we encountered no one. The silence of the ghost town was invaded only by the whoosh of my tires on the wet pavement and the steady slap of the windshield wipers.

We stopped in front of the brick two-story building with "McCauley's Furniture" scripted across the plate glass window.

"We still live upstairs," he said softly. "Thank you."

He wedged himself out the curb-side door, and then he crossed in front of my headlights. I rolled down the window, wondering if he had left something at the funeral home.

"Can we talk tomorrow?" he whispered. He glanced over at Susan and spoke even softer. "Private?"

"Sure," I said. "I'll come by."

He reached in with a damp hand and gently patted my bandaged shoulder. Then he turned and lumbered into the store like a black bear retreating to his den.

"What was that all about?" asked Susan.

"I don't know."

"Something's hurting him. Who's Brenda?"

"His daughter," I said. "She died a long time ago, but she still haunts him."

Chapter 6

On Monday the hunt for Dallas Willard was smaller in scale since most of the weekend volunteers held regular jobs and Tommy Lee had limited manpower. I planned to drop by the Sheriff's Department early and lend a hand in whatever way I could. I hoped that Reverend Pace and I would be paired together again. With the odds growing that we might be looking for Dallas' body, I preferred someone whose exuberance for the chase was not quite as overt as that displayed by Deputy Reece Hutchins. I'm sure Reece made a fine law officer, but most of my conversations with him during our search had revolved around his fantasies of how he would react to an ambush. Maybe he was just steadying his nerves, but he got on mine.

I was also unsettled by Fats' request to speak with me. Something was bothering him, and for some reason he wasn't comfortable discussing it in front of Susan. It could have merely been his old-school notion that there are some topics men should only talk about with other men. He certainly had seemed shocked by the idea of Reverend Pace having a female colleague. I suspected the terrible tragedy of little Jimmy Coleman's death lay beneath Fats' anxiety, and I decided I should see him before meeting Tommy Lee.

I had been six when Brenda McCauley was murdered. We had been in first grade together. A handyman who did odd jobs for Fats lured the trusting little girl into his car. Her body was found in a drainage ditch three days later. The killing cut our community to the quick. My classmates and I were sheltered from the grisly details, and only when I was much older did I learn she had been sodomized. The murderer died a week later in a shootout with police in north Georgia.

Losing a classmate when you're six makes a lasting impact. I couldn't see Fats without thinking of the lively red-haired girl who had once sat in the desk beside me. If I still felt some pain, what pain must Fats McCauley have had to endure every day of his life? Surely it was unbearable. Fats' wife left him on the first anniversary of their daughter's death, unable to separate her husband from the anguish of their loss. I thought about my father and his fading memory and thought at times it could be a blessing.

At ten till eight, most of the Main Street stores were still closed. Of course, P's Barbershop bustled with the usual crowd of Monday morning gossips who clustered around the central kerosene heater, drinking coffee, watching haircuts, and telling tall tales. It was the place to learn who did what to whom over the weekend.

McCauley's Furniture was three stores down from the barbershop. I parked at the curb and peered into the dim store front, but I couldn't see any activity. The "Drink Sundrop" open-for-business sign taped inside the front door announced Monday—Friday: eight-thirty to five. I guessed Fats would be up by now since the store should open in less than an hour.

I jiggled the door latch and wasn't surprised to find it locked. I banged on the window glass, but the anemic rattle did not sound as if it could be heard beyond the love seats and winged-back chairs visible in the morning sunlight.

I noticed no cars were parked at the curb. Fats' vehicle must have been kept in the rear alley. I cut through the walkway between McCauley's Furniture and Larson's Discount Drugs, dodging the boxes of trash set out by the druggist for Monday pickup. The furniture store had no exit along the side. At the rear, an old silver Buick sat snug against Fats' loading dock door. On the far side was a service entrance with an electric buzzer to signal a delivery. I had expected that. I didn't expect the broken windowpane above the doorknob. The sight of the jagged daggers of glass snapped me fully alert like no cup of coffee ever could.

I carefully reached for the inside latch, and swung the door open with my knee, leaving my good arm free should the intruder be waiting in the shadows. A floorboard creaked as I stepped across the threshold. It was the only sound other than my own breathing. I waited for my eyes to adjust. In the gloom, a packing crate became visible in the corner by the stairway to the second floor. Its lid had been pried off for a preliminary inspection of its contents. A crowbar dangled from the splintered edge where the nails had been ripped from the wood. I grabbed the flat end and balanced the cool iron in my hand. A swift swing would turn it into a lethal weapon, capable of breaking an arm or skull.

From the rear of the store, I could clearly see the silhouettes of furniture cluttered against the daylight of the front windows. The cash register at the counter appeared undisturbed. Perhaps the burglar, if he had indeed gotten inside, had fled before getting a chance to rifle the cash drawer. I decided to announce my presence in case an alarmed Fats McCauley was upstairs loading a shotgun.

"Mr. McCauley! Mr. McCauley, it's Barry Clayton." I kept the crowbar by my side and climbed the stairs, calling out with every step. I pushed open the door to the apartment and heard the sound of running water. Then I felt the wetness soak through my shoes. I crossed the small living room toward the hallway. My footsteps squished in the puddles that collected in the depressions of the hardwood floor. I found a wall switch and the overhead light illuminated the short corridor. Water flowed under the door at the end of the hall, its pink tinge offering an ominous explanation of why no one answered.

I slowly pushed the door open. In the dim light, I saw a shapeless mass quivering above the porcelain rim of the tub. I needed a few seconds to comprehend that I was staring at what once had been a human being.

The remains of Fats' head lay against the spigot, bobbing in its generated turbulence and floating just above the surface, while the rest of his body filled the tub. His flaccid mass was not round but layered in folds where the fat creased back on itself. The buoyant flesh rippled in macabre vibrations as the water swirled around the corpse and flowed over the tub's edge onto the floor.

"Oh, hell," I muttered. I saw the thick splotches of blood, hair, flesh, and brains splattered against the tile wall from the soap dish to the ceiling. A single discharged shotgun shell lay in the dry wash basin to my right. It was a number one buck Remington twelve gauge, the same kind of shell I saw ricochet off Martha Willard's casket.

"Don't disturb anything," ordered Tommy Lee. "I'll be right there."

I started to remind him I had worked in a police department, but I decided I'd probably say the same thing to anyone standing smack in the middle of a murder scene. I set the phone receiver back on the cradle, careful to hold it where I would not smudge any prints. There was nothing I could do for Fats. I took the few remaining minutes before the coming onslaught of law enforcement officials and media hounds to indulge my old police curiosity about the crime scene.

The writing desk in his bedroom was tidy. I had used the black rotary-dial phone I found squared in the back right corner. The goose-necked lamp was on the left. A plain white message pad lay in the center of the desk. Several sheets had been torn off leaving a red-gummed rim of adhesive binding sticking a quarter inch above the top sheet. Nothing was written on the pad, although I noticed an imprint from the previous notation—"Barry Clayton weather."

Just to the side of the desk was a wire-mesh waste basket, its bottom covered with wadded note sheets. I wondered if the one bearing my name was among them. On the floor next to the waste basket lay a retractable ballpoint pen with "McCauley's Furniture" gilded on the blue plastic barrel. The tip was clicked in position for writing.

Everything else in the sparsely furnished room seemed in order. The clothes I had seen Fats wearing yesterday were piled in the desk chair. The single bed was made, but the spread had been neatly folded back from the pillow. A closed black Bible rested on the crisp white pillowcase.

I returned to the hall and opened the door across from Fats' bedroom. Inside, it was as dark as if night had suddenly fallen on that half of the apartment. I fumbled along the wall until I found the face plate through my handkerchief. I flipped up the stubby switch.

In the light, I found myself staring nearly twenty-five years into the past. Against the far wall was a single bed covered with a faded peach spread. The oversized white pillow provided support for a collection of cherished stuffed animals: a teddy bear, a purple frog, a Raggedy Ann and Raggedy Andy. Stacked on the nightstand were *My First Speller* and *My First Math*, school books that had never been returned. Everything was waiting for the touch of a little hand that would never come. Fats had turned the room into a shrine.

"This changes everything." Tommy Lee slowly twirled the silver pen in his hand. Around it rotated the discharged shotgun shell he had carefully lifted from the sink. The two of us stood in the bathroom, momentarily oblivious to the floating corpse behind us. We stared at the evidence both of us saw linking Dallas Willard to another murder.

"I've got my search teams spread out through the hills, and he walks into town and shoots an innocent man in the bathtub."

"What's the motive?" I asked.

"I'll be damned if I can see it. Maybe there isn't one. Maybe he's just nuts. Maybe this didn't come from Dallas' shotgun and I'm the one who's nuts. Or simply the last to learn that Remington number one buckshot is the new weapon of choice. Well, I'll run down Main Street wearing only my holster if the firing pin mark on this shell doesn't match those from the cemetery." He slipped the shell into a plastic evidence sleeve. "If it's Dallas, and if there is no logical motive, then every citizen in this county is a potential victim."

"Let me show you something else," I said. I took Tommy Lee into Fats' bedroom and pointed to the notepad on the desk. "Looks like Fats or somebody wrote down my name and the word weather. Maybe the sheet is in the trash."

"Weather?"

"It was raining last night. Could be two separate thoughts."

"The state mobile crime lab is on the way. I want them going over the apartment before we remove the body. I'll tell them to look out for anything that might have come off this pad. No way to know if he wrote it last night or last week."

"Last night he asked to speak to me. Maybe I was on today's to-do list."

"Speak to you about what?" asked Tommy Lee.

"I don't know. He was upset by the death of that little boy. Just look in his daughter's room if you want a glimpse of Fats' private hell."

"Listen, Barry. I want you to watch your back. Dallas tried to kill you once. He may now have your name in the same pocket as his shotgun shells. Motive or not, he has moved beyond killing his immediate family."

"And there has got to be a connection," I said. "It must be about the land. Was Fats trying to buy it from Dallas' brother and sister?"

"Fats never went out of town. You think he could tote his bulk up and down the side of a mountain?"

"I meant as an investment."

"Hell, Barry, to be honest I haven't had two minutes to worry about the land."

"Then no one talked to Linda Trine?" I asked. "Remember Alex Soles told me she observed Dallas ranting at the migrant workers."

The sheriff shook his head. "One of those meant-to-do things. Since we knew Dallas pulled the trigger, I didn't waste time trying to build a case against him when the priority was to bring him in. Want to do us both a favor?"

"Sure."

"Go see Linda Trine for me. And see if she knows anything about this." He pulled a folded sheet of common white typing paper out of his chest pocket and smoothed the creases until it lay flat on the desk. An oval had been sketched with what looked like three bands drawn across it. A lopsided sandwich. The top layer was labeled L.W. and bottom layer, N.J. The initials F.W. were imprinted on the middle one. Martha Willard's signature was in the upper right-hand corner of the page, and beneath it was the date April 25th.

"Here is a photocopy of what I found on Dallas' kitchen table when I searched the cabin after the shooting. I figure this is a map. If all the Willard property is deeded in Martha's name, then this may be how she wanted it portioned up. N.J. is Norma Jean, and L.W. is Lee Willard. F.W. must be some other relative, meaning Dallas Willard got shut out completely. Must have driven him over the edge and he killed the other two."

"Then why wasn't he mad at his grandmother?" I asked. "She drew up the map, but Dallas made it a point for me to tell her he loved her when I met up with her in heaven. That's the reason he shot me."

"Yeah," said Tommy Lee. "I couldn't quite square that part either. Thought maybe you'd have some ideas."

I examined the sheet of paper. It didn't look like a legal document, more an illustration of intentions. The April date corresponded to the time Norma Jean had prepaid Martha's funeral. It was logical that if Norma Jean and Martha were making final burial arrangements, they would also update or complete a will. Perhaps all the grandchildren had received such a drawing, and somewhere an attorney would have the proper documents to turn this sketch into a surveyed and registered inheritance.

Why was Dallas excluded? And who was F.W.? Then the answer came to me. "This is Dallas," I said, pointing to the middle layer. "Remember I told you Grandma Martha had started calling him Francis."

"Oh, yeah, Saint Francis of Assisi because he talked to the animals." He shook his head. "What a family. How could she possibly be considered to be of sound mind and then will part of her land to Saint Francis?"

"Norma Jean probably went to the attorney with her. It's not considered irrational to bequeath your estate to your nearest of kin. I'm sure the official paperwork does not include the name Francis."

"Well, knowing the Willard property like I do," said Tommy Lee, "it makes sense. That center section is the highest ground, and it's the prettiest. Couple of bold streams flow off of it. I could see Dallas moving up there."

"Nobody lives on this property now?" I asked.

"You know mountaineers own land they set aside for hunting," he explained. "They settled in the valleys and surrounded themselves with ample forest for both privacy and game. It's only in the last fifteen years that developers have eyed these ridges as prized real estate. I'd say Martha Willard was just stubborn enough to hold onto her tract."

"But the grandchildren may have seen it differently," I said. "That's cause enough for a feud."

"Yep. Look into it while I try to make some sense of the madness here."

"Can I take this?" I asked, reaching for the map.

"It's yours. The original is in the case file and this copy sure as hell ain't doing me any good stuck in my pocket."

Chapter 7

Linda Trine's office was located in the limbo land between Gainesboro's commercial district and the more popular Sky High Mall several miles out at the interstate where the incoming tourists first exited. The stretch of highway included light industrial offices, fast-food franchises, and an assortment of gasoline and convenience stations.

The Appalachian Relief Center was not a center at all, but rather a loose network of charity organizations with the common purpose of serving mountain families in need. A.R.C. offices were scattered throughout the mountain cities of the Carolinas, Tennessee, Virginia, West Virginia, and Kentucky. Linda Trine had taken what twenty-five years ago had been her church social service committee and through hard work and unwavering dedication unified relief efforts into a nationally recognized operation. She accomplished all of it without creating proliferating bureaucracy and escalating overhead.

A.R.C. shared a metal warehouse building with a dog-grooming business. I drove past the first entrance. It led into the front lot where women parked their cars and carried their precious canines in for the absurd beautifications performed by the Purple Velvet Poodle Parlor. The second drive looped around the backside of the building to the offices and warehouse that dispensed food, blankets, and clothing to a segment of humanity upon which life had lavished only hard times.

The waiting room was furnished in the ever popular curbside-recyclable motif consisting of a lumpy sofa, three straight-backed chairs, and a recliner permanently jammed in the extended position. The furniture was peopled with two lean-faced women, four shaggy children, and a grizzled man, aged somewhere between fifty and seventy, who sat beneath the THANK YOU FOR NOT SMOKING poster, a cigarette dangling between his lips. They all waited in impoverished silence.

I walked over to the receptionist who, giving me little more than a cursory glance at the hand protruding from my stomach, shoved a form across the counter, turned back to her filing and said, "Fill it out and report the date of your last visit if known."

"Sorry," I said, "I'm Barry Clayton, and I'm here to speak to Linda Trine about Dallas Willard."

The woman gave me her full attention. Everyone knew about Dallas Willard.

"Mr. Clayton?" She questioned if she had repeated my name correctly. I nodded reassurance. "Let me ring her for you." After a brief word on the phone, she directed me to the back door. The hallway beyond fed four small offices before flowing out into the storage warehouse.

Linda Trine stuck her beaming face out of the last door on the left. "Barry, I heard you were in season. Remind me never to stand beside you at a funeral." She ushered me into her office, picked up a stack of files from the seat of a chair, dumped them on the floor, and bade me sit down. Organized chaos surrounded us. In addition to the piles of paper on the floor and desk, the walls were adorned with Post-It notes proclaiming a variety of names, dates, and phone numbers.

Linda pulled a wooden swivel chair from behind the desk so that she wouldn't have to stare over the mountainous mess. She was what folks in the country call a big-boned, healthy gal, probably pushing six feet in height and sixty years in age. We crossed paths occasionally if I was conducting a

funeral for one of her clients. She was always good to attend
and be of comfort to the family. Linda sported a no-nonsense
attitude, and I knew whatever I asked her, she would give me
a straight answer. In keeping with that trait, her welcoming
humor vanished and her brow furrowed with undiluted concern.

"How can I help?" she asked, getting straight to the
purpose of my visit.

"Dallas Willard," I said. "This hasn't been made public
yet, but it looks like he killed Fats McCauley last night."

"Good God," she exclaimed. "You sure?"

"Evidence needs to be checked, but I'd say the odds are
Dallas walked into town and killed Fats in his apartment.
We have no idea why."

"Have you talked to Alex Soles?"

"He said you told him Dallas acted strangely."

"Did he say I thought Dallas needed help?"

"Yes. Alex came to me in the hospital tremendously upset
that he hadn't followed up on your request."

"He never saw Dallas? I can't believe it. I was very specific
about it." Her amazement turned to visible anger.

"What made you speak to Alex?" I asked.

"I've known Dallas since he was four. He's always been
shy and reserved. Everyone knew he wasn't quite normal,
but he'd never been violent. So, it was completely out of
character when Miguel Rodriguez complained about him."

"Who's Miguel Rodriguez?"

"Oversees the migrant camps. He's an investigator for the
wage and hour division of the U.S. Department of Labor.
Compliance officer is the old term. He works with migrant
farm laborers from Florida to Virginia. He makes inspections
throughout the growing season, not only regarding wage
payments but also living conditions."

"How'd Rodriguez cross paths with Dallas?"

"It seems a few months ago Dallas verbally harassed a bus
load of workers unloading at the Bennetts Creek camp that
borders the Willard property. Stood off on the side of the road

shouting for their destruction. 'Set one foot on my land and God Almighty will consume you with hellfire.' Miguel said it was stuff like that. Most of the workers are Hispanic and speak little English, but it still unnerved them to see Dallas ranting and raving. Miguel was there that day."

"Did he talk to Dallas?" I asked.

"He tried, but Dallas turned his epithets on Miguel, then drove off in his pickup. I swung by the next afternoon when the bus brought the workers from the fields. Dallas was standing by the road, like a prophet out of the wilderness, yelling as they got off and went to their shanties."

"Did you talk to him?"

"Just for a few minutes. He knew me well enough to calm down. Told me they were plotting to take his land and that he would die first. I tried to get through to him that these were simple people with no power to do anything. He just looked at me for a few seconds, then he whispered more to himself than to me, 'Yes, the power controls them and they don't know it.' With that cryptic pronouncement, he left. Barry, Dallas seemed psychotic, and that was my big concern. I telephoned Alex Soles. He said Dallas wasn't his patient, but that he was part of an Alzheimer's support group. Alex said he would speak with him."

"Well, that explains why Alex was so upset when he saw me at the hospital."

"And since Dallas never came back to the camps, I thought everything was under control."

"Why would he think the migrants wanted his land?" I asked.

"Because there is a proposal to build a central migrant facility. It grew out of a government study that concluded better care and living conditions could be provided if everything in the county were consolidated at one location. Dallas must have gotten wind of it and thought they wanted the family property. Maybe he was actually approached, or he heard some of the farmers discussing it. That's all I know,

Barry, and I've only learned that since I spoke to Dallas. It still doesn't explain why he'd murder his own family, or why he tried to kill you."

I pulled the map from my pocket. "Did he show you this? It's a rough drawing of how Martha Willard's property could be divided."

Linda studied it for a few seconds, and then shook her head. "Have you talked to Carl Romeo?"

"No. How is he involved?" The Gainesboro attorney had drawn up my parents' wills.

"Evidently he handled Martha Willard's estate. Dallas said he'd take Carl a paper to stop them."

"This paper?"

"I don't know. Maybe you ought to drop by and see him."

As soon as I got in my Jeep, I called the law office of Carl Romeo and was told Mr. Romeo was just on his way to a luncheon meeting.

"This is Barry Clayton," I said. "I need to speak to him for one minute."

After a few seconds of silence, Carl's voice broke through. "My God, Barry, how are you?"

"All things considered, I'm fine. But I need to talk to you. When are you out of your luncheon meeting?"

"What luncheon meeting?" he said, and then he laughed. "That was just Ruth making sure I get lunch. Plus she wants my clients to think I'm always headed for some power rendezvous. I was running a few errands and grabbing a bite at a drive-through."

"Sit tight and I'll bring lunch to you. My treat. You can have anything on the Cardinal Cafe menu."

Sitting at his conference table, I wondered if Carl Romeo and Linda Trine had taken the same office organization seminar. File folders had to be swept to either side to clear a spot for our roast beef sandwiches and onion rings. Carl declined the jumbo root beer I brought him and retrieved a low-cal soda from the mini-refrigerator in the corner.

"The wife's got me on a diet," he remarked, just before popping an onion ring in his mouth and licking the grease traces off his fingers. It crossed his mind that I no longer had a wife to worry about my waistline, and he asked, "You got someone to help you, Barry? Must be a bitch tying your shoes with one hand."

"The secret is to never take them off."

He laughed. "And I thought it was the food that smelled funny."

Carl was first-generation local. For a lawyer that was a good status to claim. It meant your family hadn't been around long enough for you to know everybody's business, but you had grown up under the eyes of the old-timers. You weren't an outsider, or worse, a freshly transplanted Yankee. Carl's dad had been a doctor who moved down from New Jersey, setting up practice immediately out of residency. When your name ends in a vowel, you're a Yankee: if you're also one of ten Catholics in the county, you stick out. Getting established forty years ago had been tough, but Doc Romeo pulled enough emergency room duty and helped enough hurting folks who didn't care where he moved from or what he believed in as long as he could ease their pain, that local folks were soon eager to pass the word that he was just as good as a normal person.

Carl was several years older than me, falling on the plus or minus side of forty. He had a high forehead accentuated by an ever-receding hairline. Round, gold-framed glasses perched halfway down his nose, and he was perpetually rubbing his hand across a brown mustache that was not only salted with gray but now liberally peppered with crumbs of fried onion rings. The extra chin spreading over the knot in his tie had probably prompted his wife's dietary demands.

He had the reputation for being a crackerjack attorney. If I knew only one thing, it was that the Willard family had done well to enlist his aid.

Carl swallowed the last morsel of sandwich and swept the wrappings into a wastebasket. He completed my one-armed efforts to clean my own mess, and then sat back down and leaned across the table. "Now, Barry, what specifically can I do for you?"

"First, I need to tell you some bad news."

He sat up straight, backing away as if what I was about to say could physically touch him.

"What? Has Dallas been killed?"

"No. I gather you've been in the office all morning because I'm sure it's public knowledge by now. Last night Fats McCauley was killed in his apartment by a shotgun. Dallas Willard is the prime suspect."

"Fats McCauley?" He sighed. "What has gotten into that boy?"

"I'm hoping you can tell me. I'm trying to help run down some loose ends for Sheriff Tommy Lee Wadkins, and as you can guess, I've got a personal interest. I understand you're handling the Willard estate."

He shook his head as if I had just asked him to fix the national debt.

"I wish I'd never heard the name Willard."

"Why's that?"

"Because they've been nothing but trouble."

"Was it just bad luck they came to you?" I asked.

The length of Carl's silence told me the Willards had been more than walk-in clientele. It must be genetic that people who become lawyers cannot begin a conversation without weighing the implications of every word. When at last he reached some comfort with how to proceed, he cleared his throat and spoke in a tone that made me feel like I was taking his deposition.

"First of all, let me state that to the best of my knowledge everything regarding the Willards that I've seen has been handled on the up and up. I say that because some of the procedures may seem a little complex, but each requested action was well within the law.

"About ten years ago, a client came to me and asked for a favor. Over the years he had provided me with a hefty sum of legal fees, so, naturally I lent a receptive ear. His proposition concerned the Willard property. He was interested in acquiring it, but smart enough to know you didn't just walk in on Martha Willard and make her an offer. Selling family land would be traumatic. After all, what would all the dead ancestors think? And land values had skyrocketed during Martha's lifetime. The capital gains tax would be obscene. Martha would sooner give money to the devil than to the IRS.

"My client figured a way around these obstacles, and he wanted me to start the ball rolling by approaching Pastor Stinnett."

"Martha's preacher?" I interrupted. "You were going to get him to make Martha sell her land?"

Carl broke out in one of those "you're-going-to-love-this" grins. "He was going to get Martha to give away the land. She would gift the land to Crab Apple Valley Baptist Church. I would be responsible for setting up a trust, a charitable remainder trust to be exact. The charitable trust would receive the property, sell it avoiding the taxes, and then begin legally paying Martha an income based on the interest earnings of the trust. She could start reaping cash from an asset that was currently providing nothing.

"But what my client thought would really capture Martha's support was the creation of the trust itself, The Martha Willard Trust, because when she died, all the money left in it would revert to the church."

"How much?" I asked.

"Three hundred thousand back then. Enough to get Preacher Stinnett's attention. That's a hell of a lot of collection plates."

"That's fine for him," I said, "but wasn't Martha cheating her heirs?"

"Her son Robbie had died, and the three grandchildren, Norma Jean, Lee, and Dallas, were the only immediate family. At that time Martha was a spry sixty and never sick a day in her life. Her Alzheimer's had not yet materialized. That's where Archie Donovan came into the picture."

"The insurance agent?"

"Yes, we had figured in a premium that Martha would pay out of her new income. It would purchase a three hundred thousand dollar policy on her life with the grandchildren as beneficiaries. That would repay them the money that went to the church. Everybody wins but the IRS."

"Obviously something went wrong. Was it just too complicated for everyone to understand?"

"No, I went to see Preacher Stinnett and he jumped on the idea like a robin on a junebug. He took me with him to see Martha right away, and he suggested I let him do the talking." Carl shook his head and laughed as he recalled the meeting. "Preacher Stinnett was amazing. He presented it as if it were his idea. No, it was more of a dream he had. While he slept, God spoke to him saying that the church would always be freshly painted, that the cemetery would overflow with flowers, that the ladies' quilting circle of which Martha was a life-long member would never want for supplies. Preacher Stinnett said he asked, 'How can this be, Lord? We are a congregation rich in faith but poor in worldly goods.' And the Lord spoke majestically the words, 'My beloved servant Martha Willard can provide.' And then Stinnett said there appeared a sheaf of papers on which was written the name Carl Romeo. 'So, I sought him out and discovered he was a wise attorney and a God-fearing man who knew the Lord's will. He has shown me how those who sow unto God will themselves reap abundantly.' The preacher turned to me, and I realized that was my introduction."

"Laid it on kind of thick, didn't he," I said.

"I must have looked like a fool, sitting there in a doily-covered armchair with my mouth hanging open. 'Go ahead, Mr. Romeo,' he prompted. 'Show her the diagrams, especially the one that gives the money to the Lord instead of the tax man.'

"I managed to compose myself and drew a simple flow chart of how things would work. Martha followed pretty well and seemed genuinely interested. She asked a few questions, mainly about the insurance and could her own doctor perform the required physical. Then she announced she would pray about it and then have us return for a family meeting."

"With her and her grandchildren?"

"Yes, I got the feeling if they had no serious objections Martha would fulfill Preacher Stinnett's prophecy. A week later I was back in her small living room with my charts. Norma Jean and Lee were all for it. They had no attachment to the land, and they liked the idea that Martha had more money coming in. I'm sure their tax-free three hundred thousand dollar inheritance didn't hurt either."

"Dallas was different," I said.

"Dallas fell apart. It was awful. At first he got angry. Then he started crying. Wailing is more like it. He and his father had hunted on that land, and his dad had promised some day the ridge would be his. At sixteen, he was the youngest. His father died when he was fourteen. The mother had died when Dallas was only seven, leaving him to the maternal care of Grandma Martha. He was the baby of the family by more than five years and still held that place in his grandmother's heart.

"Well, his pathetic reaction turned Martha's mind against the plan. She wouldn't contradict Dallas' wishes. The others wanted her to give two-thirds of the land, carving out the section Dallas wanted. Preacher Stinnett looked at me, but I shook my head no. My client would not agree to buy property with the center gutted out of it. I rolled up my papers and left the room. There was nothing I could do, and frankly, the tension between Dallas and his brother and sister bordered on open confrontation. Perhaps the seeds of murder were sown that day."

"Perhaps," I agreed. I also recalled Preacher Stinnett's glare of disapproval when Dallas arrived at the graveside. He knew because of Dallas he was also burying three hundred thousand. "But you've seen the family since then?"

"Yes. About six months ago, Norma Jean brought Martha in to have her will drawn. Her general health was failing rapidly, but although her Alzheimer's was beginning to make an impact, Martha remembered me and said she knew I had only been trying to help. Norma Jean said her grandmother wanted the land to come to them intact, with equal ownership of the whole parcel."

"Not carving it up," I said. "Giving Dallas the ridge section."

"No, Norma Jean was very specific on that point."

I handed him the map from Dallas Willard's cabin. "Not like this?" I asked.

"No," said Carl. "You know Ruth said Dallas brought something like this by the office the day after Martha died. I was out of town. She told him it was not the way the estate would be settled, that Martha had directed that the land be held in common and that all the paperwork had been legally executed."

"So, what if someone wanted to buy the whole parcel and Dallas still didn't want to sell?"

"Simple majority vote of the owners."

"Did Dallas know that?"

"I assumed he did. But, given what happened the last time they tried to sell, his brother and sister could have intentionally kept him in the dark until Martha died."

"And then voted two to one against him. I understand both the power company and a migrant project are interested in the property, and it's probably worth more than three hundred thousand today."

"I wouldn't want to speculate," said Carl. "But you're right about the vote, although this document may have given Dallas a case."

I patted my bandaged shoulder. "Carl, I think it's safe to say he settled out of court."

Chapter 8

I traveled several miles outside of town and up from the valley floor to meet Tommy Lee at a local dive called Clyde's Roadside. Normally a five-minute trip, the drive took twenty because autumn tourists were as thick on the roads as—I could just hear my grandmother's voice—"ugly on a hog." She had said it in such a variety of contexts that it became a family expression for unwanted abundance.

The spectacular foliage of October kept a large number of Florida retirees in the western North Carolina mountains in unwanted abundance. And even a backwoods route did not avoid the perpetual parade of Cadillacs, Lincolns, and Buicks that crept along the winding two-lane blacktop, slowing at every break in the trees in hopes of a glimpse of some yet undiscovered panorama. My Jeep Cherokee wove through the maze as fast as the serpentine road would allow me to pass.

"Hello, sir, my name is Lindsay and did you see our specials board?" were words I would not hear inside the putrid green cinder block building of Clyde's Roadside. On the other hand, the Floridian drivers would definitely not be slowing down or stopping for this local color. At Clyde's the vehicle of choice, the pickup truck, outnumbered the cars two to one. I counted eight trucks, four cars, no out-of-state license plates, and no empty parking spaces in front.

I pulled around to the side. The site for Clyde's Roadside had been gouged out of the mountain, and a wall of dirt rose more than twenty feet above the parking lot. Naked ends of roots dangled where they had been mutilated and exposed by an earthmover's blade. Overhead, several pines at the edge of the man-made cliff leaned like green Towers of Pisa, waiting only for a windy push to topple them. Tommy Lee was parked in the V of double-stacked railroad ties which served as a make-shift dam against the torrents of water that would cascade down the slope during a heavy rain. I parked alongside him.

"Does this qualify as a rendezvous rather than a meeting?" I asked.

"My office is crawling with press. Hide at Clyde's is our safest bet if we want to talk undisturbed."

As we walked around the windowless exterior, I heard the bass notes of "Stand By Your Man" vibrate through the walls.

"At least they've got good music," I said.

"There are four copies of that song on the jukebox because they keep wearing out."

"They ought to get it on CD."

"Those are CDs," he said, and pushed the door open.

I was immediately hit by the smell of beer and peanuts.

"After you," he said.

As I suspected, someone named Lindsay was not there to ask if we preferred non-smoking. Instead, a soft gray haze flattened into a single layer and hung just below the rough-hewn ceiling planks. Neon American beer signs glowed beneath it. I would not be ordering a Newcastle Brown. As my eyes adjusted to the dimness, I spied the centerpiece behind the bar—a double-barrel shotgun which made Tommy Lee's brand of law enforcement unnecessary except for those occasional arguments which might spill out into the parking lot.

The patrons mostly drew from construction workers end-ing the day with a couple of brews, the unemployed who could afford Clyde's posted no-credit policy, and those mountain folk who tired of drinking corn liquor alone. About half the tables were filled, not with individuals, but with clusters of drinkers laughing or arguing to pass the time between swallows.

A distinct drop in the level of conversation started at the tables closest to the door and swept back across the room. Tammy Wynette's voice seemed to swell louder as the competition faded. Heads turned to the door to see what intrusion had broken the afternoon rituals. Tommy Lee just smiled and nodded his head with an unspoken "Howdy, boys." He walked over to the bar and ordered a draft of Bud for me and a Diet Coke for himself.

"Guess this means you're on duty, Sheriff," said the skinny, gray-bearded barkeeper. He slid a dirt-spotted mug of foam across the chipped Formica surface to me and an unopened aluminum can to Tommy Lee.

"Just visiting, Clyde, if that's what you mean." He popped the top, took a deep pull on the soda and turned around to survey the crowd. "We'll start a tab and camp at a back table if that's all right with you."

"Sure. Take the one under the ugly guy in the corner."

As we crunched across discarded peanut shells, the men returned to their conversations. A few said hello, and one guy with a smile sporting broken and missing teeth that looked like the keys of a basement piano loudly asked for Tommy Lee's autograph. We knew why when we saw the election poster hanging over the table Clyde so graciously offered.

"At least they didn't deface it," I said.

"Probably afraid they'd improve my looks."

We sat down. Tommy Lee grabbed a handful of peanuts from the bucket on the table, crushed them in his fist, and started sorting through the hulls.

"What did you find out?" he asked.

I gave him my report on Linda Trine and Carl Romeo.

"Sounds like the motive is pretty clear," said Tommy Lee. "When Grandma Willard died, Dallas found out Norma Jean and Lee planned to cheat him out of his inheritance."

"Cheat him out of the land," I said. "He'd get his share of the money."

"Money doesn't mean squat to Dallas. You don't have to be crazy to want revenge when the thing you love most is being stolen from you."

"You think Dallas is sane?" I asked.

"No, I didn't say that. I think the boy has mental problems. Alex Soles says he's paranoid/schizophrenic. Little late with his diagnosis to do us any good. But just because Dallas was paranoid doesn't mean someone wasn't out to get him. And now he's lost all hope."

"What do you mean?"

"He can't inherit what he stands to gain through murder. His only motive was revenge—killing his brother and sister wouldn't get him the land."

"How do you know he knew that?" I asked. "He might be crazy enough not to understand the consequences of his actions and think he'll keep the property."

Tommy Lee stared at me for a few seconds. "You know, you just earned yourself another Bud. For that matter, who else stood to gain if Dallas killed his brother and sister?"

"Carl Romeo said Martha's grandchildren were the end of the line. He's going to do a check for any legal heirs the state would recognize, but the property will probably go to auction."

"A gift to the developers," growled Tommy Lee. "Unless Carl Romeo finds an heir." He thought for a second. "I wonder if that's an angle that ties Fats McCauley in somehow." He took the final swallow from his Coke can, but before he could say anything more, a noise invaded the bar like a hundred chain saws swirling around the building.

All other sounds stopped except for Tammy Wynette and the encircling roar from outside.

"Bikers," said Tommy Lee.

The throaty rumble told me the motorcycles were not luxurious Honda Gold Wings ridden by retired couples—

Cadillacs without doors. These had to be Harleys. In quick succession, four engines died.

The door to Clyde's Roadside swung inward, spilling the brilliance of the afternoon sun around the four silhouettes of the men who entered. The jangle of chains carried across the smoke-filled air. If I closed my eyes, it might have been the sound of spurs in a saloon. One of the men leaned over the bar and spoke to Clyde. The owner pointed at us.

"Oh, no," muttered Tommy Lee. He slid back slightly in his chair, ready to get to his feet.

I looked for a back door. There wasn't one. The largest of the bikers headed toward us with his comrades trailing behind. Men at other tables stared at us, knowing we were the gang's destination.

Sheriff Tommy Lee Wadkins smiled and spoke out of the corner of his mouth. "Cover me."

"Cover you?" My voice cracked through wilted vocal cords. "I'm a damn undertaker. The only thing I can cover you with is dirt."

They were close enough for me to hear the hobnails of their boots scraping across the floor's rough planks. The leader must have been somewhere between six and eight feet tall.

Tommy Lee whispered, "Then get ready to dig our way out of here."

The smell of the man's sweat reached us first. He stopped in front of Tommy Lee. The others fanned around us, sealing our corner table as tightly as a tomb. The quartet from hell sported heavy black leather jackets decorated with studs and chain links. The curly red-haired man closest to me had the tip of a letter B showing on his neck. I could guarantee the tattoo didn't say "Born to eat quiche."

"Saw your car, Sheriff. I've been looking for you. I hear you been spreading lies about me." The leader split his lips just enough to show he had fewer teeth than cards in a poker hand. His shoulder-length black hair was pulled back with a red bandanna, and a nut and bolt pierced his ear. Ugly on a hog took on a double meaning.

"What if I am? What are you going to do about it, Jack?"

I stared at Tommy Lee like he'd turned into a stranger. If he wanted to get the crap beat out of him, fine. I'd had my stay in the hospital this month. Let Tammy Wynette stand by him.

The man called Jack turned to me. A hollow whistle sounded as he sucked in air. "He a friend of yours?" he asked me.

"Look," I said. "I'm only an undertaker and I don't need any more business."

Big Jack looked at me for a second, and then started laughing. His cronies joined in. They stepped aside and let Clyde set a tray of six bottles of long-necked Bud on the table. Jack slapped me on the back. "That's a good one," he said, and then he shook Tommy Lee's hand. "I got the job, Sheriff. Maintenance foreman said you put in a good word."

"I know you can live up to it."

Each of the bikers grabbed a beer. Jack tipped it to Tommy Lee and then to the poster on the wall. "Thanks. Now how many times can we vote?"

Tommy Lee picked up a beer bottle and clinked it down the line. "Four. But only once each."

The bikers took their beers, their leather, their chains, and my fear to the next table.

"You bastard," I whispered.

"Me?" he laughed. "My opponent Bob Cain should have a friend like you. I thought you were going to pass out."

"Who is that guy?" I asked.

"Jack Andrews. I busted him a couple years ago for drug dealing. Small time. He pulled a light sentence and is on parole. Hell of a mechanic. I got him a job in Asheville working on police cars. Figure the more he's around cops, the more he'll like them. Maybe he'll stay straight. You do what you can." He looked at his watch. "Time to go off duty," he said, and took a swig of the Bud.

I pushed my empty mug aside and grabbed the remaining bottle. "You do what you can," I agreed, and clinked his beer.

"Well now. Isn't this a sight."

I looked up to see a beefy man standing at our table. He wore a blue nylon jacket, and his white hair was buzz-cut to within a quarter-inch of his scalp. The smirk on his face begged to be wiped off.

He raised his voice above the din. "I saw your car in the parking lot and thought maybe you were actually making an arrest. But, no, a killer is running rampant through the county and our sheriff sits boozing it up in a bar."

Again, the room fell silent. Even Tammy Wynette was between encores.

"Come on, Cain," said Tommy Lee. "Why don't you take your hot air someplace else? We're having a meeting."

Bob Cain. Now I recognized him from his campaign posters. He didn't look the same without an American flag behind him.

"Having a meeting? Looks to me like you're having a drink." He glanced around the bar, expecting someone to laugh. No one did.

"Have you met Barry Clayton?" asked Tommy Lee. "He's a former police officer from Charlotte, and he was shot by Dallas Willard. He's consulting with me because unlike you I don't claim to know it all."

Cain's face reddened. "You need more help than he can give you."

"You heard the sheriff. Park your lip someplace else." Jack Andrews slid back from his table and stared at Cain.

"Butt out," said Cain. "When I'm sheriff, you and your pals will have to find some other county to stink up."

Cain may have been a security consultant, but he certainly didn't seem to think much about his own. Out of the corner of my eye, I saw Tommy Lee tense. The way things were headed he was going to have to keep his opponent from getting his ass stomped.

"You hear that, boys," said Jack. "This gentleman thinks we stink." Jack stood up. Although Cain probably topped six-foot-two, the biker had a good three inches on him. "You know what I think?"

"Can you think?" asked Cain.

"Man, you got a mouth that just won't quit, don't you? I think when your momma was pregnant, a fart got in with the baby. The baby died and the fart lived. We do take baths, but you're gonna stink every day of your life."

The room erupted in laughter. Cain went from red to purple. His right fist came up from his side in a haymaker punch that caught Jack full force on the corner of his mouth. Jack's head barely moved under the blow, but a trickle of blood streamed down his chin. Cain froze, waiting for a response.

"I'd call that an assault, Sheriff," said Jack calmly. "Wouldn't you?"

"Yep, I would," replied Tommy Lee.

Before anyone could blink, Tommy Lee leaped from his chair and snapped a cuff on Cain's right wrist. The man turned to struggle, and Tommy Lee kicked him behind the knee, sending him face first into the peanut shells on the floor. The sheriff straddled his buttocks like Cain was a ride in the penny arcade, yanked Cain's left arm behind his back and cracked the other cuff across the left wrist. He grabbed the stainless steel bracelets and lifted Cain to his feet. He spun his hapless opponent around to face him. Ignoring the blood gushing from Cain's nose and mouth, Tommy Lee stared into his face. "You're under arrest."

For a few seconds, only the sound of a Nikon motor-drive could be heard. From a dark corner of the room, a young woman had stepped forward. She had a reporter's notepad tucked under her arm and a furiously flashing camera in her hands. Evidently, she'd been the one hiding in Clyde's the whole time.

"I'll read you your rights in the car," said Tommy Lee.

"You know you just got your department in one helluva law suit," said Cain. He turned his bloody face to the reporter's camera as it continued to snap off shots. "I'm suing for excessive use of force."

Tommy Lee shrugged off the threat. "You'll get your phone call and I'll ask Judge Wood to authorize releasing you on your own recognizance. I'm not making this personal, Cain. You'll get the same treatment as anybody else who breaks the law."

"You wouldn't know the law if it bit you in the ass."

Tommy Lee turned to Jack. "Thanks for taking the punch. I'll need a statement."

"You got it," said Jack. "I'll be down to press charges later. He's not worth interrupting my beer."

Tommy Lee pushed Cain ahead of him to the patrol car and locked him in the back seat. He picked up the mike and told the dispatcher he was bringing in a prisoner.

"Ten-four. And Sheriff, we've had a call about a poisoning," said the dispatcher.

"Didn't you call poison control?" He barked the question into the microphone.

"Negative. The victim is a horse."

"A what?"

"A horse. You know. Trigger. Hi, Ho, Silver."

"God-damn-it! I've got a killer on the loose and my political opponent in handcuffs. I'm not interested in a dead horse."

The radio went silent for a few seconds as if the dispatcher was trying to build up his courage before talking to his irate boss.

"Uh, the horse, sir, the horse isn't dead, yet."

"And," asked Tommy Lee, stretching the word into at least three syllables, "what? Would they like me to drop by and shoot it?"

"And the call came from Charlie Hartley. He was quite distraught. Pitiful actually. The vet told him he thought it was poison. Charlie insisted I let you know."

Tommy Lee sighed and the anger left him. He knew as well as I now did how important those horses were to the old man. "Okay," he said. "I'm sorry. See if you can get somebody up there."

"We're spread to the limit, Sheriff. It'll have to be early this evening when the new shift comes in."

I raised my hand and caught Tommy Lee's eye.

Chapter 9

The sun was dropping behind the ridge of Hope Quarry as I drove around Charlie's house to the barnyard. Parked beside the plow was a white pickup truck with *Blanchard Large Animal Vet* lettered on its side.

I wasn't sure what I was going to do or say in the barn. I wasn't sure why the hell I had volunteered to come up here. Because it was Charlie and I liked him. Because I liked Reverend Pace and the fact that he once buried an old man's dog. I might be at a loss for words, but I could be there.

Charlie Hartley leaned over the stall railing and watched the veterinarian examine Nell. I slipped quietly beside him.

"Tommy Lee sent me," I whispered.

"Thanks," he said and turned his concentration back to the suffering animal. He didn't seem to care that I didn't have a badge or a uniform.

Sporadic convulsions rippled across the mare's flank, and her nostrils flared with every breath. Charlie shuddered with each sign of the animal's agony. All I could do was reach my arm across the old man's shoulders and give a squeeze to say hang on.

Rich Blanchard tucked his stethoscope in his jacket pocket and shook his head. He gave his patient a gentle pat on the rump, then turned to us.

"I'm afraid the foal will be stillborn. We'll deal with induced labor later."

Charlie laid his face against the back of his hands and suppressed a sob. "And Nell?" he managed to ask.

"The next few hours are critical. I've given her a heavy dose of mineral oil and an injection of a general antitoxin. I'm also flying a blood sample to the Veterinary Research Lab at NC State. In the meantime, we'll rig a sling to keep her on her feet. Keep her flushed with large quantities of distilled water. You can get it by the gallon at Ingle's Supermarket."

"You think she was poisoned?" I asked.

"Never seen anything like it. No sign of disease. Yes, I think she ingested something toxic. Charlie said she was fine until yesterday evening."

"Downright frisky when I let her out to the south pasture," confirmed the old man.

"The stallion with her?" asked the young vet.

"No. Keep them separated."

"And he is fine," observed the vet. "Must have been something she got in the pasture."

"Who'd want to poison my Nell? That's why I called the sheriff."

Blanchard shook his head. "I don't mean to suggest it was intentional. Maybe somebody dumped rancid garbage. Then she ate it, or it got in the water supply."

"Never found any dumping on my land, and the only stream in that pasture flows from the quarry. No way for anybody to get back up there since the road growed over."

"Your other horse been in that field?" I asked.

"Not for a couple days."

Rich Blanchard thought for a few seconds. "I'm going to take a sample of the creek water and send it with the blood. Might be nothing, but right now we got too many questions and no answers."

He pulled a clean vial from his black bag and walked out the back to the south pasture. Then I heard car doors slam in the barnyard. Charlie stood oblivious to the sound, staring at his beloved mare.

"I'll see who's here," I said.

Reverend Pace and a young woman were standing by his maroon Plymouth Duster, circa 1970. He smiled at me and pointed to the veterinarian's truck.

"Is she foaling?"

"No," I said in a tone that dissolved the smile from his face. "The foal's dead. The vet thinks Nell ate something poisonous. Charlie may lose her too."

Reverend Pace leaned against the hood of the car. "Oh, dear God." He squinted his eyes shut as if he wanted the sockets themselves to close up. "Don't let that happen."

He took a few deep breaths, opened his eyes and turned to the woman beside him. "Wait here. I'd like to speak to Charlie alone."

I took his words to apply to me as well, and I stayed with his companion as the old preacher disappeared into the barn to comfort his friend.

"I'm Barry Clayton."

"Sarah Hollifield. I'm an intern with Reverend Pace. Just started today. We were on our way back to town from another visit, and he said he wanted me to meet someone. Guess we came at a bad time."

"No. You came at a good time. I can't think of anyone who could help Charlie more."

"Is it bad?" She looked to the barn and her smooth forehead wrinkled with concern.

Sarah couldn't have been more than twenty-four or twenty-five. Her auburn hair framed her cherub face in a simple page-boy cut. She wore a green, V-necked sweater over a crisp, white blouse that was open at the neck and exposed a small gold cross hanging from a delicate chain. Her skirt was a muted tartan plaid hemmed just below the knee. Her black flats, dangerously close to a fresh horse-dropping, were polished to a soft finish. I imagined they had been extracted from terry cloth shoe bags assigned a special compartment in her suitcase. She was the eager angel wardrobed in a parochial school dress code.

"Bad," I said. "About as bad as it can get for the old man."

Sarah lifted her right hand to her mouth and chewed her fingers nervously. I noticed a smear of blood on the cuff of her sweater.

"Did you cut yourself?"

"No," she said absently. Then she saw I was looking at her sleeve. "It was in Reverend Pace's car. Must have been from the rabbits."

"Rabbits?"

"Yes. He said somebody left him rabbits they'd shot. Just dropped them on the front seat." She shook her head in amazement. "He said it happens all the time. People give him vegetables, deer meat, even pigs' feet." Her mouth scrunched up at the thought and she tried to pick off the flecks of dried blood. "Reverend Pace warned me to wear a different outfit next time, and that I especially wouldn't want to step in any surprises in these shoes." She glanced down and saw the pile of horse dung. "Oh, my." She edged closer to me. "And he said this skirt will never make it over a barbed-wire fence. 'You applied for field work, Sarah. That's just what this is.'" She smiled. "He told me when he first started, he rode out in the hills wearing a tailored suit, and then walked home with a load of birdshot in his rear. Learned the hard way never to dress like a Federal Revenuer."

"Where have you been?" I asked.

"This afternoon we took a sugar-cured ham to a family that lost a child."

"The Colemans?"

"Yes."

"But they wouldn't be home," I said. "Reverend Pace should have known they went to Kentucky last night."

"Oh, he knew. He said it would be easier for them to accept the gift if they just found it when they got back. He didn't even leave a note. He said they've got a long row to hoe, and they don't need to worry about thanking a preacher they don't know. I couldn't believe the Colemans didn't lock up, but I guess they don't have anything worth stealing. Reverend Pace just looped a rope around the shank bone, double-knotted it and hung the ham from the woodstove pipe. Then we closed the door and walked around their property looking for rocks."

"Rocks?"

"Yes. Do you think he's kind of eccentric?"

"No. I'd say he has a practical reason for everything he does." I also knew if Pace and his intern had been on visitations all day he hadn't heard about Fats McCauley. I'd catch him alone before I left. I walked over to his car and looked in the front window. "Did he leave the Colemans the rabbits too?"

"No. He took them out before he picked me up. He said greeting me with a couple of dead bunnies would be too much." Her brown eyes widened at the thought. "This is a lot different than seminary, Mr. Clayton."

"They both sound like they're from another era," said Susan. She lay stretched out across the braided throw-rug on my living room floor. Beside her, George nibbled a leaf of lettuce while Susan scratched the guinea pig behind her ears.

George had been my transition from married life to single life. Not that I believed a wife could be replaced by a rodent, although I know some divorced men would argue that point. Some zoologists argue a guinea pig is not a rodent. I did not mean to insult wives or guinea pigs. I had just wanted someone to come home to.

The pet store owner had assured me of the animal's masculinity, and my new companion had been thereby dubbed Curious George in honor of the playful monkey whose adventures I had enjoyed reading as a child. Within the first month, it became obvious that George had indeed been too curious because I found him one morning in the company of three miniature white and brown Georges who could only have come from what I had assumed was a guinea pig beer belly. The embarrassed pet store owner took back the offspring, but I had grown too attached to trade George in for the ballsy model. And not wanting to create a pet with an identity crisis, I decided to leave George as George, but added the appropriate surname Eliot.

"What do you mean another era?" I asked. I sat on the sofa nursing a cold beer. We had shared a late supper of roast beef sandwiches and salad. George enjoyed the green trimmings.

Susan wore a pair of my sweat pants and a UNC-Tar Heels tee shirt. No hospital rounds tomorrow meant she would spend the night at the cabin. After the day I'd had, I was grateful for her company.

"Well, how many circuit-riding preachers still exist?" she asked.

"A few, I guess. Pace is the only one I know."

"And how many goodie-two-shoes who come across like they're out of a priory school?"

"Jesus, Susan, she's training to be a minister. She's not into body piercing. You of all people should appreciate a woman making it in a man's field."

"I do. Don't be so defensive. I only said they sound like they're from another era. That doesn't mean they're not playing an important role today. They are."

"Yeah. You're right." I took a swallow of beer and thought about what was really bugging me. "Maybe I'm the one who's out of it. I feel incompetent, Susan. Last night I watched Uncle Wayne defuse the tension between that pompous power company executive and Mrs. Coleman. Me, I'm going through the motions, playing a role of somber sympathizer, standing in the background as a surrogate for my dad so that Clayton and Clayton can continue. Today, I was on the front lines with Tommy Lee and Reverend Pace. It felt more, I don't know, more important."

"Who's more important?" she asked. "Me or the ambulance driver racing my patient to the hospital?"

"You're each more important at different times."

"Very good, Mr. Deputy Reverend Clayton. And since I can't save every patient who comes to me, and since death eventually comes to every family, there will be a time when you are the most critical person in the life of the grieving. If that's not important, I don't know what is. Buryin' Barry has the respect and love of this little town, he has the respect and love of me." She got up, came over and kissed me on the cheek. "So, don't quit your daytime job."

Chapter 10

I had a restless night. Every time I moved, the pain in my shoulder conjured up the face of Dallas Willard. When I did drift off, my dreams always ended at the door of Fats' bathroom with water flowing red around my feet and horror waiting on the other side. Dallas and Fats claimed me waking and sleeping.

I heard Susan's rhythmic breathing beside me, and gently slipped from under the covers. Looking down at her slender form, barely visible in the faint light, I felt both protector and protected. A woman's strength has depths that men too late appreciate. I had first met Susan four months ago at the graveside of a patient to whom she had given every measure of her skill and talent. Her courageous dedication was to people and not to names on medical charts.

A few minutes after five, I braved the morning chill to fetch the local newspaper from the head of my driveway where I found it, as usual, tossed in the ditch. I took the paper to the kitchen, started the first pot of coffee, and assessed the damage reported in the *Gainesboro VISTA*.

The photograph dominated the front page. Cain's bloodied nose was visible, although the black and white picture made the blood look more like smudges of dirt. The caption "SHERIFF ARRESTS ELECTION OPPONENT" was less sensational than I expected, and the body of the story was carried over to a back page. The bylined reporter, Melissa Bigham, emphasized that Cain had started a verbal argument in Clyde's Roadside and then thrown a punch at an employee of the Asheville police department. Big Jack Andrews sounded like a saint in the newsprint. Melissa Bigham reported Cain was considering a lawsuit for the use of excessive force, but she had also queried a variety of high-ranking legal experts ranging from the local spokesman for the American Civil Liberties Union to the North Carolina Attorney General. They were all quoted as saying Cain had neither a case nor an excuse for his conduct.

I chuckled. Melissa Bigham had done Tommy Lee a favor. She had neatly boxed Cain in by shifting the story's focus to the appropriateness of his behavior rather than the physical fracas of two political combatants.

Fats McCauley's death was covered as a separate story, complete with speculation that the crime was linked to Dallas Willard. Tommy Lee was quoted regarding the ongoing man-hunt and the appeal for people to remain calm but vigilant. In the local section, the paper gave a brief obituary on the Coleman boy. I decided I'd read enough bad news. I got my first cup of coffee and a sharpened pencil, and lost myself in the crossword puzzle.

I walked into the Sheriff's Department at twenty minutes after eight. Reece Hutchins turned around from the coffee machine and gave me a cautious nod. "So, it's true then. The paper said you were at Clyde's consulting with the sheriff."

"Nothing official, Reece. Just reviewing how I discovered Fats."

Reece visibly relaxed. "Want some coffee? County lets us have it free."

"To keep you from sleeping on the job?"

"Sheriff didn't say that, did he?"

I realized Deputy Hutchins had no sense of humor, only a sense of importance.

The door to the private office opened, and Tommy Lee stuck his head out. "Barry, I hoped that was you. Come on in."

Reece got up from his desk to follow, but Tommy Lee waved him back. "Watch the front desk, Reece. We've got things to go over."

I closed the door. "Don't make things hard for me."

"What do you mean?"

"With Reece. I can tell he thinks I'm horning in."

"That's his problem."

"It's my problem if I'm going to keep living in this community."

"Okay. I'll give him some attention later. You see the paper?" He pointed to the *Gainesboro VISTA* spread out over his desk.

"Yes. That reporter did a good job defusing things."

"She did a great job. Cain's lawyer already called this morning saying there would be no lawsuit because quote—'Cain didn't want to muddy the issue of competent law enforcement with the personal affront he suffered.'"

"Magnanimous of him. What's the issue of competent law enforcement?"

"That Gainesboro is under a crime wave and needs big city experience for dealing with a hard-core criminal element."

"I don't know if I'd call Dallas Willard a hard-core criminal element," I said.

"But it certainly blows the murder statistics for Laurel County all to hell. In politics, it's all spin. We've never had so many homicides. Barry, the best thing for me to do is catch Dallas Willard. Then no one will remember Cain's name."

"Any word?" I asked.

"Nothing on Dallas. I did get some preliminary information out of forensics for Fats. The shell was fired from Dallas' shotgun."

"Why would Dallas kill Fats?"

"Are we back to the land?" asked Tommy Lee. "You hear anything from Carl Romeo?"

"Not yet."

"Wonder if it's too early for him to be in his office?" Tommy Lee hit an intercom button and instructed his secretary to get Carl Romeo on the phone.

"You said he was researching other heirs," said Tommy Lee. "I'd like to know what he discovered."

"Forensics find anything else?"

"Not really. I got this stuff over the phone. Full report won't be ready for a day or two. Oh, the lab man did mention one thing. You know how they like everything accounted for."

"Yeah. They don't care how gruesome the details are as long as they have an explanation for them."

"Well, forensics is interested in the notepad you pointed out in Fats' bedroom. By checking the depression on the top sheet, the lab determined your name was written in Fats' handwriting. But, the actual note could not be found. I figured Fats might have jotted down your name as a reminder that you'd be calling him and then written another note about checking the weather forecast. Maybe it would affect his plans for something. The wastebasket contained little notes for a lot of things."

"But, if he tore it off and didn't throw it away, it should have been on a calendar or the refrigerator or somewhere. Did they check his pockets?"

"Yes. And we don't have any reason to think that Fats went out after you and Susan took him home. Unless the crime lab overlooked it, or Fats destroyed it in a way we haven't traced, I'd have to say the murderer took it."

"That's real comforting."

"Yeah. Dallas still has his shotgun, and he still might want you to talk to his grandma in heaven."

The phone on Tommy Lee's desk chirped, then a woman spoke through the intercom. "Carl Romeo is on line three."

"Pull up your chair," Tommy Lee told me. He punched a button on the instrument. "Good morning, Carl. I hope you don't mind being on speaker phone. Barry Clayton is here with me."

"No problem," said Carl. "Glad you called. I just left Barry a message at the funeral home."

"Don't tell me," said Tommy Lee. "You found a Willard heir."

"I did. Spent yesterday afternoon at the courthouse going through county records."

"And the heir is Fats McCauley?" ventured Tommy Lee.

"That would be nice and neat," replied Carl. "It would also be wrong. I thought the same thing, but there isn't a connection at all. The legal heir, the one the state will recognize, is Talmadge Watson."

"Talmadge Watson?" exclaimed Tommy Lee.

He looked at me and I shrugged. I'd never heard of the man.

"That's a surprise," said Tommy Lee. "I never knew Martha and Talmadge were related."

"Oh, they're related all right. Brother and sister. At least up until sixty years ago. You have to remember that's before my time," said Carl. "We Romeos were still in New Jersey."

"I've lived here all my life and never knew that," said Tommy Lee.

We heard Carl chuckle on his end of the phone. "I did my own detective work. I asked Ruth here in the office. She called her eighty-eight-year-old aunt who said it was a double feud."

"Double feud?" asked Tommy Lee.

"Yeah. Martha ran off with a Willard when she was fourteen. Back then it was like a Hatfield eloping with a McCoy. Martha was disowned by the Watson clan."

"Including this Talmadge Watson?" I asked.

"That's the double feud part," said Carl. "A couple years later Talmadge committed an even greater crime. He married a Cherokee Indian."

"Seems like that would have brought brother and sister together," I said. "They both followed their hearts."

"We're talking mountain families here," said Tommy Lee. "Each of them would have thought the other married beneath them. You don't back off that kind of grudge."

"Would Martha's grandchildren have even known Talmadge Watson was their great uncle?" I asked.

"Talmadge Watson is not what I'd call a high-profile character," said Tommy Lee. "He rarely comes off his land. His name was probably never spoken in Martha's household."

"I know it never came up when the will was drawn," said Carl. "Dallas might not know at all."

Tommy Lee cleared his throat for an official pronouncement. "Keep it that way, Carl."

"I'm going to have to execute the estate," warned the lawyer.

"Right. Sometime. But not today, not this week, not this month. If Dallas is running around trigger-happy with a shotgun, I don't want you or me or Barry putting Talmadge Watson in his sights. I mean it, Carl. You tell no one."

"All right, Sheriff. I can take a hint."

There was a sharp rap on the glass window of the office door. Tommy Lee thanked Carl and hung up.

"Come in," he said.

Reece entered stiffly, looking past me to the sheriff. "Radio call from the Highway Patrol. They're notifying us they may be initiating traffic control up near Charlie Hartley's farm. Official request is for this afternoon. Said we're welcome to help."

"That's odd," said Tommy Lee. "What kind of traffic control do you need on that two-lane blacktop? Reece, you take a patrol car and be there. You're the best traffic man in the department."

Reece beamed and looked at me to make sure I'd heard the praise. "No problem. If they need me, I'm always ready."

When the deputy had left, Tommy Lee added, "Why don't you and I take an unofficial ride up there now. You mind?"

"Not at all."

Rich Blanchard met us outside Charlie's barn.

"We lost her. Nell died about half an hour ago."

I took a deep breath and looked at Tommy Lee.

"How's he taking it?" asked the sheriff. "Can we talk with him?"

"That would help. If you keep him occupied, I'll get my assistant and a truck, and we'll remove the carcass from the stable. He shouldn't have to see that."

"And what's all this about the Highway Patrol and traffic control?"

"I don't know," said the vet. "Must be because of the report. I expect we'll have some visitors today."

"Visitors?" asked Tommy Lee.

"Yeah. Yesterday, I air-freighted that specimen of blood and a creek water sample directly to the veterinary lab. A friend of mine is the supervisor, and he ran the tests last night. He called shortly after midnight. The toxic waste in the water makes Love Canal look like lemonade. I came right back here and found Charlie still sitting up with Nell, but she never had a prayer. My friend is required to make a full report to the EPA first thing this morning. He said don't be surprised if they're here by noon with a battery of forms and questions. To them, a dead horse is just collateral damage, if you know what I mean."

The white van beat Rich Blanchard's deadline by an hour. The vet, Tommy Lee, and I met two government officials in the front yard of Charlie's house.

The senior man introduced himself as Dr. Phillip Camas. "Is this the Hartley property?" His tone made it clear there would be no chitchat.

"Mr. Hartley is inside," answered Rich. "He lost a prized animal because of the water. I sent the sample, and I can show you around."

"Whatever," said Camas. "Can we drive to it?"

"The stream is down in the pasture. Your van ought to make it."

Once at the stream, Dr. Camas and his assistant drew a beaker of creek water. A quick test conducted in the rear of the van confirmed its toxicity.

"Mr. Hartley dump any chemicals on his property?" asked Camas.

"Charlie? He's just an old-fashioned farmer. Little fertilizer maybe."

"Well, this isn't a little fertilizer. Not by a long shot." Camas nodded to the second man, who began packing equipment in a leather satchel.

"What now?" asked the vet.

"Now, we walk upstream until we find where the hell this poison is coming from."

Fifteen minutes later we stood at the mouth of Hope Quarry, its granite walls scarred with pock-marks from the dynamite charges of years gone by. Nature had transformed the abandoned basin into a spring-fed pond that spilled over and formed the creek meandering through Charlie Hartley's pasture land.

"Nothing flows into this other than runoff," said Rich.

"Divers?" the assistant asked Camas.

"Not if we can avoid it," Camas replied. "First we've got to alert all areas downstream where we think the levels could be dangerous. Possibly as far as the stream flows before joining a major tributary. And I'll need engineers to contain and neutralize the contamination here. Tell the regional office I want a remote-cam and operator on site before authorizing any divers to go into that shit." He turned to Rich Blanchard. "This is more serious than one dead horse."

Within four hours the driveway to Charlie Hartley's farmhouse was clogged with late-model cars and vans, all cream-colored with permanent license plates and double-parked from the highway to the front porch steps. The EPA set up a mobile lab at the edge of the quarry. Government 'techies' crawled all over. Orange plastic stakes lined the creek bank for the entire distance from the pasture to the quarry. I couldn't determine whether they performed some scientific function or merely marked ground samples.

The water in the stream dwindled to a trickle. Tadpoles, newts, and salamanders lay dead in the drying mud. The last hundred yards of the creek wound up a steep grade to the lower edge of the quarry basin. The rail spur I had walked last Saturday ran down from the left ridge along the rim of the quarry and ended near the lip of the spillway. Two four-wheel-drive vehicles were parked on the opposite side. A wall of quick-set synthetic had been erected across the gouge in the basin that formed the mouth of the stream, effectively damming the water flow.

Several clusters of workers were spread around the quarry. They climbed down the jagged rocks to fill glass vials with water. An orange stake was hammered in the ground marking each specimen location, and identifying labels were stuck on the stake and vial. I counted nine such markers spaced twenty yards apart. There were still a good number of samples to be taken if they planned on covering the full circumference of the one-hundred-yard diameter pond.

Tommy Lee and I volunteered to help a young woman unload electronic equipment from the back of one of the all-terrain trucks. A television monitor and several coils of cable had been set on a portable table.

"Is this for underwater use?" Tommy Lee asked, lifting a silver metal case off the tailgate.

"Yes. It's a remote vid-cam. We submerge it from either a boat or the shoreline. Has a spotlight and sensitive chip to feed us pretty good pictures. Better than sending a diver down."

"Impressive," said Tommy Lee. "What do you think is down there?"

"Not sure. Has elements of highly corrosive sulfuric acid. Just hope we can remove it. You guys are welcome to watch."

Tommy Lee and I patiently waited while the EPA team assembled the video rig. The mini-camera was mounted in a stainless steel ball with a thick, quartz face plate. All rubber gaskets and cables were sheathed in protective alloy coverings. The unit was mounted on an extendible rod that held not only the camera but also an underwater spotlight aligned with the camera lens.

"Are the others trying to find where the pollutant is most concentrated?" I asked.

"Yes," answered Camas. "Helps narrow down the scope of the video probe. We'll cover the whole pond if we need to, but the higher the toxic count, the nearer we should be to the source. That's where we'll start."

I noticed that the sample-collecting teams had reached halfway around the quarry and were beginning to work along the bank of the rail spur. I looked up the tracks I had walked a few days ago. "Dr. Camas, you can take all the water samples you want, but the pollutant had to be dumped from somewhere. If the railroad tracks were used, I'd submerge your vid-cam at the point where the rails run closest to the water."

"You would, huh." He thought for a moment. "Miss Dodson, is the unit operable?"

"Yes, Dr. Camas."

"We'll continue gathering the concentration samples as planned. In the meantime, let's test the equipment. I suggest you follow this man's recommendation as to the best site." He gave a nod to me and went off to check on the rest of his staff.

We helped the video technician carry her equipment to the edge of the water directly below the railroad tracks. Through a series of extenders and flotation devices, she deployed the camera unit nearly thirty feet offshore and twenty feet down.

The image on the monitor was stark in its high contrast. The harsh spotlight bloomed out the near rocks and debris while darkness immediately swallowed up their shadows. The pictures could have been beamed from the dark side of the moon. Miss Dodson spent ten minutes adjusting her focus and mobility controls. Satisfied the unit was working properly, she began to make systematic passes over ten-foot square areas.

The chill of late afternoon settled over the quarry. Charlie Hartley came from the farmhouse with thermos bottles of hot coffee. I gave a cup to Dodson, who took it with a "thank you" while keeping her eyes on the screen. As she touched the cup to her lips, she let out a short shrill scream, flinging the coffee across the table and splattering my pants with the scalding liquid.

I ignored the pain and ran to her side. Her face was white, and her fingers trembled on the controls. In a few seconds, the others gathered around us and silently stared at the monitor. Slowly, Dodson backed up the camera, meticulously adjusting the focus so that no rock escaped her scrutiny.

A blurred shape passed directly in front of the lens.

"There," Dodson whispered to herself. She racked the focus sharply to the foreground.

A human hand filled the screen.

Chapter 11

Dr. Phillip Camas and his EPA team weren't prepared for a corpse. Their textbook approach to identifying and containing toxic waste disintegrated with the discovery of the body. Sheriff Tommy Lee Wadkins encountered little protest as he took control of both the priorities and resources at hand. He radioed for a rescue crew and boat, declared the rail spur off-limits until it could be searched for evidence, and commandeered the vid-cam for closer study of what lay beneath the pond's murky surface. Dr. Camas was left free to continue with his tests and make plans to siphon out the rising water into secure containers.

I stood silently beside Tommy Lee as we watched Dodson track the underwater camera.

The hand and arm stuck out from under a barrel that appeared to be at least fifty gallons or more in size. As the camera drifted over its curvature, a gaping hole crossed the screen out of which drifted swirls of a dark gray liquid.

"What's that?" asked Tommy Lee.

"I'd say it's what all the fuss is about," said Dodson. She moved the camera through the liquid, racking the focus as the spotlight was blocked by the dense fluid. "Can't tell the color, but it looks concentrated and diffuses into the water fairly quickly."

She maneuvered the camera down the other side and into a clearer field of water. The spotlight illumined the silhouettes of more of the containers. Dodson panned the lens 360 degrees. Some of the containers had streams of gray liquid leaking from them. The camera continued its arc and for a few seconds only rocks and stones were visible. Then a length of jean-clad leg appeared. No one said a word; no one breathed. Dodson inched the camera forward along the tattered pieces of cloth. A bare streak of flesh was visible beneath the torn clothing; part of an exposed calf had been eaten away by the harsh chemicals, the bone and cartilage distinctive against the darker flesh.

A severely scuffed boot drifted off screen as Dodson moved on to show more of the sunken drums.

I heard Tommy Lee whisper beside me, "The only person I know missing in the county is Dallas Willard."

I tried to recall if the boot and jeans matched what Dallas had worn in the cemetery. All I could remember was the shotgun.

The light faded quickly as the sun sank behind the mountain ridge. We had spent several hours at the site, using the camera and rescue boat to retrieve the body. The toxic acid had made identification difficult, but the hair coloring left no doubt in my mind that we had found Dallas Willard.

Tommy Lee bypassed the limited skills of coroner Ezra Clark and requested transport of the corpse to the Asheville morgue and a forensic medical examiner. He left Reece in charge at the scene, where Dr. Camas began procedures to extract the drums from the quarry.

"You know what this means," Tommy Lee said as we got in his patrol car.

"Since Dallas' pickup was by the railroad tracks, he walked to the quarry and either fell in or jumped in. You're probably looking at an accident or a suicide."

"And he just happened to disturb some chemical drums," said Tommy Lee. "I don't like coincidences, Barry. But, we won't know anything definitive until there's an autopsy on what's left of him. I hope we can get the report sometime tomorrow."

"Well, at least the county can breathe a little easier," I said. "I know I will. And Bob Cain can stop screaming so loud about a crime wave."

"That I don't believe," said Tommy Lee.

When we came to the main blacktop, he asked, "You in a rush to get back?"

"No."

He headed away from town.

"I don't like it when I don't know what's going on," he said.

"And I don't like it when you don't know what's going on," I agreed. "Particularly if I'm involved. Where are we headed?"

"To notify the next of kin that Dallas is dead. You're going to meet Talmadge Watson, the heir to the Willard land."

Tommy Lee cut on the headlights and fell silent. I left him alone with his thoughts.

"Look for a dirt road down here to the right," he said. "Three eyes are better than one."

After another quarter mile, I noticed a break in the road-side mountain laurel. We swung off on a single lane that was more gully than road. Low spots were still muddy, and Tommy Lee tried to keep up a steady momentum to avoid getting stuck. The tall hardwoods soon swallowed us up, and the blackness of the moonless night weighed down like a collapsing tunnel that pressed ever closer.

The road twisted and turned. I soon lost all sense of direction, certain only that we were climbing.

"Are we going to be able to turn around?" I asked.

"Yeah. We should be near the bridge."

The car hit a sudden dip that dropped the road out from under us. Tommy Lee braked and we slid down a muddy slope until the hill bottomed out and the tires grabbed hold of packed dirt.

With shock absorbers creaking and the headlight beams bouncing up and down in the trees, the patrol car came to an abrupt stop.

"Maybe the county ought to buy you some tires with tread," I said.

I peered over the car's hood at a split-log bridge spanning a black void. The sound from a whitewater creek rose up from its depths. There were no safety railings and the width couldn't have been more than a foot or two wider than that of the car.

"You call that a bridge, huh?"

"Gets us from one side to the other," said Tommy Lee. "It's not more than twenty feet above the water. Wanna take the wheel? Anybody who can drive around the expressways of Charlotte shouldn't give it a second thought."

I declined the offer. The timbers groaned and the washboard surface racked every joint of me, but the bridge held. When we stopped on the other side, I remembered to breathe.

"Tell me we don't come back this way," I said.

"Not unless you want to walk back to town. Relax, we're just going to the top of this hill."

I counted four hairpin turns where the road snaked back on itself to make it to the top. When we reached the crest, Tommy Lee stopped the car and killed the engine. He left the headlights burning and pointed to a soft, yellow glow shining through the woods off the side of the road. "There's our man. Get out with me slowly, and then stay visible in front of the headlights."

I followed his lead. We walked about twenty-five feet in front of the patrol car where the low beams converged in a broad pool of light. Tommy Lee held his hands out to his side and turned once around, then he faced the yellow glow in the woods. I mimicked the action, raising one arm and turning so that the lights caught the empty sleeve of my wounded one. My eyes adjusted to the darkness, and I saw the outline of a window with a thick brown shade that diffused the light behind it.

A sliver brightened as someone pulled the shade back a few inches. I stood still with my face angled to the headlights so that whoever was inspecting us would have a clear view. The shade was released, and a few minutes later, a ball of light started moving toward us.

I made out the shape of a kerosene lantern. Its reflector plate threw its beams forward and shielded the bearer in the night shadows.

"Who you done brought with you, Sheriff?" The voice croaked out like aged timber bending in the wind.

"This here's Barry Clayton. He runs the funeral home in Gainesboro." Tommy Lee shot me a glance to keep quiet.

"Jack Clayton's boy?" he asked me.

"Yes, sir," I answered, hoping it counted for something.

"What happened to your arm?"

"Dallas Willard shot me at his grandma's funeral."

"He did, huh. All them Willards is a strange lot." He made the statement as if it explained everything. "Ain't seen your Pa since Lottie passed over. That's been nigh onto six years. Jack's a good man, for an undertaker." With that judgment pronounced, the speaker crossed into the light and walked up to me. He said nothing, merely nodded and waited. Tommy Lee knew to provide the formal introduction.

"This is Talmadge Watson. I been knowin' Talmadge long as I can remember."

I caught how Tommy Lee eased into the mountain dialect, but I knew if I tried to follow now, I would make it mockery. "Pleased to meet you, Mr. Watson."

"Talmadge," the old man corrected.

I risked a glance up and down the mountaineer. His face was covered with stubble and his leathery lips were drawn tight, masking whatever teeth he had. He wore no shirt; only the upper half of his long-johns covered his chest. He had skipped a button hole and the yellow fabric was bunched up where the mismatch created an extra fold. Cigarette ashes stained and splotched the front. Brown suspenders hoisted dark baggy trousers over his scrawny waist, and the scuffed work boots made his feet look too big for his body. But the most prominent feature about Talmadge Watson was the rifle resting in the crook of his right arm.

"Talmadge," I repeated. I sensed a handshake was not expected.

The mountaineer turned back to the sheriff. "Reckon this ain't a raid," he said.

"Now you know I believe in live and let live," Tommy Lee said. "But, Talmadge, it is official business. I got some bad news. Earlier this afternoon we found Dallas Willard's body at the bottom of Hope Quarry. It lay with some dumped chemical drums. We don't know what happened."

Talmadge took a sharp breath and looked away. For a long moment, there was no other sound except for the night crickets and the distant hoot of an owl. "Live and let live," he said. "Seems like there's been more dying than living lately. You know Martha Willard was my sister."

"Yes," said Tommy Lee. "I'm sorry."

"Well, things have a way of gettin' said by people too stubborn to take them back. Me included." He shook his head. "You boys want a swallow?"

"That would be fine," said Tommy Lee.

"Wait here."

Talmadge stepped out of the light and walked back to the cabin. He returned a few minutes later, and I noticed he had exchanged his rifle for a long, gray coat.

"Give this to your pa," said the old man. He held out his hand and stuffed a wad of bills in my palm. "Tell him my cash money's as good as anybody's, and I won't hear it no other way. Now, Sheriff, we'll have to get it from the creek.

You boys turn your car around up in the yard, and I'll meet you at the crossing."

Before he started the engine, I asked Tommy Lee, "What's this money for?"

"I'd say it's for Lottie's funeral. She was his wife. Talmadge probably didn't have money for the burial, and your father didn't charge him much, if at all. Talmadge knows that and is going to pay what he thinks is fair if it takes the rest of his life. Now, you don't argue with Talmadge, and you don't keep him waiting. We'd better get to the creek."

Tommy Lee eased the cruiser down to where Talmadge stood with his lantern in his hand and signaled us to park just short of the log bridge. He waved us out of the vehicle.

"I'm gonna show you boys the spot in case you come by and I'm huntin' or cookin'. Not that there's a still around here." He stepped down the bank to a narrow footpath that ran along the water.

I walked right behind him as we traveled single-file upstream from the crossing. After no more than forty yards, the creek took a sharp bend, and the car, headlights left burning, was lost from sight. Talmadge swung the lantern's beam into the woods.

"There's a couple of sittin' rocks for you. They're what attracted me to this place."

The way he said it sounded like he was describing a favorite restaurant. Tommy Lee and I did as he instructed and sat down on two dry boulders. Talmadge set the lantern on the creek bank and grabbed a tangle of vines that grew out from a base of exposed pine roots and formed a thick mesh at the edge of the stream. He lifted them like a loosely woven carpet and revealed a backwater eddy notched into the bank.

A rusted chain looped around one of the tree roots and disappeared into the water. Talmadge reeled it in, careful to raise the links straight up so that whatever was tied to the submerged end would not be dragged across the rocky bottom of the stream. There was the clink of glass as Talmadge lifted a wire net out of the water.

"Nice and cold. Don't need no refrigerator. Good thing too cause I still ain't got no electric." He untied a line that cinched the top of the netting so that it formed a closed sack. He removed what he wanted, secured the line again, and lowered his cache back into place. He spread the vines over the hidden pool and joined us.

I saw he carried a mason quart jar, the metal lid a bit rusty from its underwater storage. A liquid just tinged with amber refracted the light of the kerosene lantern and cast a mosaic of dancing shadows across the face of the mountaineer.

"This ain't corn. Cooked it from apple. She's smooth, but the fruit will stay in your head if you drink too much." He twisted off the top and handed the jar to Tommy Lee.

The sheriff held the moonshine aloft in a ritual of admiration. "You've never lost the touch." He closed his eyes and took two deep swallows, the gulps clearly audible above the sound of the rushing brook. His shoulders shook in reflex, and he let out a long sigh as he passed the jar back to Talmadge, who drew a steady swig before giving the communal cup to me.

I knocked the jar back like it was a shot of Scotch, but I wasn't prepared for the tidal wave that poured out of the wide-mouthed container and slammed into the back of my throat. The fire exploded into my nose and set my ears ringing. For a moment I was too paralyzed to even swallow, and I panicked that I would cough or gag. I handed the jar to Talmadge and hoped neither the old man nor Tommy Lee noticed the agony on my face. Just when I thought I could hold out no longer, the pain subsided, and I forced the potent brew down my throat, feeling every drop as it burned its way to my stomach.

Talmadge again offered the jar, but both of us declined. The old man took another sip, then said more to himself, "All the Willards gone, a whole family gone."

"Talmadge," said Tommy Lee. "We don't know how it happened. Maybe an accident, maybe he killed himself."

"I heard the boy had gone crazed."

"He also killed Fats McCauley."

"Fats McCauley? That don't make no sense at all."

"I know. I was hoping you'd see a reason. Was Fats connected to the Willards or the Watsons in any way?"

"You mean like blood-kin?"

"Blood-kin or even close friend."

"No. The McCauleys hailed out of Tennessee. They've always been town people." He thought for a few seconds. "Why are you askin' about the Watsons?"

"Because the Willard land now comes to you."

"It does? What do I want with it?"

If there was any suspicion that Talmadge was somehow even remotely involved with the killings, it evaporated with his question.

"Well, it will get figured out," said Tommy Lee. "But till then, I'm not gonna tell anybody you're Martha's heir. No sense having you pestered by the press." He rose from the stone. "Thanks, Talmadge."

"Thanks for coming in person, Sheriff." He turned to me. "Here." He passed me the sealed jar of moonshine. "Want you to keep this. Sheriff's runnin' for office. I don't want to cost him the election."

I slipped it into my jacket pocket.

We returned to the car in silence. As I opened the door, I felt a firm slap on my shoulder.

"You boys come back," said Talmadge.

After we reached the paved road, I said, "Talmadge is an interesting fellow."

"He's an original all right. He likes you. Don't think I've ever seen him take to anyone so fast."

"He hardly spoke to me."

"He slapped you on the back. Believe me, touchie feelie, he ain't."

When we got back to the department, Tommy Lee pulled alongside my Jeep.

"Is there anything else I can do for you?" I asked.

"Yeah. Take tomorrow off. I'll let you know what I find out."

As I grabbed the inside door handle, Tommy Lee added, "And thanks for indulging my drink with Talmadge. He and his sister may have been estranged, but family is family. I didn't want him hearing the news any other way."

"I know," I said. "Family is family."

I started the Jeep and felt the need to make my own visit.

I let myself in through the back door and walked to the kitchen. As expected, the old white counters gleamed from Mom's after-supper cleansing. An ironed blue-checked cloth covered the Formica table where I had eaten daily meals until I went off to college. Worn paths criss-crossed the gold-flecked linoleum, etched into the floor by the thousands of footsteps taken between sink, refrigerator, and stove. The hands of the round red clock above the table showed eight-thirty-five. I heard the murmur of voices coming down the back stairway. Mom was probably watching a television talk show since such a continuous conversation had not occurred between her and Dad in the past year. I didn't want to startle her so I called up from the base of the stairs.

She sat in the upstairs den, watching a gardening show on PBS, wearing an apricot-colored, quilted housecoat and holding her knitting needles and the beginnings of what looked like a new sweater in her lap. She looked up with a smile that could not quite chase the exhaustion from her face.

"Hi, son. You want to spend the night here? I changed the sheets after Reverend Pace stayed over."

I shook my head, then bent over and gave her a kiss on the cheek. "No. I just stopped by for a few minutes. You heard about Dallas Willard?"

"Yes. Terrible, terrible thing. Don't know what this world's coming to. Wayne says the body is going over to Buncombe County for a full autopsy. It won't be released till tomorrow afternoon." She glanced down at the knitting and stifled a sob. "And poor Travis. After all that man has been through."

"Tell Uncle Wayne I'm available to help."

"He's accustomed to it. He used to tell your Dad, 'birthin' and dyin' are the two things man's got no control of.'"

"You know Susan has Wednesdays off. I was thinking we might come by for lunch, if that's not a problem."

"No," said Mom. "That would be nice. What time?"

"How about one? We've got something to do in the morning."

"One will be fine."

"Is Dad asleep?" I asked.

"Maybe, but I heard him stirring a little while ago."

I walked down the hall to my parents' room. The door was open and the lamp between the twin beds turned on. The spread and blanket on my father's bed were pulled back from the pillow, but he was not there. The bathroom next to the bedroom was dark. Beyond it, a sliver of light split the gap between the door and jamb of the guest room which had once been mine.

Time had settled the old house on its foundation so that the door swung closed on its own. My father did not like to be alone in a room with the door shut, but he was probably in there, unaware of his confinement.

The creak of the hinges should have alerted him someone was entering. Instead, I found him standing in front of the bureau in his green and white striped pajamas. His back was to me, but I saw his reflection in the mirror, saw the gaunt face and disheveled gray hair, saw the watery blue eyes staring down with bewildered fascination.

"Dad," I said. "It's me, Barry."

Slowly, he turned around. He looked at me and smiled the old smile, the one that used to break just before he made some teasing remark. "My son," he started, and then faltered as the rest of the sentence left him. The smile wavered with confusion, and he lifted up his hands to show me the gold-framed photograph he held. I was eight years old, in my Cub Scout uniform, grinning through two missing front teeth. This was the son. He did not recognize the man standing in front of him.

He looked around the room as if by seeing the remnants of my childhood—the books Mom left on the shelves, the model cars and ships he and I had spent Sunday afternoons building, the small trophies from Little League baseball and youth football—by seeing these he could tell the friendly stranger about his boy. It dawned on me how much of a museum my room had become. Not for my benefit, but for my father. Suddenly, Fats' shrine to Brenda did not seem quite so strange. When you lose someone, you look for them where the memories are strongest. But what do you do when you are losing yourself? How frightening it must be to reach out for those memories and grab a handful of fog. And what of Mom and me? Our memories were strongest in the visible presence of a husband and father whose personality was dying, whose spark of identity flickered weaker and weaker until one day it would be extinguished completely.

For the first time in my life, I fully realized Clayton and Clayton Funeral Directors provided a service far greater than just chemically preparing a body for burial. We enabled the ritual of grief to be expressed and offered a family the closure of a casket and the memorializing of a life which could be fondly remembered. But what can we do when the body still walks among us?

I took the photograph from his hands and set it on the bureau. Then, as gently as I could, I led him by the arm back to his own room. As soon as we crossed the threshold, he hurried to his bed and sat on the edge, clutching the spread as if the familiar texture of its ribbed fabric gave him comfort. I sat on Mom's bed across from him and started to talk in a quiet, steady voice. I told him about Dallas and Fats, about Talmadge and his moonshine and burial money, about Tommy Lee and Bob Cain. Occasionally, my father would meet my eye and smile, but I could only hope that my words registered with any meaning, however briefly that may be. At last, while I was still speaking, my father lay down and curled up in a fetal ball. I leaned over, kissed his forehead, and turned out the light. In the hallway just outside the door, I leaned against the wall and cried.

Chapter 12

Talmadge's moonshine left an arid wasteland of dehydrated tissue that still clung to my teeth and gums the next morning. The false dawn gave just enough light for me to see my watch. Five-thirty. Earlier than I wanted to get up, but the drive for a drink of water became overpowering.

I tiptoed out of the bedroom and gulped three glasses of cold water at the kitchen sink. They cured the cotton feeling in my mouth but left me wide-awake. I accepted I was up for the day and put on the clothes I had shed by the hearth. A sheet of paper was in the front pocket of my pants. I fished it out and unfolded the copy of the drawing Tommy Lee had found in Dallas Willard's cabin. I stared at it.

"I enjoyed the bed, but breakfast service seems a little slow." Susan stood in the hallway, wrapped in a heavy, gray terry-cloth robe.

"I'm sorry. I didn't mean to wake you on your day off."

"Tell me why you're up and maybe I'll grant you a pardon." She bent down and kissed me, unconcerned that the loose robe opened to the morning chill.

"Thinking."

"About Dallas Willard?"

"About where I'm taking you to breakfast."

"Right answer." She nestled into the sofa beside me. "What's this?" she asked, pointing to the drawing.

"The way Dallas thought his grandmother's land was going to be divided. When he learned his brother and sister had gotten legal control to sell it all, he killed them."

"And they told him?"

"What do you mean?

"Well, seems strange they would have sprung the news any sooner than they needed to. You told me Norma Jean said Dallas left the room when Martha died and they hadn't seen him since. Did Lee and Norma Jean bring it up as the woman expired? I doubt it. If Dallas had been aware of the will earlier, why wait till the cemetery for revenge? And why didn't he try to reach you as soon as his grandmother died?"

"Maybe someone else told him," I said. "Told him between the time Martha died and the funeral."

"Could that have been Fats McCauley?"

"I don't see how Fats knew anything about it. If he did, it's a stretch to make that a motive for Fats' murder."

"Carl Romeo?"

"Carl hadn't spoken to him. His secretary said Dallas showed up at their office because he learned the will had been changed."

"Do you think that it's important now who told him?"

"I think you ask good questions," I said, squeezing her hand. "And I think Tommy Lee is lucky you're not running for sheriff."

"So, where are we going for breakfast? Not Herbie's House of Pancakes. They go straight to my hips, syrup and all."

"No, 'Barry's House of the Lord.' And if that's not good enough, we're having lunch with Mom and Dad. I'll check your hips later."

The discovery of Dallas Willard's body had one effect on me I hadn't fully anticipated. Tremendous relief. I didn't comprehend the pressure I had been under until that pressure was released at Hope Quarry Pond. The string of deaths I had witnessed underscored the fragile nature of life, a fragility we cannot consciously bear all the time or all alone. That is why funerals are communal rituals. At some point, we must all feel connected to something larger than ourselves: there is no point quite as dramatic as when we are forced to face our own mortality. Had Dallas Willard aimed six inches more to his left, I would surely have perished.

I am not a particularly religious person. As a kid, I attended the First Methodist Church of Gainesboro with Mom and Dad, went to Sunday school and summer vacation bible school, and endured the prayers and preachers that always seemed to fill the funeral home. Two years ago when I first returned to help Mom and Uncle Wayne, we would go to church as a family. But, as Dad's condition deteriorated, the Sunday morning ordeal of worrying whether he would be able to follow the continuity of a worship service caused Mom to limit our attendance to special occasions and holidays.

We replaced pew time with quiet hours together on Sunday afternoons. Mom would fix a special lunch, and then she and I talked while Dad nodded off in his chair with either cartoons or football on the television. These were the good Sundays now.

While I'm not religious, I am spiritual. There is a mystery to life that is made all the more real when tear-streaked faces bend over the casket and see the remnant of someone whose love will never leave their hearts. It is proof to me that the kingdom of heaven intervenes in our world in ways that religion prefers to contain and control, to package for dispensation on defined terms, when really the only term acceptable is unconditional love. In short, why make the simple complicated? Religion is to spirituality as lawyers are to handshakes.

My cathedral for spirituality was Pisgah National Forest. This "House of the Lord" had its genesis in the George Vanderbilt Estate. At the end of the 19th century, when the railroad heir chose the site to build his summer castle near Asheville, he wanted a mountain view. He also wanted to own everything within that view. His purchase of 125,000 acres with the nearly six-thousand-foot-high Mt. Pisgah as the tract's pinnacle would have impressed even an English feudal lord. It certainly impressed the U.S. Government when, after Vanderbilt's death in 1914, a major section of the Estate was deeded to it and became the core of Pisgah National Forest, including the trout-rich Davidson River that tumbles and rambles off the crest of the Blue Ridge Mountains.

Susan and I entered the lush forest preserve traveling along a two-lane highway that paralleled that wide, white-water stream. Behind us the commercial scars of civilization encroached right up to the forest's entrance. I turned left onto the road leading to the Pisgah fish hatchery and then made a quick right into an unpaved clearing barely large enough to swing the Jeep around. A short walk into the woods brought us to our destination, a single picnic table on the point where the stream flowing from the trout hatchery merged with the river. Across that broader, rushing body of water lay the main road, hidden from sight and sound by a thicket of mountain laurel. "Beautiful," said Susan. "I love it."

"Good," I said. "I'm real tight with the maitre de. I'll tell him you approve."

We unloaded the Jeep. I had gone on a shopping spree on my way there. In my right hand, I toted two lounge chairs with price stickers still glued to the metal legs. Amazing what one can buy in a twenty-four-hour drug store at seven-thirty on a Wednesday morning. My sling-encumbered left arm easily managed the bag of apple cinnamon muffins. Susan brought the thermos of coffee and three newspapers. I had picked up *The Charlotte Observer* because I like the sports section, Susan wanted *The Asheville Citizen* for the calendar of regional events, and we had agreed to fight over the crossword in *The New York Times*.

The coffee and muffins were great, and the temperature hovered in the comfortably cool range. I lost myself in the sports page until my attention was diverted to Susan's slim form walking by the edge of the stream. She moved with such grace, like a deer coming to the water to drink. Watching her against the backdrop of nature's beauty pushed the horrors of the past week into another time, another life.

I came up beside her and wrapped my good arm around her waist. She leaned against me.

"A penny for your thoughts," I said.

"No," she whispered. "Today they're priceless."

A trout broke the surface a few feet away, and the silver tail sparkled in the sunlight an instant before disappearing. The water gurgled across brown and gray stones, hurrying along to join the river just fifteen yards away. Even over that short distance, eddies pulled twigs and leaves out of the current to loop back against the bank where they became trapped in the counterflow of turbulence.

Susan bent over, grabbed a stick, and tossed it in. Bobbing along the rapids, it wove around the stones and floated into the river. I broke a second stick and launched it from the same spot. A few yards downstream, it coursed off to the right and wedged against a tree limb dangling in the water.

I heard Susan sigh. "What?" I asked.

"I was just remembering. There was a game my brother Stevie taught me where you threw a stick in the rushing water and tried to make it strike a particular rock downstream. We would take turns and the first one to hit it won."

"Not easy," I said. "I dropped my stick in the same place as yours and wound up going a completely different route."

"Unpredictable," she said. "Like the weather. Too many variables affect the water flow. Did a trout underneath flip his tail and shift the current, or did a bear four hundred yards upstream wade across? No two sticks ever go the same way. Stevie and I would play for hours." Her voice caught on her brother's name.

I pulled her close and rested my cheek against her silky hair.

How many unpredictable, random events occur to create the pattern of our lives? What sends one stick safely through the rapids and another into a snag? How many connected events result in sending one man into a cemetery to pray and another to kill? And for Dallas Willard, was this chain of events forged at random, or specifically programmed?

Mom placed a pot of hot tea and a platter of pecan cookies on the low table in front of the sofa where Susan and I sat. As she went to retrieve her knitting basket from the corner, I leaned forward and scooped up three of her homemade delights.

"Remember your hips," I warned Susan.

She gave me a hard kick on the ankle.

Dad pulled his chair close to the TV and watched as the roadrunner ran circles around the coyote. He enjoyed the colors and action without any need to follow the plot or hear the sound. Sadly, even the old cartoons were fresh.

Mom steadied herself with the armrest as she eased into the rocker across from us. It was in those small movements that I realized that although her mind was as sharp as ever, she too was slipping under the weight of time.

"Lunch was delicious," said Susan. "I insist you let me clean up."

"Nonsense," said Mom. "You relax. Barry has told me you often work eighteen-hour days." She sorted out yarn from needles and began knitting.

"And she's still got work to do today," I said.

"Back at the hospital?" asked Mom.

"News to me," said Susan.

"Campaigning. Tommy Lee was supposed to have dropped off some posters this week. I told him I'd put them up at the intersections near my cabin."

"I saw them by the back porch," said Mom.

"I might just want to sit here and eat cookies," said Susan. "Broaden one's voter base, so to speak."

"No comment," I said. "But, I figured as my doctor you wouldn't want me on the side of the road with only one good arm trying to hold a poster, a hammer, and a nail."

"That's true," said Susan. "You'd probably lose three fingers and a thumb."

The needles in Mom's fingers halted. "Sheriff Wadkins sure has his hands full. All those murders."

"That he does," I agreed.

"And coming at the time when he is running for re-election," continued Mom. "Just gives that other fellow something to pick on."

"Cain," I said.

"Cain," she repeated as if the word tasted sour in her mouth. "Seems every day the mail brings more of his ads. Must be spending a lot of money."

"I think he has got money behind him," I said. "He's in the pay of the power company."

"Still, I look at it this way," said Mom. "If he were qualified to be sheriff, he'd know Tommy Lee is doing a great job and he wouldn't run against him."

"I like your logic," said Susan. "You should be Tommy Lee's campaign manager."

Mom laughed. "I don't know about that. If he asked me to serve, then I'd doubt his judgment as well." She looked at me. "You're helping with these murder cases, aren't you?"

"Some."

I saw her eyes fill with tears.

"I'm being careful, Mom. Nothing dangerous. Especially since Dallas is dead. Now we're just going to brainstorm a little."

"Brainstorm?" she asked.

"Yeah. Possible motives. I'm not in the line of fire. Been there, done that. I don't want to be a target again. I'm not that crazy."

"Nuts," said Dad.

The three of us looked at my father, surprised that he had followed and joined the conversation.

"Nuts," he repeated and held up his half-eaten pecan cookie.

We had to laugh.

"That's right, Dad," I said. "Nuts."

The telephone rang. Mom answered the extension in the hall.

"It's the sheriff for you, Barry."

"Let me catch it downstairs," I said, as I walked out of the den. "You and Susan can visit without me bothering you." I did not want to have Mom overhear whatever news caused Tommy Lee to track me down. A knot tightened in my stomach, telling me that today's peace and tranquility was about to come to an abrupt end.

"Stabbed?" I asked, not sure I had heard Tommy Lee correctly.

"That's what the medical examiner said. I haven't gotten the full written report, just a briefing by phone. He said no doubt about it. Clean penetration at the base of the sternum, then a twist under the rib cage that punctured the heart. Death was nearly instantaneous."

I backed away from the kitchen counter, stretching the phone cord until I could sit down at the Formica table. "People don't commit suicide by stabbing themselves in the heart."

"No, not that I've ever seen. But here's the really strange part. The M.E. couldn't give me an exact time of death, but he did determine Dallas had been in the water around five days."

"But that can't be," I stammered. "How could—"

"Yes. How could Dallas have been killed Thursday and murdered Fats McCauley Sunday?"

"I'll be right there as soon as I take Susan home."

I placed the phone back in the wall cradle. My knees wobbled as I started for the stairs. Fats McCauley had been murdered by Dallas Willard's shotgun, but Dallas Willard's body had been at the bottom of Hope Quarry at the time. A murderer was still on the loose, and he probably had my name on a note in his pocket.

Chapter 13

Tommy Lee was on the phone, but he waved me to a seat. I slid into a chair and sipped my cup of free county coffee.

"It's two-thirty now. Give me the rest of the afternoon," he told someone. "I want to see how he reacts to the news. You can move in after that."

He hung up, visibly satisfied by the call.

"That was Dr. Camas," he said. "Last night they brought in work lights and a magnetic crane. All the drums have been removed from the quarry."

"They didn't find a shotgun, did they?"

"Shotgun? You mean Dallas'? No."

"Good. Then at least Fats wasn't killed by a ghost carrying a ghost weapon."

"No, Fats was killed by someone who wanted us to think Dallas had killed him and who never expected Dallas' body to be found."

"Camas give you any leads?"

"Just that those old ruptured chemical drums indicate a possible criminal disposal of toxic waste. The EPA won't be releasing any official information for at least a week, but they want to begin their investigation immediately. I got him to hold off till tomorrow."

"Why hold them off at all?" I asked.

"I went back to Hope Quarry at dawn. Dr. Camas was bringing up the last of those containers. The insides of the broken metal shells were lined with some kind of non-metallic material. Looked almost like the glass of a thermos bottle."

"To hold what?"

"Camas said acid. Acid that would have eaten through metal. Indications are the containers were dumped along with Dallas' body. Most were damaged, and the acid ate through their rusted exteriors and contaminated the water. I saw one of the drums. The only markings on it were the stenciled letters 'PPM.'"

"What's that mean?"

"I'd bet it means Pisgah Paper Mill. Funny thing is they've been out of business for ten years."

I remembered where I'd heard of the company. "Have you seen him yet?"

Tommy Lee smiled. "That's why I'm holding off the EPA. Come on, Barry. This should be interesting."

"He's not expected until four," said Fred Pryor's secretary. "He's been at a corporate meeting in Charlotte the last few days, but he called this morning to say he's driving back after lunch."

Tommy Lee leaned over the desk in the cramped mobile office and glanced at the open appointment book. The brunette appeared flustered, not sure whether she should close it or not.

"Wednesday, October twenty-fourth," said Tommy Lee. "The meeting is not marked for today."

"It ran over. He normally drives back the end of the day, but Mr. Ludden scheduled an executive committee meeting for this morning."

"Is that Ralph Ludden?" asked Tommy Lee.

"Yes," she said. "The CEO. His office is in the tallest skyscraper in Charlotte." She looked around the dingy room. "I hope we'll be there someday."

"Mr. Pryor is in line for a promotion?"

"Well, it's not my place to say, but Mr. Ludden is sixty-three. He'll be stepping down in a few years. Mr. Pryor has worked for the company for thirty years. Nobody knows Ridgemont Power better."

"And you'll go with Pryor if he gets the job?" asked Tommy Lee.

She smiled. "It's customary."

"Well, I hope your days here in the wilderness pay off, Miss—"

"Cummings. Jane Cummings."

"Jane, my associate and I are going to grab a burger." He tapped the calendar. "Pencil us in."

As we walked toward the car, a voice called behind us. "Is there a problem, Sheriff?"

We turned and saw a workman hustling across the parking lot to catch us. He wore a green John Deere cap, blue flannel shirt, and dusty jeans.

"Somebody die?" he asked as he stopped in front of us.

"Why would you say that, Odell?"

I didn't recognize the man until Tommy Lee spoke his name. Odell Taylor, the construction foreman who had stayed glued to Pryor at the Colemans' visitation. Last time I'd seen him he'd been more formally dressed.

"Ain't he the undertaker?" he said looking at me. "I thought maybe y'all had come to tell somebody their kinfolk was dead."

"No, not this time. We came to talk to Pryor."

"He ain't here. Something I can do?"

"Thanks, but we'll be back."

Taylor cut his eyes back and forth between us like he wanted to ask another question. Then he shrugged. "Suit yourself. Well, I got to get to work."

When we were in the patrol car, I asked, "What do you know about him?"

"Not much. I run into Odell around the county now and then. Couple years back he put in a driveway for Reece."

"Seems like he doesn't want anyone getting too close to Pryor. At the Coleman visitation, he was like a guard dog around his boss."

Tommy Lee laughed. "Maybe that's something he picked up from Reece. Of course, I didn't say that."

At the junction with the main highway, Tommy Lee said, "You don't want a burger, do you?"

"No."

"Good, because we aren't going anywhere." He looked right and left. "Pryor should come in from the south, from the expressway. Let's see if we can find a cozy spot to wait."

About a quarter mile from the entrance to the Broad Creek site, Tommy Lee found a gravel road where we could park with some degree of secrecy.

"You remember the cars by Pryor's office?" he asked.

"Just that secretary's Subaru. Only one I saw."

"I mean from last Friday."

"You're kidding." I thought for a few seconds. "Your pal Bob Cain's car. You pointed it out to me."

"Beside it was a blue Buick Park Avenue. A typical executive-mobile. That's what we're waiting for."

Tommy Lee's memory didn't fail him. Within twenty minutes, the Buick zipped by. The sheriff's tires sprayed loose rocks as he kicked the patrol car in pursuit. We caught up with Pryor as he turned into the project entrance, and Tommy Lee rode the man's bumper all the way to the trailer.

Pryor quickly opened his door and stepped out. This time he looked the board-room part. Gone were the jeans and cowboy boots. He wore a well-tailored, blue pin-stripe suit and a natty yellow tie, and carried a slim, smooth, black leather briefcase. Gold cufflinks flashed above his wrists.

"Good afternoon," said Tommy Lee. "How was your trip?"

He stared at us in bewilderment. People like Pryor fear not having control, hate not knowing what is going on. Pryor obviously despised this situation.

"We need to talk a few minutes," said Tommy Lee, and he started for the door of the trailer. "Glad to see you have power today. Maybe Jane can make us a cup of coffee."

When Pryor entered his private office, he assumed his executive posture behind his desk. He had used the last few minutes to regain his composure and now felt confident to deal with our unannounced visit.

"I'm very busy, Sheriff. Is this a social call or can I help you in some manner?"

"A little of both," answered Tommy Lee. He took a cup of black coffee from Jane and sat down in one of the two guest chairs as if he had all the time in the world. I followed his lead and set my cup on the edge of Pryor's desk.

"So, how's the project going? Is my friend Mr. Ludden pleased?"

Some of the regained confidence ebbed out of Pryor's voice. "You know Ralph?"

"We've done some charitable work together. Veteran causes." Tommy Lee touched the patch on his eye. "Ralph has been very supportive, but you probably know all about that."

"Yes, I understand he was in the Marines."

I knew Tommy Lee had been active on issues for veterans, but he never dropped names. A CEO, a Congressman, or an unemployed vet all received equal treatment from him.

"Yeah, Ralph's a hell of a guy," he said. "Must be great to work for. Gives you the independence to do your job your way."

Pryor nodded enthusiastically.

"Wants you to have your own mind. I know he'd tell me 'Tommy Lee, if Fred Pryor wants to support Bob Cain, that's his business.'"

I thought the man would choke. He spit coffee back in his cup and his face turned neon red.

"That's not true," sputtered Pryor. "I just use Cain as a security consultant. I don't think he'd make a good sheriff."

"Well, thank you for your support. You may want another security consultant since somebody stuck Cain's bumper sticker on the back of your Buick." He paused and took a sip of coffee, savoring the man's discomfort. "So, the project is on schedule?"

"Ahead of schedule," Pryor said, anxious to move to another topic, "and under budget. The utility commission, our stockholders, and the Ridgemont customers will be glad to know that."

"Then you don't need to excavate as much as planned?"

"We are excavating more. Our work force has done an excellent job, and we've been able to go deeper. The volume of the lake will be over ten percent greater without flooding any more land or exceeding the specs of the dam. It's now a four-hundred-acre battery."

"Battery?"

"I've started calling it that. You've probably always heard it referred to as a pumped-storage project, but since power-generating potential will be stored in the water of the new Broad Creek reservoir, it's like a battery. We charge it at low-demand times and tap it at high-demand times."

"Wasn't there some question about energy efficiency?"

"Opponents tried to make something out of that. Yes, it will consume more power than it generates because Broad Creek is not a large enough body of water to feed the reservoir fast enough to run the generating units. That's why a tunnel is being dug to help fill the reservoir from Lake Montgomery fifteen hundred feet below."

"That's quite a distance," said Tommy Lee.

"It's true the electricity required to get water up into the reservoir is greater than the power generated when that same water falls down through the powerhouse chamber. But that's not the point. We pump the water with excess electricity at night or other times when our other facilities are under-utilized. A significant percentage of what would be lost generating capability is stored for use at times of peak demand. It's clean, it's safe, and it's responsible energy management." He punched this last phrase with all the PR tones of a television commercial.

"I'm just a local sheriff and you have to make it real simple. You're saying, at night, when there is plenty of extra electricity, you use it to pump water up out of Lake Montgomery and top off the reservoir?"

"That's right," said Pryor.

"Then when your customers are really pulling the system, say air conditioning on a hot day, then you use the reservoir water to make extra electricity, even though it puts out less than the power it originally took to pump that water up the mountain."

"Exactly."

"The water just flows back into Lake Montgomery?" asked Tommy Lee.

"Yes. We control that lake too. It is an inexhaustible, reusable supply."

"It's also the drinking water for many of the small foothill towns—the heart of their watershed."

"Plenty of water is available. Three years of drought conditions did not seriously affect Lake Montgomery."

"I was thinking of the water that is recycled and stored in your newly created basin. What safety measures have been taken to see there is no contamination?"

"The tunnel and the turbines will be as clean as the equipment at any treatment plant."

"And the land to be flooded? Has it been checked for any pollutants, either natural or unnatural?"

"Hundreds of tests have been run, soil samples taken. The EPA has crawled over the ground like ants."

"If they found something, would the project be stopped?"

"No. Just delayed until any cleanup is completed and the EPA standards are satisfied. But I assure you, we have been given full clearance. Our working relationship with the federal government is exemplary. Ralph Ludden even helped the Administration with energy policy."

"I know my buddy Ralph would want everything done by the book," said Tommy Lee.

"Broad Creek is a pet project of his. I don't mean to brag, but it is unusual that someone at my level of management would be on-site. This project is very important, and Ralph has entrusted me to personally see that every step is taken precisely by the book."

"Then will there be a thorough recheck of all the basin land in light of the Hope Quarry problem?"

Both of us saw the puzzled look cross Pryor's face.

Tommy Lee looked at me. My turn.

"You do know about the chemical spill?" I asked. "The EPA has been up there since yesterday." I caught the flash of panic in Pryor's eyes and the flick of his tongue as he moistened his lips.

"I've been out of town, you know. First I've heard of it."

Tommy Lee leaned forward in his chair and the chatty tone of his voice disappeared. "Mr. Pryor, containers were dumped in the quarry lake—containers filled with highly concentrated acid waste. The EPA thinks they may be chemicals used to process wood pulp into paper, or the toxic runoff collected from such a process. I'm surprised you haven't been notified."

"Why should I be? Hope Quarry is a good ten miles from here. That water is isolated from our operation."

"I saw the containers being pulled from the quarry. Each was stamped with the letters PPM. The Broad Creek Project does encompass all the land formerly occupied by the Pisgah Paper Mill, doesn't it?"

"You know it does." A defensive edge crept into Pryor's voice. "What's your point, Sheriff?"

"My point, Mr. Pryor, is that Ridgemont Power and Electric is clearing land once the site of a major paper mill. It now appears that toxic waste associated with that mill has been disposed of in a most irresponsible manner. I thought you might be concerned, especially since you are flooding Pisgah Paper Mill land with the water which will eventually flow from the taps of thousands of your customers. I know Ralph will be concerned."

Pryor chose his words very carefully. "Well, you are the first to bring it to my attention. If what you say is true, then I and Ridgemont Power and Electric certainly decry and condemn this outrage. We want to assure you and all our customers that since filling of the reservoir has not yet begun, we have complete access to the land and will reinspect a site that has already been thoroughly examined. There is no way toxic waste can remain undetected like that which has been submerged at Hope Quarry all these years. We hope those guilty can be found and brought to justice no matter how long ago the violation occurred."

Tommy Lee stood quickly, forcing the man to look up at him. "That's the interesting part. I don't think the EPA will be looking for guilty parties of long ago. They'll be focused on here and now. You see, along with those drums of chemical waste, the EPA found the body of Dallas Willard. You've heard of Dallas, I believe. And less than a week ago, he was very much alive."

Pryor's face turned to paste.

The sheriff paused long enough to make sure the executive was indeed speechless. "I won't trouble you for further comment at this time. We'll be in touch."

We left him at his desk and closed the door behind us. As I passed by Jane Cummings' phone, I saw that Fred Pryor had already put one of the lines in use.

Chapter 14

"What do you think he knows?" I asked.

"More than he's telling," said Tommy Lee. He started the patrol car and we drove away from the Broad Creek office. "I'm not sure he was surprised about the toxic dump, but there's no question in my mind that Pryor was surprised to learn we found Dallas Willard's body."

"Surprised that we found it or surprised that Dallas had been killed?"

"That's the critical point. What do you think?"

I tried to reconstruct Pryor's reactions as Tommy Lee told him about the Pisgah Paper Mill waste. Pryor's PR speech of bringing polluters to justice was canned, and I'm sure he'd given it before. It was the kind of thing he would say whether he thought his company were involved or not. However, if he knew a dead body was linked to the waste, he should have been more nervous when the sheriff first mentioned the pollutants.

"I think he was stunned that the body was with the contamination," I said. "Everyone has anticipated that Dallas could be found dead, most likely a suicide or case of exposure. But since those drums have a link to Broad Creek, Pryor is desperately trying to convince himself no one from his company is guilty."

"I agree. I just hope if he discovers what happened, he has got the sense not to cover it up."

"What are you going to do now?" I asked.

"Head back to the office. The M.E. report should be there by now. I want to see it."

I skipped to the "CONCLUSIONS" section and paraphrased aloud. "Probably no chance for defense. There were no other discernable marks on the body to indicate a struggle. Victim was standing at the time of the attack. Assailant had to be within a foot or two."

"Know that from the angle of the wound," said Tommy Lee.

"He says a four-inch blade. Something like a folding knife."

"Yeah. That's bad. They're so damn common."

"No indications of alcohol or drugs in Dallas' system." I read the rest of the report in silence, and then laid it in front of Tommy Lee. "Sure turned this out fast."

"Government pressure. I think the EPA is hoping Dallas could be blamed somehow for the toxic dumping."

"Why?"

"If it was an accident that happened while disposing of the drums, then I no longer have a murder investigation and I am no longer in their hair."

"A knife wound changes that," I said. "What do they say now?"

"Nothing. Clamps are coming down. I talked to someone in the criminal division. They're tracking former employees of Pisgah Paper. Another main probe is Broad Creek and Ridgemont Power. Ralph Ludden has a lot of Washington political clout and will be pulling PR strings, but basically he'll cooperate with the investigation. I've made it clear the murder is the most serious offense of all, and we have jurisdiction. I demanded their full assistance and any information pertaining to Dallas Willard that they might uncover."

"You see anything else in here that surprised you?" I asked.

"The coat."

"What coat?" I looked again at the report. "There is no mention of a coat?"

"Exactly. Where is the long gray coat he wore in the cemetery to hide the shotgun? It wasn't in the pickup and it wasn't on the body. Was he killed elsewhere, say inside, and then moved to the quarry? But you know how rough that road was. How did the murderer bounce him around in the pickup without some blood seepage? We went over that truck carefully and there were no blood stains."

"Someone not only has the shotgun but the great coat as well."

"That's what I think," said Tommy Lee.

"So, where are you going to start?" I asked.

"With a return visit to our new best friend, Fred Pryor. We'll see him bright and early in the morning. He thinks he's got troubles with the EPA. Wait till he hears in no uncertain terms his company is the subject of a murder investigation. And I'm gonna be in his hair like a hungry cootie."

"Really? I've always thought of you as more of a louse."

"You're confusing me with my opponent."

"Do you think Cain's involved in this somehow?" I asked. "He's in charge of security."

"Certainly a possibility. But I've got to be careful not to look like I'm persecuting him, especially since I've already arrested him once."

"That Coleman boy who died of the snakebite. His father is part of a group that works at Broad Creek. Wonder if they would know anything?"

"Maybe," said Tommy Lee. "They back yet?"

"I don't know. Last Sunday night the Colemans and their preacher went straight to Kentucky from the visitation. They might drive home today. Reverend Pace said they all live close together, like a compound. You ever seen it?"

"Once. Went up there trying to straighten out why their kids weren't in school. They've spread their shacks out along some acreage the power company owns. Not really an organized compound like those Branch Davidians in Waco. More of a migrant workers camp, except they had to build their own shelter. The site is not far from the power project. We can stop by on our way to rattle Pryor's chain."

A little before nine the next morning, Tommy Lee pulled behind an old maroon Plymouth. Reverend Pace's car. He and Sarah Hollifield were just getting out as we parked. Gone were Sarah's tartan skirt and black shoes. Now she wore jeans and a pair of hiking boots. Pace was making progress with his new charge.

"Got a new congregation?" joked Tommy Lee.

"Can you believe it?" asked Sarah. "That's their church."

We walked over to a circle of wooden benches surrounding a hand-hewn, six-foot cross erected in the center. It was an outdoor amphitheater carved in the woods where twenty or thirty worshipers could gather.

"From catacombs to cathedrals, it's the people who make the church," said Pace. He turned his attention back to us. "They in trouble with the law?"

"No," said Tommy Lee. "We're just following up some things. The Colemans back yet?"

Pace pointed to a shack barely visible through the trees. "Don't know. Sarah and I dropped by to see."

We walked thirty yards through the woods. Pace led the way, followed by Sarah. I stayed close behind, sticking to the narrow path which had been worn from the outdoor church to the compound of makeshift houses clustered on the ridge. Tommy Lee brought up the rear. As we stepped into the open, a voice broke the stillness.

"Wouldn't be thievin' now, would you?"

Leroy Jackson stepped around the corner of the first shack. He carried a gym satchel in one hand and his Bible in the other. Without a word of greeting, he strode to us, his face darkened with suspicion and anger.

"I truly hope you haven't suffered any theft or vandalism, Mr. Jackson," said Pace. He forced himself to present a smile and an attitude of concern. "We only came by to see that everything was all right with the Colemans. Figured you and them would be back from Kentucky."

Leroy Jackson paused a moment, not sure how to react to Pace's disarming words. "I drove all night to get back," he said flatly. "Luke and his wife are coming in tomorrow. Now I got to go to work."

"Power project?" asked Pace.

"Yeah. Hard, honest labor. I don't have any rich, liberal denomination sending me a paycheck."

Pace let the criticism pass unanswered.

"Well, we don't want to hold you up," said Pace. He nodded to us. "I believe you know Mr. Clayton and Sheriff Wadkins, and this is my associate, Reverend Sarah Hollifield."

"A woman? A woman preacher? I suggest you read your Bible, Miss Reverend Sarah Hollifield. First Corinthians 14:34—'Let your women keep silence in the churches: for it is not permitted unto them to speak; but they are commanded to be under obedience, as also saith the law. And if they will learn anything, let them ask their husbands at home: for it is a shame for women to speak in the church.'"

Sarah's face bloomed scarlet at the admonishment, but a fire leapt in her eyes. "'Let your women keep silence,' Mr. Jackson. I have good news to preach. Was it not Mary Magdalene to whom the Risen Lord first appeared and commanded she tell the others? Was it not also St. Paul who wrote we are all one in Christ, 'there is neither male nor female.' Yes, I do read my Bible, thank you, with my mind and my heart."

She turned away from Leroy Jackson before he had a chance to argue further. Reverend Pace whispered an "Amen" and followed, trying not to show the pride I knew he felt for his spunky sidekick.

"Let's go," Tommy Lee told me. "Mr. Jackson, I'm sure we will be meeting again."

"The Colemans have suffered enough," he said. "Leave them alone."

As we walked back to the patrol car, I had the feeling Leroy Jackson's eyes never left us.

"But I understood Mr. Pryor just returned from Charlotte yesterday." Sheriff Tommy Lee Wadkins made the statement sound like an accusation.

Jane Cummings simply shrugged her shoulders and said, "Mr. Ludden phoned Mr. Pryor last night. Mr. Pryor left me a message this morning that he was driving to Charlotte and would not be in the office today."

Tommy Lee looked at me and I could tell he was disappointed. Evidently Ridgemont Power and Electric was circling the wagons, and Pryor was being indoctrinated with the company line. I hoped that would mean full cooperation.

"When is he coming back?" asked Tommy Lee.

"He said he'd call when he got there. It's a three-hour drive. I don't expect to hear from him before one. If the meeting only lasts this afternoon, then he'll probably drive home tonight. He has rented a condo over in the Mica Valley resort."

"Well, when he phones in, let him know I want to speak with him first thing in the morning. Would you check his calendar?"

The woman flipped the pages of the date book on the corner of her desk. "I can't confirm his schedule until I speak with him, but it looks clear."

I edged closer to her desk, trying to get a better view of the appointment book. "What was Mr. Pryor's schedule last Thursday and Friday?"

She reviewed the pages. "He was in Asheville Thursday. That's where our main office was before we came here full time. Then he was here on Friday."

"Would you check his Friday morning appointments?" I asked.

"Nothing noted here. Perhaps it's on the daily log. Mr. Pryor has me keep a project journal. He likes a detailed record on a day-by-day basis." She hesitated and wondered whether she should be telling the police about her boss' private diary.

"I suggest you get it," said Tommy Lee. He anticipated her wavering. "The journal is just your chronological report of project activities. We're not requesting privileged information."

With that official assurance, she retrieved a loose-leaf notebook from the top of the credenza behind her desk. She opened it and found the days in question. "Here's last Friday." Several paragraphs were typed on clean white paper that had been hole-punched and reinforced so as not to tear out of the three-ring binder. She turned back a page. "And this is Thursday. Yes, Mr. Pryor spent the day in Asheville."

Thursday's report was handwritten on a sheet of lined yellow legal paper. "I forgot to re-type this one," Jane said. "Power was out that morning."

"Thursday?" I asked. "It was also out Friday when we first came by looking for Dallas Willard."

"That's the morning I mean," explained Jane. "I always type up the daily report on the following morning. But someone had backed into the utility pole Thursday night and knocked out the electricity to this trailer. Mr. Pryor was quite upset about it."

"Did he find out who did it?" asked Tommy Lee.

"That's part of why he got so angry. No one stepped forward and admitted it. Security's pretty tight. Someone had to have a gate pass-key to get on-site. And then it took longer than it should have that day to rehook the power. Some of the men were late to work."

"Do you mind?" I asked. I picked up the notebook before she could object and flipped a few pages. Stopping at one of the entries, I said, "On Saturday, Pryor met with Bob Cain. Does your boss work Saturdays?"

"Sometimes. He always has me log it. I think he wants the corporate office to see how dedicated he is."

"We saw Cain's car here the day before." Tommy Lee grabbed the journal. "Three to three-thirty, Saturday. No topic or reason listed. Do you know why Cain returned?"

"They meet frequently. Mr. Cain handles our security."

"Was it Cain who left someone free to knock over your power line?"

"Maybe that's why Pryor saw him last Saturday," suggested Jane.

"Maybe," said Tommy Lee.

As we stepped out of the trailer, he whispered, "I hope Pryor saw Cain last Saturday and tore him a new asshole."

"Really?" I asked. "Can an asshole tear an asshole on an asshole?"

"Good question. I don't know. But there's its shadow."

I followed Tommy Lee's gaze to the edge of the parking lot. Odell Taylor stood beside a yellow bulldozer, staring at us.

Chapter 15

When we returned to Broad Creek the next morning, a second trailer had been parked about twenty yards from Pryor's. A gray sedan with black-on-white federal plates was parked in front.

"I heard CEO Ralph Ludden has given permission for an EPA investigator to have an office on-site," said Tommy Lee. "Let's pay our respects to the Feds first. I want them to understand their information is my information."

We were surprised to find Miss Jane Cummings seated at a desk just inside the door. She had a stack of files and notebooks in front of her.

"New job?" asked Tommy Lee.

She shook her head. "I'm assigned to assist in the collection of any and all relevant materials," she said and rolled her eyes. Then she lowered her voice. "Mr. Pryor ordered me to grin and bear it. He said our guest will soon see there's nothing wrong." She glanced through the office door at the far end of the trailer where a young government agent was already going through a pile of books.

The man looked up from his work and immediately reacted to Tommy Lee's uniformed presence.

"Sheriff Wadkins," he stated and hurried out to greet us.

Tommy Lee saw Jane Cummings look at her watch, then grab her purse. "I need to speak with you," he said. "Don't leave for lunch yet."

"Kyle Murphy," said the agent, and he firmly shook our hands. "Phillip Camas told me to expect you. I'm in charge of the investigation in so far as the power company may be involved. Miss Cummings has provided the project journals, and Mr. Pryor is lending assistance during crew interviews and site analysis. If there is any way I can aid your murder case, just let me know."

"Thanks," said Tommy Lee. "Has the Pisgah Paper Mill connection led anywhere?"

"Not yet. We're not surprised. It's a defunct company, and no former manager wants to admit he improperly or illegally disposed of those cylinders."

"That's what I figured. Well, I can't think of anything I need right now. Don't let me keep you from your paperwork. I just have a few questions for Miss Cummings." He turned to the woman who sat fidgeting with her purse. "We can talk on the way to your car, can't we?"

Outside the new trailer, we walked ahead of the woman until we reached her vehicle. Tommy Lee leaned against the driver's door, making it clear she would have to get through him and his questions. "Did Mr. Murphy ask you anything unusual?" He folded his arms across his chest as if he could stand there all day.

"Guess not. Lot of questions about Mr. Pryor. Did his habits change recently? Does he drink on the job? Is he seeing people at the office not tied to the project?"

"What did you tell him?"

"That I haven't noticed anything. I just try to do what Mr. Pryor wants. He's not one of the easiest people I've ever worked for."

"He is a tight-ass, isn't he?"

Jane Cummings didn't smile. "Getting tighter by the hour."

I got the distinct feeling the lure of being in a Charlotte skyscraper with Pryor was losing its charm. He struck me as one of those men who lash out under pressure. Jane Cummings would be an easy target.

"He ever have any arguments with the men? I've known construction guys to be a hotheaded lot."

"Not really. The subcontractors are specialists. Ridgemont bids and buys the best. Odell Taylor handles the general laborers. He and Mr. Pryor seem to get along fine."

"What about Bob Cain? What does he do?"

"I don't know. He has meetings with Pryor and reviews our security arrangements. He doesn't come to the site that often." Jane looked at her watch for the third time. "Can we talk later? I'm meeting a girlfriend for lunch."

Tommy Lee ignored the plea and pressed forward to the main point of his inquiry. "We were here last Friday when the power was off. Someone knocked out the electricity."

"Yes. Right over there." She pointed to the far end of the gravel parking lot where the fifteen-foot pole supported the cable feeding the trailer.

"Put in a new one?" asked Tommy Lee.

"No. It didn't actually fall down. Just got bumped enough to snap the wire. The guys straightened it and restrung the power line."

"The guys. These the men who came in late?"

"Yes."

"Remember who they were?"

"Odell and some of the Kentucky crowd. Faron Thomas and Junior Crawford."

"Luke Coleman?"

"Don't remember. Think he was sick last Friday."

"Pryor must have blown his stack when they were late. He sure seemed hot when we talked to him."

"That's kind of funny. He was angry when he first got here, but when Odell and the men finally showed up, he joked about it. Didn't even dock their hours."

Tommy Lee didn't ask any further questions. He stepped aside and opened the door. "Thanks for your time, Miss Cummings. I'll be back in touch."

As her car drove away, we walked the length of the parking lot to the utility pole. One section, about three feet off the ground, still showed splintered damage. A streak of blue paint marked the spot where a fender or tail-gate had wedged against the treated timber.

"Pryor drives a blue car," I said. "Could he have done it himself?"

"Maybe," said Tommy Lee. "He could have been too arrogant to admit to us or Jane Cummings that he did something stupid like that. Easier to blame it on the crew." He looked at Pryor's empty parking spot. "I see he skipped on us. Probably saw us go into Kyle Murphy's trailer and now will claim he had a meeting and couldn't hang around."

I followed Tommy Lee back into the EPA investigator's office. Kyle Murphy looked up from his papers.

"I'm heading out," said Tommy Lee.

"Was she any help?" asked Murphy.

"Not particularly. Mentioned a few possibilities. I guess you're already checking into Bob Cain?"

Murphy's face went blank as he struggled to place the name.

"Cain," repeated Tommy Lee. "The outsider who consulted on security. Miss Cummings didn't know why he kept coming by for special weekend meetings." The sheriff let the words "special weekend" roll off with an ominous inflection. "It's awkward for me to investigate. Cain is challenging me in next month's election."

"Oh, yes. He's on our list. Appreciate your sensitivity. We'll keep you out of it, but we're going to have to make him a priority."

"Whatever you think best," said Tommy Lee. "We'll stay in touch."

He chuckled to himself as we stepped outside.

"Whatever you think best," I repeated. "You're wicked. By tomorrow morning, Cain will be a bug under a huge federal microscope."

"Yeah," said Tommy Lee. "A bug I hope gets squashed."

Since there was nothing I could do to help Tommy Lee on Saturday, I decided to enjoy some normalcy and get as far removed from a multiple murder investigation as I could. At nine-thirty I turned into Fletcher's pasture, which serves as the park-free zone for all the archery tournaments at our club. Although my wounded shoulder would not allow me to compete in my favorite hobby, I thought walking the course as a spectator would do my spirits some good.

Susan rode beside me in the Jeep, dressed in lightweight, wheat-colored jeans and a red cotton blouse. She'd rolled the cuffed sleeves back from her wrists. A novice at her first tournament, she had taken my warning about ticks to heart and left little skin exposed.

Breakfast had been a treat, not only because Susan had given into Herbie's House of Pancakes and their buttermilk flapjacks smothered in real Vermont maple syrup, but also because she was a wonderful diversion from the cyclone of events usurping my life. Now she and the tournament promised to take me away from those problems for awhile.

I parked between a 1963 Impala and a new Range Rover. The vehicles epitomized the socioeconomic span of the participants. Trunks and car doors stood open as archers selected their equipment for the day. To the uninitiated, it appeared to be a tailgate party or impromptu flea market. Susan saw everything through fresh eyes, and as we walked along, she didn't hesitate to barrage me with questions.

"Why are there wheels on the bows?" She pointed to two men sitting on the tailgate of a pickup truck. Each held a compound bow. The cam wheels at the tips and the multiple strings linking them together certainly gave the impression of a contraption that would have caused Robin Hood to shake his head in disbelief.

I overheard enough of their conversation to recognize the endless arguments that keep archers jawing for hours: magnesium vs. wood vs. aluminum for bow construction, the ideal arrow weight, the perfect flight speed, ad nauseam.

"The wheels act like pulleys on a block and tackle rig," I explained. "Draw back the bow and sixty pounds of effort can be reduced to thirty pounds. The more power in a bow, the harder it is to pull. This design lets even a woman shoot a hunting bow."

"Even a woman?" Susan drenched me with sarcasm.

"Did I say woman? I meant even a wimp like myself."

"Barry!"

I heard my name on the open air.

"Barry," shouted Josh Birnam. He stood at the end of the row of cars, waving his bow over his head.

Josh and I could pass for brothers. The color of our sandy, curly hair matched perfectly, and we both cut it the same. Josh wore glasses and stood a couple of inches taller at an even six feet, but we drew the same length arrow which, in an archer's eye, made us the same height. He was thirty-five, five years older than me, and he looked it, thank God. As we walked toward him, I enjoyed watching the curiosity grow on his face.

"Josh, you know Dr. Susan Miller."

He shook her hand and then looked at me. "So, you brought a doctor along just to back up this phony sling as your excuse to get out of the tournament?"

"That's right. I did his surgery myself," said Susan.

Josh didn't miss a beat. "Well, that explains it."

"Explains what?" asked Susan.

"Why you're with this turkey. Professional duty, right? No good-looking woman would hang around him voluntarily. And I apologize, Barry. Obviously, you're severely injured."

"Tell me, Josh," she said. "Do you shoot arrows as well as you shoot bull?"

"Unfortunately, no." He laughed. "But maybe my arrow shooting will improve. I got the new bow, Barry." Josh held out his prize for me to admire. The high-gloss silver and camo finish enhanced the image of its technical wizardry.

"So, you went with the Lightning," I said.

"Yeah, Darton makes another bow I liked, but this one just has such a great feel. I jumped to a sixty-pound pull, and at full draw, it's no heavier than my old one. Want to try it?"

"With what?" I asked. "My feet?"

"Hey, that might improve your scores," he said. "Surely something can. I brought you my old bow and arrows."

He reached into the rear of his SUV and pulled out another camo-colored bow and quiver of arrows.

"Josh is a certified archery addict," I said to Susan. "He has to get the latest and greatest."

"Why are you giving Barry your arrows?" she asked.

"My new bow takes a stiffer spine. And who said anything about giving. Shoot them, Barry, and if you like them, we can work out something on next year's tax fee. The fletchings are in good shape. I'm not just giving you the shaft."

"This will be a first."

"Why do arrows have to match a bow?" asked Susan.

"It's all very scientific," said Josh. "The arrow has to bend a little as the bow releases its stored energy, but the arrow can't flex too much or it wobbles. Either way accuracy suffers. Barry has a wimpy bow, so he'll have to use these arrows with this bow."

"I guess even a woman could shoot Barry's," said Susan.

"Yeah, even a woman," agreed Josh, not realizing he was trampling through a flower bed.

Susan smiled at me. "So, show us what a real man can do."

We transferred Josh's old bow and arrows to my Jeep, and then followed him to the practice range that hugged the boundary of the pasture and woods. Six targets lined the edge of the forest. Multiple stakes marked the distances from them. Archers waited in line for a chance to set their bow sights because once on the actual course, the distances would be unknown, just like in hunting. The archers would have to estimate and adjust their sights against the tested reference points.

These targets were not the multi-colored concentric rings around the gold bull's-eye that most people remember from a few hours of practice at summer camp. Instead the only clear spot to aim at was a small black circle on a white field. I realized as Josh sent four arrows inside that sweet circumference that he would be hell to beat whenever I started shooting again.

"Okay. Ready as I'll ever be," he said, after nailing another four from sixty yards. "Let's go join up with Doug and Sally Turner. We go off at ten. I knew they wouldn't mind you tagging along, and the total number of entrants worked out so that we can stay a threesome without adding someone who may object to my little entourage."

Normally, tournament rules allowed four archers to shoot the course together, much like a foursome in golf. A path wound through the woods, passing by thirty different three-dimensional targets. Thirty molded replicas of deer, bear, and a variety of small game animals constituted the challenge. Clean "kills" scored ten points. Other hits counted for eight or five. A perfect round was three hundred.

We stopped at the registrar's table where Josh picked up a scorecard. Doug and Sally Turner waited along the pathway to the first target. Like church door greeters, they welcomed everyone and wished them luck on the round. Silver-haired and crinkled from years of outdoor activities, both would never see seventy again. Yet they lived as if their whole lives stretched before them, looking forward with excitement to whatever the next day held in store.

Sally captivated Susan immediately. Who wouldn't be fascinated upon meeting a storybook grandmother armed to the teeth. Battle gear included a quiver of twelve arrows hanging from her waist and a leather arm guard strapped to the inside of her left forearm with a matching, right-handed finger glove to keep the bowstring from slicing into the skin during the thirty times Sally would draw, aim, and release. The bow at her side gleamed black in the sunlight, uniquely wicked-looking with its high-gloss finish where most archers chose the greens and browns of traditional camouflage design.

"Stay with me, honey," Sally told Susan after I made the introductions. "We'll show these men what we can do with their precious phallic symbols."

"Don't mind her," joked Doug. "It's my fault she's over-sexed."

"A legend in his own mind," said Sally. She stepped up to the first stake and stared down the cleared forest avenue to the model grizzly reared up on hind legs. The menacing target looked a good seventy yards away. "Ladies first, I assume." Then she said to Susan, "They always say that to make me take the first shot. I'm the guinea pig to get the distance, but then I fib about where my sights are set."

She slid her needle-pointed sight lower on its track, nocked an aluminum arrow and drew back until its small conical tip was flush with the front of the bow. Broadhead hunting blades were not permitted as the targets would be shredded before half the archers went around the course. Sally's left arm elevated a few inches, and then held steady. A full five seconds elapsed. At last, the string twanged its solitary note of relief as the arrow leapt forward, hurled by the pent-up energy into arced flight. We watched the white feathers curve downward and slam into the frozen creature's chest. A second later the smack of the impact returned to our collective ear.

"Bravo, Sally," cheered her husband, the spotting binoculars held to his eyes. "A perfect shot. Did you go at sixty-five yards?"

"See what I mean," she told Susan. "Gee, I can't remember, dear. It was either sixty-five or seventy-five, I guess."

Josh shot next. The power of the new bow propelled his arrow in a much flatter trajectory, but Doug sighed behind the binoculars. "No, just outside the kill area, up on the neck. Better not allow for much drop."

Doug's own arrow arced more than Josh's but struck lower. Sally had spotting honors and announced, "You just raised his growl three octaves. He's alive, but you killed his future children."

The banter continued throughout the entire round. I had expected Josh to carry the day; but Sally, inspired by Susan's presence, made kill after kill. As we walked away from the last target, Doug double-checked his math and proudly declared his wife had set a new personal record. She finished only three points behind Josh and stood a good chance of winning the Woman's First Place Trophy.

"Drinks are on me," said Sally, and led us over to the volunteer fire department's concession stand.

We commandeered an empty table. Josh tossed several bags of shelled peanuts in the middle to keep us going while the tournament rankings were tabulated.

Doug Turner tore open a corner of one packet and poured salted nuts in his hand. "You know what I like about goobers? That."

He pointed to an adjacent picnic table where a young mother served slices of watermelon to three carrot-topped boys whose ages probably ranged from three to eight. The youngest shrieked, tears gushing down a face as red as his hair, and waved a pudgy hand at the yellow-jacket wasp that belligerently strutted across the juicy pulp.

"Goobers don't interest any bees or bugs I know of." He tossed a peanut high in the air and caught it in his mouth.

"I once performed an emergency tracheotomy at a baseball game," said Susan. "The guy caught three peanuts in his windpipe. I don't worry about someone catching a watermelon in his mouth."

"See, Doug. I've told you that a thousand times," said his wife. "You don't want me to go cutting on your throat, do you?"

"Aren't you kidding?" Doug asked Susan, taking an extra chew or two for safety.

"Yeah, I am."

Sally laughed. "Child, you've got a devilish sense of humor."

Josh asked, "How long are you going to keep Barry looking like a goony bird with a busted wing?"

"Probably five or six weeks. Then he'll be out here losing his arrows like old times."

"Barry, she's seen you shoot before," said Doug.

Sally wiped the flecks of peanut dust from her hands and looked across the table at me, her face suddenly aged with worry. "Why, Barry? Why would Dallas Willard want to kill you?"

I shrugged. "I don't know. Guess I was at the wrong place at the wrong time. He was upset his grandmother had died. And he may have thought his brother and sister were selling the family land out from under him."

"Waylon Hestor's project," commented Doug, as if we all knew what that meant.

"What?" The intensity of my single syllable caught everyone's attention.

Doug reacted as if he had said a cuss word at the church barbecue. "There was nothing wrong with it. Josh, your name was mentioned. Look, Waylon was a general partner bringing in limited partners to develop property. I've invested with him before. So have you, Josh."

"No, not exactly," Josh corrected. "I've audited some of his deals in the past. He's clean enough, Barry. He's a real estate developer who lives in Asheville, but he has holdings in our county."

"This limited partnership, it wouldn't by chance be to develop land adjacent to migrant work camps?"

"Yes, it would," Josh said. "If and when the county consolidated the worker camps, the limited partnership would begin development of land tracts owned by Waylon. The low profile was kept because of the politics involved, but nobody did anything illegal. Waylon already owns the property."

"Yeah, but I bet he'll be first in line to buy up the old camps as they are closed."

"Probably," said Josh. "It's public record, Barry. Carl Romeo handled all the legal filings."

"Carl Romeo? But he—" I stopped myself from blurting out that he hadn't told me anything about it. Instead, I continued—"but he would make sure everything was in order."

"Exactly my point, Barry."

Chapter 16

I dropped Susan off at her condo, declining her offer for lunch and claiming I needed to review some files at Tommy Lee's office.

Fifteen minutes later, I turned down Vance Avenue. Down aptly described the sloping street whose sidewalks each hid behind a row of white pines that guarded the Saturday strollers from the Saturday cruisers. Vance Avenue dissected the heart of Gainesboro's vintage neighborhood of choice. The houses were set back in generous lawns. Most were two-story brick or stone built in the 1930s. An occasional ranch sprawled across an acre, breaking the pattern.

Carl Romeo owned a neo-Victorian he had constructed on the ashes of a client's fire-gutted disaster. Suing the electrical contractor and insurance company for faulty wiring had not rejuvenated his client's incinerated invalid mother, but it had provided enough cash for the client to move to Florida and Carl to buy the scorched, empty lot.

A bronze plaque embedded in the stone column that marked the entrance to his driveway summed up the story: "PHOENIX HOUSE." Fifty feet from the curb, the driveway split with one lane looping behind the house and the other ending in a brick-lined terrace used for guest parking. A powder-blue Cadillac occupied a third of the space. I pulled to the far right, allowing as much clearance as possible.

Prior to that day, I would have turned my car around and driven off, not wanting to encroach upon someone's Saturday afternoon company by arriving unannounced. But now social conventions and courtesies carried no significance because although I wasn't sure where my action was taking me, action was required, no matter what proper etiquette decreed.

I walked between purple and yellow pansies lining the Romeos' sidewalk. This horizontal sea of blossoms rippled in the late afternoon breeze. The air moving over my skin felt neither hot nor cold, a curious lack of sensation blending me into the world around me. The phrase thermal harmony popped in my mind. It was the only harmonious thought I had.

A wide, covered porch extended across the entire front of the house. Two Adirondack chairs and a cane-bottom rocker held sentry duty, their empty frames huddled in silent homage to some past conversation.

As I reached the front door, I heard muffled voices at a distance farther than just the other side. Most likely, they were in the dining room if I remembered the layout of Carl's house correctly. Too early for a dinner party. Perhaps a neighbor had dropped by, and Carl could easily excuse himself.

A brass knocker in the shape of a gavel tempted me to enthusiastically call the court to order. Instead, I used the doorbell which sent out a mellow chime proclaiming a wanderer at the gate.

There was a faint sound of a door closing, then footsteps. No window or peephole offered advance warning that I stood on the threshold. The latch clicked, and I gave Carl a tight-lipped smile as he stood in the half-opened doorway, his eyebrows arched in unrestrained surprise.

"Barry?" He stopped, clearly not sure what to say.

"Carl, I need to talk to you."

"I've got company, Barry."

"I'll just be a minute or two."

He hesitated a second and then opened the door wider. Perhaps he intended to step out, but I took the move as approval and slipped into the foyer beside him. On the left, closed French doors screened me from Carl's company, which was just as well as it relieved the need for introductions and my awkward request that Carl and I speak in private.

He led me through the archway on the right into the living room. I knew next to nothing about antiques, but I speculated the furnishings in the room were of significant value. Carl sat in an armless, velvet-cushioned chair and motioned me to the adjacent small settee. Now that we sat face to face, I wished I had rehearsed this conversation. Carl allowed no time to craft an opening sentence.

He folded his arms on his chest and asked, "So what's this about?"

"It's still about Dallas Willard and the Willard property. It's about your not telling me about your involvement in a venture to get the land."

He paled and his tongue flickered across his upper lip. Reading his face proved difficult. A tangled mixture of anger and fear. He leaned forward, placing a hand on each of his knees. The fingers whitened slightly as he gripped his khaki pants.

In a voice barely above a whisper, he said, "That's not fair. You asked me to speculate on the value."

"I didn't think we were splitting legal hairs, Carl. The context was what could have caused Dallas Willard to behave as he did. Any individuals or situations that could have pressured him were certainly relevant to my questions."

"I was not splitting legal hairs. I was respecting legal ethics. I don't go around giving out my clients' names or discussing their business any more than you go around saying how much somebody spent on a funeral. You should understand that."

His words stung and the blood rushed hot in my cheeks. To hell with thermal harmony. Frustration pushed my decibel level to a near shout. "We've had enough god-damned funerals. And what about your responsibility to Martha Willard, and Norma Jean, and Lee, and Dallas. They were your clients too, and the bodies don't stop there, Carl. Something is going on I don't understand, but if there is a connection, any connection, between what happened in that cemetery and Dallas Willard's and Fats McCauley's death, I'll be god-damned if I'm stopping until I'm satisfied that I know all there is to know even if it creates a problem for you, or Doug Turner, or some hot-shit wheeler-dealer named Waylon Hestor."

The flicker of fear on Carl's face burst into outright panic. He looked to the dining room doors as they split apart.

"Just who the hell do you think you are?" shouted a steel-haired man who strode across the foyer and into the living room. He stopped only a few inches away, towering over me, the wealthy tan on his face broken with blotches of fury. We recognized each other. He had been the distinguished mourner at Grandma Willard's funeral.

I sat in stunned silence and then guessed the obvious. "Carl," I said in the quietest, most civil tone I could muster. "Why don't you introduce me to Mr. Waylon Hestor?"

Carl Romeo got to his feet, and for a split-second, he looked like he would bolt from his own house. I stayed seated, leaving both men to realize my level suited me perfectly. I was content to look up to them and found nothing intimidating in our relative positions. Psychological power stayed on the settee with me.

"Mr. Hestor, this is Barry Clayton."

Carl waited, but neither Hestor nor I said anything. I wasn't expecting a handshake or a "glad to meet you." He had just heard me call him a "hot-shit wheeler-dealer."

Carl filled the silence. "Barry, that is Mr. Clayton, was shot by Dallas Willard."

"I know," said Hestor. "I was standing beside him."

Carl looked surprised for a second, and then continued, "Barry came to me thinking I might know why and could it involve Martha Willard's land. I told him how attached Dallas was to the ridge sections of the property based upon an earlier effort to buy it. Now he apparently believes I was less than truthful because I didn't mention your development plans."

Waylon Hestor studied me for a few seconds. His eyes focused on my left arm and shoulder while he relived the horror of the cemetery. I assessed him as well. He looked to be in his early fifties. The green pullover short-sleeve shirt and yellow cotton slacks tagged him as the country club set. His body was trim and lean, the result of a disciplined diet and regular exercise. I suspected he took an active role in whatever interested him. I also suspected he wielded formidable economic and political power, and that he did not like to lose.

Waylon Hestor cleared his throat in an effort to reset his vocal cords to a more conversational mode. "You're an undertaker, aren't you?"

He asked the question without sarcasm or any implied condescension. More for confirmation.

"Yes. And I've had more business than I want."

"That was a terrible tragedy up there. I hope you have a speedy recovery, Mr. Clayton. I can understand why you want answers." He looked at Carl and frowned. "I appreciate your concern with confidentiality, Carl, but, under the circumstances, I want Mr. Clayton to know I do have an interest in the Willard property. Frankly, that's why I attended the service—to pay my respects, sign the register book, and begin a relationship with the heirs."

I slid over. "Why don't you have a seat?"

"I think the dining room is more appropriate, don't you, Carl?"

Our mutual attorney gave an audible sigh of relief.

Five or six tubes of rolled documents were stacked at one end of the dining room table. Two copies of *Architectural Digest* on either side of this elongated pyramid kept it from collapsing. An inch-thick pile of unrolled charts and survey reports fanned across the center of the table. Most looked like topographical mappings of land tracts, although their exact technical description was unknown to me. Several of the larger sheets had black and white aerial photographs clipped to them. Hand-drawn red lines on each photo

identified an area of particular significance, probably corres-
ponding to the attached surveyor's plot.

I walked full circle around the table, looking for anything
that would put me on familiar ground. Even the aerial shots
offered nothing in the way of recognizable landmarks.

"This mess is a process," said Waylon Hestor. "A process
of prioritization."

"Housing developments?" I asked.

"One residential community to start with." He walked to
the table, rolled back the top two sheets of drawings and
pointed to an aerial composite.

Across the upper left corner ran a two-lane highway with
a cleared circular area beneath it. There I saw the roofs of
migrant shanties and an old school bus parked in a dirt lane
connecting the camp to the paved road. A dotted line had
been drawn from the highway through the school bus and
shanties into the middle of the wooded terrain.

Waylon Hestor's broad hand and stubby fingers swept an
ellipse around the picture. "As things stand now, most likely
my land out on Walnut Hollow Road. You see, my investors
and I don't have the kind of capital to take on more than one
project at a time. Sure, I own three tracts, but it is the investment company that's got to put in the roads, survey the lots,
create a marketing plan, and sell the real estate. Carl and I
are determining which tract will have the lowest start-up costs,
whether it be road construction, sewer and water lines, or
environmental impact studies."

"And how about return on investment?" I asked. "Isn't
that what it's all about? Keep your costs down and your prices
up? The Willard property has more than a little to do with
pricing, particularly if the migrant camp beside it is closed."

"Indirectly." He looked back at Carl, who still stood just
inside the double doors.

"We're willing to lay that out for you, Barry," said Carl.
"There's nothing to hide."

"Then let me take a stab at it," I said. "Mr. Hestor, all your property borders migrant camps. No coincidence. In fact, you probably bought it cheap because of that proximity. A migrant camp is not a desirable neighbor to an exclusive residential community. You're smart enough to take the long-range view that someday, when those camps are gone, the value of your land jumps immediately. So, regardless of those development costs you've just outlined, the lot prices increase without you spending an extra nickel. A government recommendation for centralization can make that happen. You work quietly behind the scenes so the politics come together, and you and Carl start working on the Willards to sell their land. It's a tract you don't own, but fits in with your plans. Only Dallas won't budge. In fact, he thinks the migrant camps are directly tied into the deal somehow and begins taking out his hostility on the workers."

I looked from Hestor to Carl Romeo. Neither seemed concerned. They simply waited patiently for me to finish.

"So, his brother and sister get the grandmother to leave the property in such a way that Dallas can be out-voted. And you don't tell him anything about the new will, Carl. Then Grandma Martha dies. Dallas thinks everything is like his grandmother promised in that sketch, but someone tells Dallas the truth. That causes him to come to your office, where your secretary confirms his fears. When he finds out his brother and sister can sell the land, he makes plans to kill them."

"That's an interesting theory, Mr. Clayton." Waylon Hestor actually smiled. "Part of it might be true. I can't know what Dallas Willard thought or what his family told him. I don't know why he should think the migrants had anything to do with it. I do know I neither spoke with him nor instructed anyone else to."

He waved his hands over the table. "This is what I like to do. Take something from an idea to a finished project. Sure, I want to make money. And yes, bottom line, that's why I have an interest in the government consolidating the migrant camps so that property like the Willards' becomes more valuable. At least that's the way it started."

"What changed?" I asked.

"Everything changed. Now buying the Willard land also means buying lakefront property when the new reservoir is filled." He gestured toward another aerial photograph. This larger one included several ridges with a blue-coded oval superimposed over the valley between them. It depicted the expected shoreline when the Broad Creek dam was completed. "That means double maybe even triple appreciation," continued Hestor, "and now I'm competing with Ridgemont Power and Electric who wants the property just as badly. Hell, they don't want to protect the watershed, they want to sell lakefront lots and homes like they've done with every other hydro-electric lake they've ever created."

I heard the anger come back in his voice.

He heard it too and sighed. "But, the money isn't life or death to me. As for the government, you flatter me that I exercise any control. I've been to a few hearings and seen the county and federal bureaucrats in action on the migrant camp consolidation. Yes, they'll probably agree on a centralized site, but I had nothing to do with it. If anything, my lobbying would have hurt that proposal. Others would draw the same conclusion you have and figure I was only out to make a quick buck."

Waylon Hestor spoke with conviction. If pressed for a judgment, I would have said he told the truth. I had also heard so many good liars that I refused to suspend my skepticism. Hestor admitted the Willard land made a difference to his bottom line. For a business man driven to succeed, there might be no other priority.

"Carl had a buyer for the land at three hundred thousand ten years ago," I said. "What's it worth today?"

"Ten times that. I've offered three million."

"Your other investors, the limited partners, how many are there?"

"Thirty. Each has put in an additional fifty thousand. I've made up the rest."

I turned the numbers in my head. One and a half million from the partners, the same from Waylon Hestor. Dallas stood between his brother and sister and three million dollars. Three million dollars that went to Talmadge Watson as soon as the gun smoke cleared in that cemetery.

"Would any of the other investors have approached Dallas? Tried to get him to sell?"

"No one would have gone around me," said Carl. "The limited partners are legally prohibited from any management or strategic decisions. That protects their liability to their original investment."

"Yes. That's the downside, but on the upside, what do you estimate the removal of the camps and the lake frontage to mean?"

"A thirty to fifty percent increase in the price per lot," said Waylon Hestor. "Throw in the more expensive homes that will be built on the more expensive property and the total revenue from the development jumps ten-fold. We're talking a thirty million dollar deal."

"Well, you may not be greedy, Mr. Hestor, but out of thirty people who plopped down fifty thousand for the Willard property, you're saying none of them wants to earn as much as he can? That no one would engineer steps to make that happen?"

"I'm afraid you still don't understand," said Hestor. "Engineer what steps? When I say everything changed, I mean everything changed up in that graveyard. With no Willard heirs, the property will eventually be auctioned off. Ridgemont Power and Electric has pockets as deep as that reservoir. We can't compete."

I shot a glance at Carl Romeo and felt guilty about my accusations against him. He had kept Waylon Hestor in the dark about Talmadge Watson.

"How did you expect to compete at all once the power company became interested?"

"I'm a real person," he said. "Yes, I've been financially successful, but I was born up on Yellow Mountain and had the good fortune to develop my family's property instead of simply selling off when the first land speculators came in thirty years ago. The Willards liked talking to a homegrown, not an institution of suits. I thought I had a chance to work out a deal even Dallas would have been happy with, until I realized he was mentally ill. Then we tried to work around him."

I looked down at the tract surveys. They could as easily have been the locations of lost gold mines given all the money at stake.

"And you're sure none of your investors would have thought they could intimidate Dallas into selling and thereby aggravated his unstable condition."

"No, I can't say that with certainty," conceded Hestor.

"I think it's important the sheriff know who those thirty people are. You have my word any inquiries will be handled discreetly."

"And if we refuse?" asked Carl.

"I expect Sheriff Wadkins will decide how he wants to incorporate you and your limited partners into his open investigation of Dallas Willard. Discretion will become a public inquiry."

"Make up the list, Carl." Hestor pulled a slim billfold from his hip pocket. He extracted a business card and handed it to me. "Here are phone numbers for home, office, and car. In return for my cooperation, I'd appreciate a call if you learn anything."

I looked at the string of numbers under HESTOR ENTER-PRISES before slipping the card in my own wallet. "Certainly," I said.

It was after 5 P.M. when I left Phoenix House. Carl Romeo handed me a folded sheet of white paper which I tucked unopened into the front pocket of my slacks. On it, he had written the names of the thirty investors, and although I was eager to read them, I waited until the first stoplight on Vance Avenue before unfolding the paper against the center of the steering wheel.

I scanned the list. Most were unknown to me, probably cronies of Hestor in Asheville. A few were familiar, moneyed individuals who lived in Gainesboro. Doug Turner's name was near the top although I didn't believe Carl had listed them in any particular order. The last name surprised me. Dr. Alex Soles. Did the psychologist have a very practical and profitable reason for not helping Dallas Willard? Or was there more to it than that? What kind of mind games could he have played if he had seen Dallas after Martha Willard died?

I called Tommy Lee and laid the whole thing out. Dr. Alex Soles would be getting an unexpected visitor.

Chapter 17

The breakfast crowd came in shifts at the Cardinal Cafe. Most of the construction workers arrived between six and six-fifteen, wolfing down tankards of hot coffee and platters of eggs and grits. They were replaced by the shopkeepers and tradesmen whose livelihood enjoyed a more leisurely start on the workday. Finally, the retirees arrived, meeting a crony or two and lingering over morning coffee and sweet rolls; by nine-thirty, the bustle had faded to a few tables of gossip and refills.

At seven forty-five Monday morning, the triple bells over the front door announced our arrival. Helen, the head waitress, glanced back over her shoulder and saw Tommy Lee and me entering the diner. The sheriff raised two fingers and pointed to an isolated booth along the wall. We were between the shifts of shopkeepers and retirees, and the restaurant would fill up again before eight. With a nod, Helen grabbed a pot of coffee and two cups from the counter.

I followed Tommy Lee's example and kept my voice low. We also avoided names whenever possible. "So, what did you learn from our doctor friend?" I asked.

"Not much. I called on him at his house yesterday afternoon. As soon as I mentioned the Hestor project, he started blubbering about how he didn't mean to avoid Dallas. He started psychoanalyzing himself. Subconscious motives he didn't recognize. He was more concerned I would report him to a licensing review board than that he was a murder suspect. Psychologists! They're all crazy."

"Crazy like a fox. He had a conscious motive to push Dallas to sell. I'm concerned he did see him and tried to manipulate him. I don't know much about dealing with someone like Dallas, but I suspect it can be playing with fire. He would have a good reason to lie to you if he talked to Dallas right before Dallas shot his brother and sister."

"Yeah, maybe," Tommy Lee said. "Our doctor said he hadn't seen Dallas since he quit the Alzheimer's meetings. Kept saying Dallas was not his patient. And I heard the tape of Dallas Willard's voice, the messages he left trying to reach you the night before the funeral. Dallas didn't say a thing about him."

"Okay," I admitted. "That's a point in his favor."

"He was also aware that with Lee and Norma Jean dead the power company holds the cards and the cash if the property goes to auction. You told me Carl Romeo has kept mum about Talmadge Watson's connection."

"That's right," I said. "Waylon Hestor didn't know anything about Talmadge. I'm surprised someone in the Ridgemont Power and Electric legal department hasn't discovered Martha had a brother."

"Why should they look? The line of descendants was uncontested down to Dallas, Lee, and Norma Jean. No one anticipated a whole family would be murdered."

"But they will look now," I said. "There is too much at stake."

"Probably. Carl Romeo found Talmadge because he went back to the hard records. The county hasn't computerized those early twentieth century birth certificates yet. Maybe Martha's birth record will be entered when her death certificate is being processed. But birth records don't list siblings and Martha was born before Talmadge."

"Without an heir, the benefactor will be the power company, and it's the least likely to be a murder suspect."

"We're talking about people," said Tommy Lee. "Not an institution."

"Then who personally benefits?" I asked.

Tommy Lee stared into his coffee cup, as if the answer were to be found there. "I'm afraid the Feds are going to have to break that case for us. We need to learn if Dallas was killed because of his land or because he witnessed the dumping of the toxic waste."

"Again, that comes back to the power company. We've got Fred Pryor, Bob Cain, and those Kentucky men who were late Friday morning."

"Yeah. Pryor doesn't want the EPA delaying construction. That could cost hundreds of thousands, maybe even millions of dollars at a time when he needs to look like the corporate heir apparent. We know Cain is a hothead who acts first and thinks later, and we know those Kentucky families depend upon the power company for both a paycheck and housing. Pryor's right-hand man, Odell Taylor, tells them what to do. That could include loading and unloading the drums."

"Taylor," I said. "He's the guy Pryor depends on when dealing with the crew. Have you heard anything from that EPA investigator Kyle Murphy?"

"No. Finish your coffee and let's see if he had a nice weekend."

Kyle Murphy pulled a report from a file on the desk where Jane Cummings had organized materials. Evidently, Jane was attending to her normal Monday morning duties for Fred Pryor in the other trailer.

"They all said they were with Leroy Jackson at a morning prayer meeting," said Murphy. "They just ran long."

"On a Friday morning?" I asked.

"That man keeps them in line," said Tommy Lee. "I hear even Odell Taylor's fallen in with them. What else have you got?"

"We were busy all weekend working through the federal computer networks. I'm not going to give you the written files, not unless it's needed for prosecution, but I will tell you we traced a path that had some interesting turns and twists."

"Money," said Tommy Lee. "You followed money."

"Too bad I don't live here, Sheriff. You just got my vote."

"What do you have?" I asked impatiently, anxious to hear names.

"Where does this path begin?" asked Tommy Lee.

"Excellent question," said Murphy. "Where it starts is always as important as where it ends. This trail begins with a discretionary account controlled directly by Fred Pryor. Now there is nothing wrong with that. I made a quiet inquiry in their Charlotte office and learned project managers often have access to funds not earmarked for any particular budget line. Ridgemont Power audits them quarterly and the expenditures are assigned to a job cost. It gives the manager of a major project like this one faster reaction time without being tied to purchase orders and computer checks, especially when you're isolated in the mountains, three hours from the home office."

"How much money are we talking about?" I asked.

"Only six thousand. That was the budget for the quarter. It is wired into the local branch and Pryor can manually write a check for cash."

"So, what's unusual?" asked Tommy Lee.

"He isn't a full month into the quarter and the account's nearly depleted. We got photocopies of the canceled checks. Only one stub has a reference, a hundred dollar check to Luke Coleman for bereavement written Sunday, October twenty-first. Two checks were written Friday the nineteenth. One for a thousand dollars, the second for two thousand. Both made out to cash. The last check was issued Wednesday the twenty-fourth. It was also for two thousand dollars."

"Any endorsements?"

"The Coleman check cleared Friday with Luke Coleman's signature on the back. All of the other checks were cashed by

Fred Pryor. The local teller remembers the one last Wednesday. Pryor came running in just at closing, and she had to get the funds from the vault."

"That was the day he came back from Charlotte," said Tommy Lee. "And it was late that afternoon when he learned about the dumping and Dallas Willard's death."

"Then he was called back to Charlotte the next day to help set the strategy for dealing with you guys," I said.

"It doesn't cost two thousand dollars to drive to Charlotte," said Tommy Lee. "He must have needed it for something that night."

"So, not counting the Coleman check, five thousand dollars has disappeared," I said.

"No," said Murphy. "The FBI did a routine check on the bank accounts of the people who came in contact with Pryor during that period. Sheriff, your mention of Bob Cain turned up a cash deposit last Monday in his personal account. One thousand dollars."

"One of the checks Pryor cashed on the previous Friday," I said.

"I'd bet on it," said Tommy Lee.

"Four thousand is still missing," said Murphy. "We haven't said anything to Cain or Pryor because we don't want to tip our hand until we trace more possibilities."

"And you've examined all Pryor's personal accounts?" asked Tommy Lee.

"And then some. In the last six months he has borrowed the maximum on his 401k, taken a second mortgage on his home, and depleted his savings."

"What's he buying?" I asked.

"Nothing yet. The money has gone into a holding account for a limited liability company, a real estate venture named New Shores."

"Who else is in it?" asked Tommy Lee.

"We're running the name through the North Carolina Secretary of State's office now."

"New Shores," said Tommy Lee. "We know of some new shores soon to be created, don't we, Barry. I smell a sweetheart deal. A little inside profiteering."

"If that's the case, I'll be turning the information over to the SEC," said Murphy.

"And if that doesn't lead anywhere?" asked Tommy Lee.

"When it looks like a dead-end, we'll confront Cain and Pryor with the checks."

"How was Cain normally paid?" I asked.

"Monthly retainer. That's not due until the first of November and he is not paid in cash but by check."

"Hush money?" I asked.

Kyle Murphy shrugged.

Tommy Lee smiled. "Maybe. Or maybe he actually earned it in a way Pryor wants to keep hidden."

"Toxic waste dumped in a quarry," I said.

"Toxic waste and a body. Two bodies—Dallas Willard and Fats McCauley. And I still can't see the connection."

"I'm glad I don't have your problem, Sheriff," said Murphy. "That's why I'm giving you all we've got."

Tommy Lee shook the younger man's hand. "You're all right, Murphy. For a Fed. Think I'll drop in and brighten Fred Pryor's Monday morning."

We actually brightened Jane Cummings' day first. At least she had to smile when Tommy Lee said, "Would you tell the tight ass I'm here to see him?"

She picked up the phone and buzzed his extension. "Mr. Pryor, Sheriff Wadkins is here to see you."

We heard some garbled, muffled reply come from the receiver. A tinge of color spread over the woman's cheeks. She hung up the phone.

"I'm sorry, Sheriff. Mr. Pryor says you'll have to make an appointment for later this afternoon. He's reviewing material he has been ordered to give to the EPA immediately."

"Did he really say that, Miss Cummings?"

"Not in those exact words. More like if I can't get rid of you, he'll get rid of all of us."

"Nice guy." Then Tommy Lee took in a deep breath and bellowed, "Tell Mr. Pryor he will be charged with impeding the investigation of a double homicide. Tell Mr. Pryor if that door doesn't open in ten seconds, I will place a phone call to *The Charlotte Observer* and report that a senior executive of Ridgemont Power and Electric is stonewalling evidence which links a public utility to the brutal murders of a mentally deranged young man and an elderly furniture store owner. Tell Mr. Pryor the EPA acknowledges the magnitude of the crime of murder even if he does not. And tell Mr. Pryor—"

The door opened and Pryor stood shaking with fury.

"What do you want? Just tell me and then get the hell out of here."

"Good morning," said Tommy Lee. "Thank you for clearing your busy schedule. I want to ask you a few questions."

Pryor closed the door behind us and we sat in the same chairs as during our earlier visit. The office décor was beginning to grow on me.

Before Tommy Lee could say a word, Pryor stated, "I know nothing of how those containers wound up in Hope Quarry. I have no idea who killed Dallas Willard or why his body would have been dumped either separately or with the toxic waste. I had never heard of Travis McCauley. His murder is regrettable, but I challenge you to find any connection to this project. Furthermore, I know of no direct links between work done on this site and any of the deaths that occurred. Frankly, such a suggestion is unsubstantiated and irresponsible."

"Are you finished?" asked Tommy Lee.

"I am, but the legal counsel of Ridgemont Power and Electric may not be," he said with undisguised contempt.

"I doubt they are finished or will be for quite awhile. Especially with the real estate hanging in the balance."

"Real estate?" Pryor's curiosity got the better of his self-righteous indignation.

"Yes, although he forfeited his legal claim when he shot his brother and sister, Dallas Willard definitely can't inherit the property as a dead man."

"Well, the state will take care of that," Pryor said. "I imagine there will be a buyer."

"The state?" Tommy Lee asked.

"With no heirs."

"Who told you there were no heirs, Mr. Pryor?"

"Well," he stammered for a few seconds, "I don't know that anyone told me. I must have read it in the newspaper."

"Ah, well, I wouldn't believe everything I read in the paper. I suspect the Willard land will stay in the family. These mountain people love to hunt on their own ground. Hell, they'll be able to fish in your new lake. You know, with all those new shores you will be making for them."

If I hadn't been staring intently at Fred Pryor's face, I probably would have missed the quiver of his lower lip as Tommy Lee casually said "new shores."

"Are you here to question me about real estate?" he asked.

"No. Something you know something about. Electricity, or the lack thereof. When we first met, your power pole had been knocked down."

"That's right."

"I want the names of every man who was late that Friday and their employment records and applications. And, I want the same for every person supervised by Odell Taylor whether they were working that Friday or not."

"I don't see what that has to do with anything," Pryor protested.

"Mr. Pryor, there are a lot of things you don't see. Like the fact that there is a link between that toxic waste and death. An old man lost a prized horse because of somebody's illegal action."

"A horse?" asked Pryor. "Like that nag I saw when I went up to inspect the quarry yesterday?"

"Yes," said Tommy Lee. "That nag had sired the unborn foal that was also killed by the contaminated creek water."

"Tell you what, Sheriff, just to show you I'm not the hard-hearted bastard you claim I am, I'll send that old farmer—"

"Mr. Charles Hartley," Tommy Lee said.

"I'll send Mr. Hartley a check for his loss, even though we bear no responsibility. If we're finished that is."

"For now," said Tommy Lee and stood up. "I'll tell Kyle Murphy to expect those employee files by mid-afternoon. He has offered the full resources of his department."

As we passed Jane Cummings' desk, Pryor yelled from his doorway, "Jane, draw up a check for Charles Hartley." He paused, then said, "Hey, Sheriff, how many cans of dog food you think that horse was worth? Fifty?" He slammed his office door.

Jane Cummings looked up at us. "You know," she said, "he's beginning to piss me off."

Tommy Lee and I stepped down from the construction trailer into the late morning sunlight.

"I hope I didn't overplay my hand," said Tommy Lee.

"You mean with the new shores comment?"

"That and dangling the prospect of an heir in front of him. I'm just trying to make him jump because he's probably got everyone else toeing the company line."

"His stunt with the check for Charlie Hartley reminded me of somebody else."

"Who?"

"The Coleman child. Maybe I'll have to help someone step out of the company line."

"What do you mean?" asked Tommy Lee.

"I need to revert to my daytime job. An undertaker consoling a family. Some ol' time religion wouldn't hurt either."

"Barry, should I be having a bad feeling about this?"

"Don't worry. I'll be careful."

I do my best contemplating while lying on my sofa with my eyes closed—not a nap but a relaxed reflection, as I like to call it. However, this time all I saw was a grieving mother and Fred Pryor handing her a hundred dollars for the life of her son. Was Jimmy Coleman collateral damage, nothing more to Fred Pryor than Charlie Hartley's horse? And there was Fats, hovering over Harriet Coleman. What did he say? "Too cold. It was too cold." I sat straight up on the sofa. Fats' other words sprang to mind, the words he had written on the note pad—"Barry Clayton, weather." "Weather" and "too cold." I telephoned Mom to find out how to reach Reverend Pace. He had also heard Fats' words and would know more about any religious rituals that might be involved.

"'Too cold,'" I said when I reached him. "I know what Fats meant when he said it. The weather was too cold for the snakes." I waited for the voice on the other end of the phone to respond, but the silence told me my point was being thoughtfully considered.

"Yes," Pace said at last. "No rattler would have been out on a rock at that temperature. I knew something bothered me about Luke Coleman's story. I even looked for rocks around his house. I didn't think about the cold."

"We can't prove it," I said, "unless someone tells what really happened. You've probably witnessed snake-handling before. Do you think that's how the boy was bitten?"

"No. I been in these hills forty years and never heard of any church or sect letting kids handle serpents. Maybe he was with his dad when they were ousting the rattlers from their den."

"Maybe," I said. "Maybe a lot of things. What we do know is they probably lied about how the boy was bitten. So what else are they lying about, and how far would they go to keep their snake-handling a secret?"

"You think Luke Coleman or that Leroy Jackson killed Fats McCauley?" asked Pace. "They heard Fats say it was too cold for the rattler to be out of its den."

"What proof did Fats have?" I asked. "He just mumbled 'Too cold' and went on home. Luke Coleman and Leroy Jackson went to Kentucky that night. They weren't in town.

No, I was thinking if we don't know the truth of how the snake bit Jimmy, we might not know the truth of when the snake bit him. They could have been afraid to bring the boy to a doctor and they tried to care for him themselves. Remember Friday morning several of those church members were late. Maybe that's the reason."

"They were praying over Jimmy Thursday night? But that could give them an alibi for Dallas Willard's death and the chemical dumping," said Pace.

"Possibly, and I want to establish that fact so we're not wasting time on the wrong trail."

"Where do you want to start?"

"I only know of one place," I said. "Harriet Coleman. Someone has got to get her to tell what happened."

Pace sighed. "Well, way I see it, it's not a problem of the law, it's a problem of the spirit. She needs a comfort."

"Yes," I agreed. "Would you go with me?"

"A preacher and an undertaker?" He laughed. "Guess we're not so far apart at that. I'll pick you up at eight tomorrow morning. My old Plymouth might be a little worn, but it will look more at home in the Colemans' woods."

Chapter 18

From the edge of the trees at the Kentucky workers' compound, Reverend Pace and I watched Harriet Coleman hang a pair of jeans on the clothesline stretched across her front porch. The washtub of milky rinse water had just yielded up the last garment for drying in the morning sun. Harriet stepped back and looked along the fifteen feet of cord at her Jimmy's clothes fluttering in the breeze.

I could only imagine how the finality of this never to be repeated cycle of washing and drying for her little boy must have torn at her heart. Suddenly, she whimpered and slid down against the porch post.

She didn't hear Pace calling her name. She did feel my hand on her shoulder and the squeeze which brought her to her senses.

"Mrs. Coleman, are you all right?"

She squinted against the sun to make out the two men standing over her. She looked at Pace. "The preacher. From the funeral home," she stammered. "I'm all right." She struggled to get to her feet and willingly accepted my arm.

"Yes. We met at the visitation for your son. I'm Reverend Pace, Mrs. Coleman. This is Barry Clayton. He was there as well."

Harriet Coleman gave me a nod of acknowledgment. "I remember. You were very kind."

"We came by just to talk for a few minutes," said Pace. "If you have the time." He let his eyes wander to the string of drying clothes and the empty washtub.

"I was just finishing up. Jimmy's things. I know it's not right to keep them when some other boy could wear them."

Her act of charity, coming from one who had lost so much and had so little, touched us both. I saw Pace's eyes glistening. Without hesitation, he reached out and wrapped his arm around her shoulders. The woman fell against him, and all the unspoken sorrow boiled over as she cried against his chest. I opened the front door and motioned for Pace to bring her inside.

We seated Harriet Coleman in a plain rocker with a blue plaid cushion. The small front room had no sofa. Two other chairs were pulled around the kerosene heater. Four old framed photographs were clustered on one wall. Family portraits of another, more prosperous generation.

"I'll get you a glass of water," Pace said. He sought out the kitchen and returned with an iceless glass.

Harriet took a sip and held it in her mouth a few seconds before swallowing. Then she gulped more rapidly until the glass was drained.

"Another?" asked Pace.

"No, thank you." She set the glass on the floor beside her. "You missed my husband. He won't be back from work till four."

"You can help us, Mrs. Coleman," said Pace. "There're some things we know aren't right. You're better to confide in me and Barry, and that way maybe we can keep anyone from getting in trouble."

"You'd best talk to Luke," she answered, and set her lips in a tight line.

Pace crouched down by the chair and took her hand. "Mrs. Coleman, your son was bit by a snake on a day too cold for it to be out on a rock ledge. We suspect snakes are used in your church service, and that snake was one of them. We're not claiming it was anything more than an accident, but we are going to notify the sheriff, and he will have to investigate.

Barry and I wanted to speak with you first. Barry's been around enough deaths to know Jimmy's doesn't make sense the way we've been told it happened. I know men-folk can be hardheaded at times, and your husband and the others may not see things the way you and I do. I don't want Jimmy to be disturbed if we can avoid it."

"Disturbed?" she asked. "What do you mean disturbed?"

Pace looked to me to deliver the news. "He means a judge may order his body exhumed," I said.

"Dig up my Jimmy's body?"

"Yes. If they think something is being hidden from them."

"Body or soul," the woman whispered. "Body or soul." She started to cry softly.

"We should never be afraid of the truth," said Pace. "Jesus says, 'The truth shall make you free.' The loss of your son is burden enough, Mrs. Coleman. At least free yourself of any other burden."

"Leroy Jackson said it was God's will. That's why Jimmy died."

"Your heart will tell you God's will," said Pace. "I don't claim to understand the mysteries of Life and Death, but I cannot and do not believe God wanted your boy to die. There are tragedies that happen. God's will is to bring Good out of Evil, and to bring you peace. Jimmy is in His care now. You are the one we are concerned about."

"It was God's will," she said. "If Luke and I told what happened, God's punishment would be on Jimmy. I couldn't endanger my boy's soul."

"So that's what Leroy Jackson said. And what does your heart say?" asked Pace.

"I've been listenin' to my heart since we buried Jimmy. Jesus says, 'Suffer the little children to come unto me, for of such is the Kingdom of Heaven.' I know my Jimmy is with Jesus."

"Then you have nothing to fear for his soul, my dear," counseled Pace.

"There were no rocks, no snake on a ledge," began Harriet Coleman slowly. "That was what Odell told us to say. Otherwise, he said we would get everyone in trouble."

"Where was Jimmy bitten?" asked Pace.

"Under Leroy's house. In the crawl way. It was early Friday morning."

"Friday?"

"Yes. Luke had to work Thursday night. Some of the men were helping Odell Taylor at Broad Creek. Jimmy and I woke up Friday morning and found Luke still gone. That day was a teacher workday to get report cards ready. Jimmy didn't have no school. I let him walk up the ridge to Leroy's and wait for his daddy. Sometimes the men share rides. Luke had ridden in Leroy's truck. 'Bout an hour after Jimmy left, Luke and Leroy come running up. Luke was carrying Jimmy. Leroy said they'd found Jimmy lying underneath the house by the pit where they keep the snakes. The slat cover was off."

"Why didn't they take him to the hospital?" asked Pace.

"I pleaded with them. Luke did too, but he was so scared. Leroy said them was anointed serpents. God would cure Jimmy if we had the faith. Leroy stayed right with us at the bedside, but it weren't no good. My boy just slipped away before my eyes. Saturday morning he was gone."

"And where was Odell Taylor?" I asked.

"He'd gone back to work Friday. Didn't know about the accident till that evening when he came to see why Luke didn't return to the job. The men who worked Thursday night were supposed to get a few hours sleep, and Odell cleared it so they could punch in late."

"Didn't he think Jimmy should go to a hospital?"

"Odell agreed with Leroy. And he told Luke there would be a lot of questions. That Luke was in it as much as any of them. He wouldn't want someone else to get hurt. That's when he told us to tell the story about the snake being on a ledge."

"Do you know what he meant about someone else getting hurt?"

"I guess about the snakes."

"Thank you, Mrs. Coleman," said Pace. "I know this hasn't been easy for you."

"I swear it's the truth. They won't bother Jimmy, will they? Luke and I don't care what happens to us, as long as they don't bother Jimmy?"

"No, Mrs. Coleman," I said. "I can't think of why the sheriff would want to do that when I tell him what you've told me. And for right now, I'd advise you not to say anything to your husband. No sense involving him unless there's a reason. Are you comfortable with that?"

"Yes, sir. I'd never lie to him, understand, but I'd rather he didn't know I talked to you unless something's going to come from it." She turned to Pace. "You would tell me that, wouldn't you? So as I could speak to him myself."

"You have my word on it," he promised. "And I'll be glad to talk to Luke with you, if that time comes."

As Pace steered his car onto the highway, I said, "We'd better get straight back to Tommy Lee. That was pretty damning testimony."

"Do you think they'll be prosecuted for not taking the boy to a doctor? It's sensitive where religious beliefs and medical treatments cross paths."

"I was thinking of what she said about Odell Taylor's Thursday night work party. That's the night before Dallas Willard's truck appeared. Taylor and the men lied about where they had been. And then Harriet Coleman said Taylor told her husband there would be questions and 'he was in it as much as any of them.' He may have been talking about more than snake-handling."

"Murder?" asked Pace.

"What do you think?"

The old reverend shook his head. "I don't know, but if there is a hell of fire and brimstone, the majority of its population must consist of preachers who have bent the simple faith of good folks like Luke and Harriet Coleman to their own purposes. And Leroy Jackson has got to be earning a place for himself on those fiery sulfur shores."

"I think I ought to bring Luke Coleman in for questioning." Tommy Lee made the matter-of-fact statement in the confines of his office. Reverend Pace and I sat across the desk from him. The sheriff had listened silently as we related our interview with Harriet Coleman, and he pronounced this judgment without hesitation.

"I don't agree with you," I said and looked to Pace for support.

He nodded his approval. "You know I'm as mad as you are about Jimmy Coleman being denied medical treatment, but Barry is right. The boy's death will get into a freedom of religion issue, and if Luke witnessed, or worse, participated in the murder of Dallas Willard, he's not likely to admit it. And it sounds like Taylor has coached his story."

"A story we now know is a lie," protested Tommy Lee.

"Exactly," I said. "I suspect they killed one of the rattlers right after the boy died on Saturday so it would be fresh in the truck. It was a conspiracy held together by fear. We know what happened, but they don't know we know. Why give up that advantage?"

Tommy Lee conceded the point. "Yeah, when someone thinks he's in the clear, he's more likely to screw up. Looks like we move straight for Odell Taylor then."

"Is he your main suspect?" asked Pace.

"Well," said Tommy Lee, "he had his men on the job the night Dallas died. Then he didn't want Jimmy Coleman to go to a doctor because of the questions that would raise. I think Taylor feared questions concerning Thursday night, not the snakebite on Friday morning. Luke would be asked why he wasn't home. Taylor couldn't trust that Luke or his wife would hold up under examination."

I jumped in to state the obvious. "By then, Leroy Jackson had scared the Colemans into relying on faith healing, and that served Taylor's own interest. Why risk going to a doctor? If the boy survived, everyone would be in the clear. When the boy died, it was just a tragic accident. God's will. Neither the chemical dump nor Dallas' body had been discovered, and no one had any reason to doubt the events the Colemans described. After all, the boy had died on Saturday, but we now know it was the day after he was bitten."

"Why would Taylor kill Dallas Willard?" asked Pace.

"Maybe he was in the wrong place at the wrong time," I said. "Let's assume the grading or tunneling at the Broad Creek Project uncovered the cache of containers buried by Pisgah Paper Mill. If only a few people knew about it, Fred Pryor had three options. He could immediately report the discovery to the EPA and make arrangements for a proper examination and disposal, he could check the contents himself, weigh the toxic risk, and then notify the EPA, or he could sneak them off the premises without alerting the EPA."

"That all makes sense," Tommy Lee said. "If Pryor indeed found them, we know he didn't notify the EPA. I don't think he even bothered to check the containers because it didn't matter what they held. He didn't want his construction schedule buried by a costly and time-consuming site reevaluation. Even if the material was relatively harmless, the EPA would be alarmed that waste had been disposed of in such a manner. It was just the kind of development Pryor was anxious to avoid."

"So he entrusted the problem to Odell Taylor," I said.

"Odell Taylor," agreed Tommy Lee, "and maybe Bob Cain. One of Taylor's crew probably unearthed the drums in the first place. Taylor knows the area. He has access to a rail spur and a work engine. Taylor and his men load the stuff on a rail car, sneak out to the main line and travel to the abandoned spur where they can transport the drums to the quarry and dump them in the water."

"He and his crew would never have to go out on a highway," I said.

"Right. Fred Pryor may not have known the exact solution to the problem, and probably didn't want to know. He kept his hands clean and paid off his security chief Bob Cain to ignore whatever Taylor devised. I'll bet a guard wasn't even assigned that night. It was perfect."

"It was perfect until Dallas Willard showed up on the same stretch of track," said Reverend Pace. "A terrible coincidence."

Tommy Lee shook his head. "I don't know about that. I keep saying I don't like coincidences. And we don't know why Fats was killed with Dallas Willard's shotgun unless that was the whole point. The killer made sure the shell was left in the bathroom because Dallas provided the answer to who-dun-it. Mystery solved. A convenient way to murder Fats for whatever reason. It might not tie into Dallas Willard in any other way."

"Whoever killed Fats had to know it was Dallas' shotgun," I said. "He probably took it from him."

"Yes, and he felt confident enough to stand close to a homicidal maniac and stab him. I don't buy a coincidence that Dallas just appeared on the tracks. I think he was taken there alive. He had to hole up somewhere for a week. He might not have been alone."

"Who would help him?" asked Pace.

Tommy Lee leaned across his desk. "Someone who wanted a three million dollar tract of land. Someone who turned Dallas against the migrants to spoil the Waylon Hestor deal, and then against his own brother and sister when he discovered Dallas couldn't stop Lee and Norman Jean from selling to Hestor."

"The power company," I said.

"No, I'm beginning to think Fred Pryor kept the power company in the dark. I think he was setting up a way for New Shores to control the property."

"Dallas would never talk to a man like Pryor," said Pace.

"Dallas probably didn't even know Pryor existed. But Odell Taylor is another story. Taylor is a worker, a regular guy. He and the Kentucky group wouldn't be a threat to Dallas. Taylor could ingratiate himself on Pryor's behalf. Maybe even incite Dallas to murder his brother and sister while all the while Fred Pryor pulled the strings."

"And now Dallas is a dead witness," I said.

"Convenient isn't it. Get rid of him after he's served his purpose."

"How can you prove it?" asked Pace.

I looked at Tommy Lee. "You've already laid the groundwork, haven't you?"

"Yeah, and I want you to get his permission. I've got to set up a surveillance plan."

"What are you talking about?" asked Pace.

"The best evidence is to catch someone in the act of committing a crime," said Tommy Lee. "I'm going to give Pryor a new problem. Someone who will be just as stubborn as Dallas about selling the property. The newly discovered legal heir, Talmadge Watson."

I heard the dull thuds of an axe on seasoned wood. Turning the corner of the cabin, I saw Talmadge Watson by a pile of cordwood. His back was to me, his concentration directed on the log standing end-up on the chopping stump.

Talmadge lifted the axe even with his shoulder, gave a half swing, snapping his wrists with precision born of practice, and cleanly split the wood in two. He tossed the pieces into the growing stack, positioned another log and swung again. His fluid motion never faltered as he worked like some mechanical man in a hardware display.

I watched for a few minutes until Talmadge leaned the axe handle against his leg and mopped his brow with the hip-pocket red bandanna.

"Wood for the stove, or wood for the still?" I asked.

Talmadge looked over his shoulder. "Little of each. They both keep me warm. You come for some?"

"Thanks, but no. Came to talk, if you got the time."

Talmadge embedded the axe head in the stump. "It'll wait on me. Let's go inside."

I followed the old man across the threshold into the front room. In the funeral business, I'd been on enough house calls that the sparseness of the mountaineers' living conditions no longer surprised me. I expected the wood-burning cooking stove and the wellspring right in the middle of the kitchen with the heavy metal dipper hanging above it. What I didn't expect was the neatness of a man who lived alone. The cabin's plank floor was swept clean and a braided throw-rug lay in the middle. A few odd chairs and a sofa flanked off the fireplace. Every arm was covered with a doily. Lace curtains framed in the two front windows, and a white tassel hung from the center of each pulldown shade.

Shelves lined the walls. A few held cooking utensils, but most were filled with birds, birds perched on branches or mounted in flight—birds hand-carved from solid wood and painted in realistic detail. I could not take my eyes off them. My hands went behind my back with the reflex of a kid whose momma had trained him in the shops where the breakable merchandise was more than we could afford.

"You can touch 'em," said Talmadge. "This ain't no museum."

"These are fantastic. You carve them?"

"For my wife Lottie. She loved her birds. Guess they were her children. Many a winter evening's up on these shelves. The carving part was easy. I always whittled, ever since I was a kid. Lottie did the paintin'. She had the eye for it. Her Cherokee grandmother taught her to make the dyes. Showed her the roots and berries."

"She made her own paints?"

"Indians been making paints for hundreds of years. Lottie took to it like a duck to water." Talmadge chuckled. "And my moonshine made a thinner much better than store-bought. Lottie was agin my distillin', but she had to confess it put life in them colors. Never seen a bird's markings she couldn't match." He looked around the room as if appreciating the collection for the first time. "I sure do miss her."

I picked up a big blue jay with his head cocked to one side and a tuft of feathers cresting his head. The bird eyed a wood beetle carved atop the branch near his talons. It was a frozen moment capturing the split-second before Nature's food chain offered one less wood beetle.

"You're too modest, Talmadge. If I had this talent, I'd have my birds in galleries all over the country."

"Why? We made 'em for our enjoyment. Why trade that for money?"

I didn't have an answer. I set the blue jay up on the shelf.

"You come to talk birds?" Talmadge pointed me to the sofa and eased himself into a cane-bottom chair.

"No. I guess you could say I'm on official business. We think we're closing in on who murdered Dallas. That may lead us to who killed Fats McCauley."

"How do I figure in?"

"There's a possibility the deaths are related to the Willard land, who will be able to buy it."

"Sheriff said it was coming to me."

"That's right," I said. "But nobody knows that yet. The assumption is the land will be auctioned."

"Cause Martha and I disowned each other," he said. "Only a few of the old timers remember we was kin." He thought for a moment. "So, I'm the meat in the snare."

"Yeah, I guess that's as good a way of putting it as any."

"When is this snare gonna be set?"

"Tomorrow," I said. "If we have your permission."

"Well, I guess a man can't let another man kill his family no matter how distant and then go on as if nothin' happened. What do I need to do?"

"Sit tight. The sheriff will assign a deputy to watch you."

"Watch me do what?" Talmadge Watson chuckled softly at the thought of having a guard. "Well, tell him to send a young one who don't know me. The old deputies will just keep pesterin' me for a swallow."

The offices for the *Gainesboro VISTA* were in a brick building at the north end of town. A line of five parking spaces in the adjacent lot had been stenciled VISITORS. All were open. The news business on a Tuesday afternoon must not have been bustling.

I entered a modest reception area. Bookshelves on either side touted the various awards and trophies the small daily had earned since its founding seventy-five years ago. Across the room, a woman as old as the paper sat at a multi-line telephone. The headset hung around her neck and she read the large-print version of *Reader's Digest*. On the front of her desk were two signs with arrows pointing in opposite directions: Editorial to the left, Advertising to the right. The lettering for Advertising was twice the size of Editorial.

The woman looked up and shoved the magazine out of sight. "May I help you?"

"I'd like to speak to Melissa Bigham, please."

"She's a reporter in Editorial," answered the woman, and the smile which briefly appeared for a potential advertiser vanished.

"Yes. I have information for her."

The receptionist looked at a pegboard mounted alongside her phone. Six or seven sets of initials were listed in dry marker. "M.B." had a blue peg sticking out of the In hole.

"Melissa's here but she's on her line. You can go on back," she instructed. "I can't leave my post. She's in the third cubicle on the left."

I saw the top of her head first, short brown hair cut for easy maintenance. She heard me step behind her and glanced over her shoulder. She must have been in her late twenties, cute now that I could take a closer look and I wasn't intimidated by Jack Andrews and his biker pals. She sat in front of a computer terminal. Her Nikon rested atop the monitor and her notepad hung from a suction cup stuck on the metal cubicle wall.

"Hey, what's up?" She tucked the phone against her shoulder and kept her fingers speeding across the keyboard to complete her thought.

"I need space on the front page of tomorrow's paper," I said.

"Expanding the funeral home to handle all the bodies?"

Just the irreverence I expected from a reporter, no matter how small the paper.

"We're going to trap a killer," I whispered.

Melissa took her hands off the keys and said, "Gotta go" into the receiver.

"I can wait a minute," I said.

She hung up the phone. "Just a call from the school system. Next week's lunch menu. Country-style steak is not the kind of thing to yell stop the presses over. Barry Clayton, right?" She stood up and rested an elbow on the top of her cubicle. "Are you serious about trapping a killer?"

I looked around the deserted newsroom.

"There's nobody else here," she assured me. "But we can talk in the conference room if you like."

"No. If we're alone, this is fine. I am serious, but you've got to print what I say and no more."

"You know I can't agree to that. I'd be compromising the paper, not to mention my own ethics. I do have a few."

"The paper won't be publishing anything that's not true. Just consider me an anonymous source with limited but accurate information."

"I can't make any promise for placement. I don't make up the front page."

"Then tell whoever does it's the inside, exclusive track on a major story."

Melissa's eyes brightened at the carrot dangling in front of her. She cleared the screen with a single key stroke. "Give it to me now. I'll take it straight to the editor as soon as I finish."

Chapter 19

Except for the time I spent at college or working in Charlotte, P's had been the only shop where a barber had ever touched my head. Since my first wailing episode in the toddler's booster chair to the trim the week before my gunshot wound in the cemetery, P.J. Peterson had clipped my curly locks. P.J.'s dad Pete had founded the barbershop/gossip emporium in 1935. Twenty years later, Pete Jr., aka P.J., had joined his dad and his older cousin in the family business. In the early 1970s, P.J. acquired me, red-faced and screaming, as a new customer. P Senior died in 1978, and although the surviving Petersons hired another barber, no one sat in or worked old Mr. P's chair. It reigned near the storefront window as a constant reminder that eventually we all get that final haircut.

Melissa Bigham's story had been in the newspaper's version of primetime—the front page, above the fold. Reading it had given me the urge to get a haircut.

The shop chatter abruptly ceased as I walked in. All eyes turned to me, formerly Jack Clayton's boy, now town celebrity.

"Mornin', Barry," P.J. called from behind the balding pate of Mayor Sammy Whitlock.

"Mornin', Barry," echoed the mayor. "How's the arm?"

"Mending fine," I said.

There was a round of "that's good" from the six other men, only half of whom were waiting for haircuts.

"Guess you saw the paper this morning," said P.J.

"No," I lied. "Something special?"

"You'll never guess who has come forward to claim the Willard property," said P.J.

"I haven't a clue," I said and eased into a plastic chair beneath the shelf stacked with vintage Butch Wax.

"Wait, don't tell him, let me read the article." Mayor Whitlock fumbled his hands free of the barber's cloth and reached out for a newspaper. One of the assembled court passed him the front page. No one loved the sound of the mayor's voice more than the mayor.

"'The aftermath of Dallas Willard's murderous rampage that ended in his own death took a surprising turn yesterday. An exclusive investigation by the *VISTA* has uncovered a previously unknown heir who stands to inherit the entire tract of land in the Willard estate. Talmadge Watson, the reclusive brother of the late Martha Willard, plans to file his claim as sole surviving heir at the Laurel County Courthouse tomorrow. When asked why he had not stepped forward sooner, Mr. Watson said, "Martha and I had some distance between us and hadn't talked in over sixty years. But that was our business, nobody else's."'

"That sounds like ol' Talmadge, don't it?" commented the Mayor.

"Yeah," agreed P.J., "except everybody knows his business."

The men laughed. Mayor Whitlock said, "He'll keep making shine till he drops dead in the fire. With all that acreage, he'll have plenty of new places to hide a still." He glanced back to the article and paraphrased. "Says he's not concerned whether county records prove his claim or not. He's got the family Bible with his and Martha's birth dates entered in their grandmother's handwriting."

"Talk about an old testament," said P.J.

A wheezy voice from the corner piped up, "Shoot-fire, probably has Jesus' autograph in it."

That got an even louder round of laughter. Mayor Whitlock handed the paper back, P.J. resumed his scissor snips, and the talk wandered to property taxes and how much land Talmadge would probably have to sell to keep the best. I enjoyed the free entertainment while awaiting my turn. My only commitment wasn't until noon.

"See you got your ears lowered." Tommy Lee gave his review of P.J.'s handiwork as I sat down across from his desk.

"Undercover work. Talmadge was the talk of the morning."

"Good. I'd have been surprised otherwise."

"Anything happening?"

"Not yet. Cain is spending the day politicking. I called in some favors from Buncombe County and a couple of their people are shadowing him. I've got tails in place ready to pick up Taylor and Pryor when they leave Broad Creek. I expect Kyle Murphy to call soon."

"Sounds good."

"And while I was at it, I asked Buncombe County to keep an eye on Waylon Hestor and Alex Soles. Just because we couldn't see a connection doesn't mean there isn't one."

"Especially Soles," I agreed. "Psychologist for a man whose land he wants."

Tommy Lee had set his plan in motion yesterday while I called on Talmadge and Melissa Bigham. He contacted Murphy and learned Odell Taylor was scheduled to spend this morning with his men doing general clean-up. Grading had been halted pending the outcome of the EPA investigation and further soil tests. Murphy reported the EPA had not discovered any additional contamination, but they still had ground to cover. Ridgemont Power claimed that if the suspension lasted much longer, Taylor and his men would be laid off.

That prospect wouldn't be the only problem on Taylor's mind. Murphy had been instructed to tell Pryor the sheriff would be by at noon to ask Taylor a few questions about

Dallas Willard. Pryor knew he had to fully cooperate, and the sheriff was free to take as much time as he required. Taylor had all morning to wonder what prompted Tommy Lee's return visit. He had made his statement once already, and his men had all corroborated they had not been on the site the night Dallas died.

The morning hours would pass slowly for him. At a quarter to twelve, Taylor was to break his men for lunch and walk from the gravel base of the dam construction to the EPA's trailer. Kyle Murphy would give Sheriff Wadkins the use of his office for the private interrogation. Except Tommy Lee never planned to be there.

At ten after twelve, the call came in from Murphy. Tommy Lee put him on the speaker phone. "How'd it go?"

"Like we expected," said Murphy. "Taylor found me sitting in Jane Cummings' vacant chair, reading the *Gainesboro VISTA*. I sent Jane to lunch early. I acted surprised when Taylor came in. He asked where you were and I said I was sorry. I forgot to send word you had to cancel."

"How did he react?" asked Tommy Lee.

"At first he was relieved. I could tell he had been nervous about talking to you."

"Good. I want him nervous."

"Then it dawned on him this was probably only a postponement. He would still have to face a new round of questions. He asked me what happened. I said you had a development you had to check out and I slid the paper over to him."

"Had he already seen it?"

"I don't think so. He read it. Repeated Talmadge Watson's name to himself, then looked at me like I had some explanation."

"What did you say?"

"I laughed and said sounds like this old coot is going to be a real estate tycoon. Taylor asked if you thought Talmadge had killed Dallas for the land and was that why you canceled. I said I had no idea. You were tight-lipped with me, but you told me you'd be back to see him in a day or two. He said if

Talmadge Watson was the killer, then you had no cause to bother him again."

"Right," said Tommy Lee. "He wishes. Interesting he tried to immediately peg Talmadge Watson as the man who killed Dallas Willard."

"I guess that's natural," said Murphy. "Talmadge gets quite a windfall."

"Also natural for someone who is looking for a fall guy for his own crime. I think Taylor doesn't like the heat. If Talmadge could be convicted for the murder, then the property is back on the auction block and he's off the hook. But, Taylor knows that's not going to happen. Then what did he do?"

"He gave me back the paper and said, 'Murder's a terrible thing, ain't it?' I agreed and apologized he came up to the trailer for nothing. I told him to take an extra fifteen minutes for lunch and I'd clear it with Pryor. I waited until I heard the gravel crunch of his footsteps fade, and then peeked out the window. Taylor went straight to Pryor's office."

"We should have had it bugged," said Tommy Lee.

"He only stayed about five minutes, and then went back to his men. I'm going to hang in here until everyone leaves."

"Murphy, you ever want the quiet life, I'll find you a job up here."

We could almost see the Fed smile through the speaker phone. "Quiet life? Sheriff, I've never been in the middle of so many dead bodies in my life."

I waited with the dispatcher in the radio room of the Sheriff's Department. Communication was essential and the network of surveillance needed a nexus for efficient operation.

The two-way crackled. "I'm ready for him," said Tommy Lee. "Won't press him too closely. I don't expect anything to happen until after nightfall anyway. No sense taking chances. Once I know he's headed home, I'll ease back."

"Want some company?" I asked.

"Sure. Just don't drive up here with rap music blaring. There's an abandoned barn on adjoining property. Looks right down on Taylor's. If he stays put, you can probably come in after dark. Bring a fresh thermos of coffee and—hold on, I see him. He's at the main highway. At least he's turning in the right direction."

Two hours later, I pulled my Jeep Cherokee beside Tommy Lee's patrol car. The sheriff had parked broadside against the rear of the dilapidated barn. Missing slats of siding afforded a view through the back wall and out its open doors. I joined Tommy Lee in the front seat of his car, bringing a thermos, binoculars, and a white paper sack.

"Here's a bag of doughnuts. This is an official stake-out, isn't it?"

"It is now," said Tommy Lee, "although I never eat these things. I'd weigh four hundred pounds. Just pour me a cup of coffee."

"Anything going on?" I asked.

"No. And that's unusual. I would have thought he would run out somewhere. Pick up a few groceries, beer, or cigarettes. He just came straight from work. Maybe he spotted me."

"It makes sense he wouldn't leave," I said. "If he wants to get to Talmadge, he's got to be making a plan and getting his arsenal together."

"Maybe," agreed Tommy Lee, "or maybe he's just not sure what to do."

The two-way radio crackled as the dispatcher's voice broke through our conversation.

"I copy you," replied Tommy Lee. "What's up?"

"I've got a phone call for you from Kyle Murphy. I can patch him through if you like."

"Okay," said Tommy Lee.

"Wonder what he wants?" I asked.

"Sheriff, do you hear me?" Murphy's voice was tinny but clear.

Tommy Lee paused a beat, then depressed the mike key. "Yeah. What is it?"

"I just got a report faxed from Somerset, Kentucky, but your deputy says I shouldn't bring it to you."

"No. Any more cars up here and we'll look like a parking lot. What's the bottom line?"

"We ran background checks on the men who came in late on the Friday morning after we think Dallas was killed. They all came back clean."

"Dead-end, huh?"

"Not exactly. It's interesting that we found Taylor's tracks go back to Kentucky. He migrated here fifteen years ago with enough money to buy a grader and bulldozer. Started putting in roads and driveways for developers and retirees who were building their mountain homes. He did good work and got picked up on the Broad Creek Project."

"Well, that explains the Kentucky connection," Tommy Lee said. "He brought Luke Coleman and the rest of Leroy Jackson's flock down to join him."

"But you also wanted checks on all the men Taylor supervised, not just the ones who clocked in late. Turns out Leroy Jackson did time. I mean serious time, like more years in prison than out. His sheet goes back to teenage theft and larceny, then various assault charges, some of which were violent enough that he went into observation and evaluation for mental problems. A borderline psychopath. He was a prime suspect in two capital murder cases but the D.A. didn't have enough evidence to prosecute. He has been out eight years now, his longest stretch of freedom. The last conviction was for aggravated assault with a knife. Bar fight over a twenty dollar pool bet. Served eighteen months and his cell mate was an old con man called The Preacher."

"The Preacher," repeated Tommy Lee. "So he found himself a mentor."

"Yes," said Murphy. "Evidently, Leroy Jackson had a conversion experience. He was released from jail a self-proclaimed prophet and over time attracted enough Kentucky hill people to found his church."

"Interesting."

"It gets better," Murphy continued. "Prison records and parole applications name next of kin for notification of emergency situations. Jackson has only one listed relative, his brother Odell Taylor."

Tommy Lee pressed down the key, stepping on Murphy's words. "Leroy Jackson is Odell Taylor's brother?"

"Half-brother. Taylor's father died when he was an infant. Couple years later his mother remarried long enough to have Jackson before the marriage broke up."

The nerves in my neck tingled. "The drive to Kentucky," I said.

"What?" asked Tommy Lee.

"Pace and I remembered that only the Colemans and Leroy Jackson were present at the funeral home when Fats said 'too cold.' But they left the visitation and drove straight to Kentucky. Fats was killed later the same night, after they had gone. We've not considered Jackson because we assumed he went with the Colemans."

"Except the day you and I were at their compound with Pace and his intern, Leroy Jackson showed up and said he'd driven all night to get back and the Colemans were returning the next day. He had driven his own truck."

"Exactly. Jackson could have stayed late enough Sunday to kill Fats and still have made the burial service in Kentucky."

"What about Taylor?" asked Tommy Lee.

"Maybe he and Jackson are tied into everything together. Blood is thicker than water."

"Tell that to Norma Jean and Lee Willard," said Tommy Lee. "Blood is flowing like water and we may have a psychopath at the spigot."

"And not a soul watching him," I said.

"No one to blame but myself," said Tommy Lee. "God damn it. Leroy Jackson has a free hand and we don't know where he is." He keyed the mike. "Thanks, Murphy." Then he told his dispatcher, "Have Talmadge Watson brought to town immediately. I don't want to take any chances that Leroy Jackson can get anywhere near him."

I sat quietly while Tommy Lee finished radioing his instructions. Thoughts darted through my head like trout in a mountain stream. "Maybe we should confront Taylor now."

"Why's that?"

"At lunch, you made sure Taylor saw the newspaper story. Did he tell Jackson about it? Does he know what his brother plans to do? Maybe he's waiting for Jackson to come to him. Our angle can be you pick Taylor up for questioning. You were supposed to see him today, right? You start asking him about his brother."

"You mean overplay my hand," said Tommy Lee.

"Yes, if he seems shaken. He might be expecting only to defend himself. You hit him with a lot of accusations about his brother—even if it's conjecture, enough might be true that Taylor won't be able to figure out what we know and what we don't know."

"And if Leroy Jackson is the triggerman, Taylor might not want to go down for murder. His record seems to be clean. All right. Let's squeeze him a bit. Right now it's the only bone this ol' bloodhound's got, and I aim to gnaw on it. You got a gun?"

"In the Jeep."

"Get it. I've been sheriff long enough to know something goes wrong with every plan. You use it if you have to."

I followed Tommy Lee's patrol car out to the highway and we drove the short loop down to Odell Taylor's double-wide. One car passed us, a Camaro loaded with costumed teenagers shrieking obscenities. They nearly swerved in the ditch when they realized they had mooned the sheriff.

Taylor's trailer was only thirty yards off the highway. I could see him sitting in the living room. The bluish glow of a television screen reflected off his face. He moved to the window and stared out at the two vehicles that had just invaded his bare dirt yard.

Tommy Lee sat for a moment in the patrol car. I could see him talking into the two-way. He probably radioed his new location to the dispatcher, and I hoped he told him to send backup if he didn't hear from us in ten minutes. Then Tommy Lee got out of the car and slammed the door loud enough for Taylor to know we were not sneaking up on him.

I jammed the holstered revolver in my jacket pocket and wiped my sweaty palms on my pants. I left the Jeep door open for a quick get-away.

Taylor's silhouette crossed in front of the window. A yellow bulb came on outside the door throwing a pool of light to the edge of the driveway. Tommy Lee and I stopped at its outer rim and waited.

The metal front door opened and Taylor walked out onto the cinder block step.

"That you, Sheriff, or somebody with a helluva Halloween costume, patrol car and all?" He gave a nervous laugh.

"We need to talk, Odell." Tommy Lee spoke casually, calmly. All the while he watched Taylor's hands closely, ready to jump if there was a sudden movement.

"I looked for you at lunch. Kind a late now, don't you think?"

"I'm afraid it's later than you think, Odell. Things have changed since lunch. I thought it was important to you that I pay a friendly visit."

The Adam's apple of Taylor's narrow neck bobbed. I realized he was close to panicking.

"Come on in then."

"No, Odell. We'll talk by the car. I need to be by the radio."

"Let me get a jacket."

"The car is warm. I've kept it running behind the barn up on the hill where I've been watching you."

Tommy Lee's candor unnerved Taylor. "Why? I ain't done nothin'."

"Then you ain't got nothin' to be afraid of, do you?" Tommy Lee motioned Taylor away from the trailer. He kept him in front of us as we walked to the car, where he instructed him to sit in the back seat.

"You puttin' me under arrest?"

"Just putting you in back so that all of us will be more comfortable," said Tommy Lee.

I opened the car door for him and stepped away.

"Suit yourself," he said and crawled in.

I walked around to the front passenger side and felt little comfort at the steel mesh hanging between Taylor and me.

Tommy Lee slid in the driver's seat and turned around. "Tell me, Odell. When's the last time you saw your brother?"

In the glow of the interior car lights, I saw the man's lean, wolfish features flinch. "My brother?"

"Yeah, brother Leroy. Not in the church brother sense. The kin brother sense. Family. Blood family. Like Dallas Willard and his brother."

"I told you I don't know nothing about Dallas Willard."

"Yeah, you did. And that's where I'm getting confused. I'm hoping you can help me sort out the truth. Like you said, you ain't done nothin' wrong, so there's no reason for you and me not to help each other get to the truth, is there?"

"No."

"Good. Suppose I told you someone claims to have seen you and Leroy with Dallas Willard."

"Who said that?"

Tommy Lee didn't answer. He left Taylor's question hanging and asked another. "What do you think of Fred Pryor? Should I believe him?"

"Pryor?" The name came out as a cracked whisper. "Did he say Leroy and I talked to Dallas Willard?"

Again, Tommy Lee ignored the question. I couldn't help but admire the way my friend was manipulating Taylor's responses.

"You know, I've made no secret of the fact I don't trust that man. I've told you that, haven't I, Barry?"

"Since the first day you met him."

"Yeah, the Friday morning the power was out at the construction trailer. Reminds me, we got to get the paint match back on the vehicle that hit the pole that night. The night Bob Cain seems to have let any and everybody onto the site. But, we were talking about Pryor. Yeah, I believe the prick would sell his mother out before taking any responsibility for something that could hurt his career. Like admitting he knew anything about the toxic waste dumping. Man, his whole New Shores scheme would blow up in his face. That's probably why he suggested the drums could have been moved by the utility engine. Without his knowledge, of course. He's trying to appear helpful."

"When did he say that?" asked Taylor.

"Say what? That man talks a lot. Frankly I was surprised he told me you came to see him this afternoon about Talmadge Watson. But like I said, I don't trust him. What's your version?"

"Look," said Taylor. He sounded like he could jump out of his skin. "I don't know what he told you, but I just asked him if he heard some old mountaineer named Talmadge Watson was inheriting some land he wanted."

"So, he did tell you about his real estate scheme. So, if he told me that he knew you and Leroy had talked to Dallas Willard, it was because he had asked you to. And then he tries to make it look bad for you because it will be only your word against his. What a snake."

"I only did what he told me. He's my boss." Taylor looked out the patrol car window as if he expected Pryor to be standing there listening.

The action did not escape Tommy Lee's eye. "You expecting company?"

"Nah. I'm not exactly a trick-or-treat kind of guy."

"Really? Would it surprise you if Pryor said you were planning to trick-or-treat Talmadge Watson tonight? What would he mean by that? Another one of those talks like you all gave Dallas Willard? Help him understand what's expected of him?"

"You'll have to ask Pryor. I ain't no mind reader."

"Come on, Odell, you just told me Pryor is your boss and you do what he tells you. Does that mean he can leave you twisting in the wind while he goes back to the comfort of his country club and boardroom? I think you've been given a new assignment. You and Pryor talked about Talmadge Watson all right. Who was going to take care of him, you or your ex-con brother Leroy?"

Taylor shifted in the seat, sliding away from the window. He spit the words out in a harsh whisper. "I never done nothin' but talk. If Pryor said something different, it's a lie. We were going to talk to this Talmadge Watson. Pryor was coming too."

"He must be getting desperate. When?"

"Tonight. Pryor is going to make him an offer for the land. Nothing illegal about that."

"And when he won't sell, cause trust me he won't, what then?"

Taylor said nothing.

Tommy Lee dropped the friendly tone and barked out questions without giving Taylor time to answer. "How about your brother Leroy? Does Leroy only do what Pryor tells him? Is that why Leroy murdered Fats McCauley with Dallas Willard's shotgun? Is that why Leroy knifed Dallas Willard? Listen, Odell. Fred Pryor has denied any part of your brother's killing spree. Pryor understands conspiracy charges. Premeditated murder applies to everyone who can be proven a conspirator, and North Carolina is not in the least bit shy about capital punishment."

"I had nothing to do with any of that," Taylor said. Fear tightened his throat and I got the feeling we were not going to get anything more.

"Maybe you didn't, Odell. But what do you suppose a jury is going to think when they hear the description of how little Jimmy Coleman died in agony because you wouldn't get medical help? What will a jury think of a piece of shit who denies treatment to an eight-year-old boy? I'm not supposing anymore, Odell. You do the supposing now. What do you suppose will come out of the foreman's mouth when he stands up to deliver the verdict?"

Through a muffled sob, Taylor said, "The Colemans agreed. They agreed with Leroy. That's all I got to say about any of it."

"That's all you got to say, huh? Well, I wonder what brother Leroy will say or do when I put the word out you've been talking to me."

"No, don't," he pleaded.

The radio crackled to life. "Sheriff?" I recognized the anxious voice of Deputy Reece Hutchins.

"What is it?" snapped Tommy Lee.

"Kyle Murphy just telephoned. He found Fred Pryor by the construction trailer at Broad Creek. He said the man has been nearly cut in two by a shotgun blast."

"Oh, God," wailed Odell Taylor and buried his face in his hands. "He's out of control. He killed them all."

"Who?" shouted Tommy Lee. "Who's out of control?"

Odell Taylor lifted his head and looked out the window, his eyes wide with fright, his jaw clenched shut.

"Who, Odell?"

The man had become a statue.

Chapter 20

"Give it to me quick, Reece."

"Murphy heard a shot. Ran outside. Found the body around the side of the construction trailer. Called immediately. Shooting occurred less than five minutes ago."

"Osteen still in position at the front gate?"

"Yeah. He was waiting to tail Pryor. Nobody has come out."

"Split the manpower, Reece. Cover all roads in and out of Broad Creek and the Kentucky compound. And put out a BOLO for Leroy Jackson. He's driving—" Tommy Lee looked back at Taylor. "Come on, Odell. What is it?"

Taylor refused to speak. He just stared out at the night.

"It's a blue pickup," I said. "I saw it at the funeral home. Has a lot of rust and a camper on the bed."

Tommy Lee repeated the description and added, "Jackson could be armed and extremely dangerous. He could also be mentally unstable. I'm headed to the scene. Whoever killed Pryor must still be on site. Barry Clayton will be bringing in Odell Taylor."

I wanted to blurt out "I am?" but realized Tommy Lee was right. He needed all his resources concentrated at Broad Creek and the compound.

"Clayton? He's with you?"

"Yeah, Reece. And be damn glad he is. Now you do your job."

Tommy Lee got out of the car. A light rain had begun to fall. He opened the door for Taylor and ordered him out. "I've got a lot more questions for you, and I don't want any trouble. You know you're probably safer in jail anyway."

Taylor didn't argue. We walked to my Jeep and Tommy Lee cuffed Taylor's hands behind his back. He put him in the front passenger seat and buckled him in.

Tommy Lee handed me the key. "And keep your gun out where you can get it." He looked at my wounded left shoulder. "You okay with this?"

"Yeah. Just take care of yourself."

"I want to hear this Jeep engine start, and then I'm gone."

I took my Smith & Wesson out of the holster and laid it on the seat beside me. As soon as the engine caught, Tommy Lee peeled out of the driveway. I watched his flashing blue lights fade into the rain and fog.

My shortest route into town was over Hickory Nut Mountain. The two-lane road was narrow and curvy, but I doubted I would encounter much traffic. The light rain became a torrent as a storm front moved into the region dumping water by the bucket load. I dared not go over twenty-five miles an hour for fear of outrunning my visibility. The windshield wipers whipped across the glass at high speed, and the more I ascended the mountainside, the thicker became the enveloping clouds.

The single headlight first appeared soon after I passed the barn where Tommy Lee and I had watched Taylor. It just didn't register at the time. On a down-slope straightaway, the reflection in my rearview mirror caught my eye. Someone was coming up fast behind me. A motorcycle in this flood?

Then Taylor shouted, "It's him. He's just got one headlight. He's chasing us."

I looked back in the mirror and saw the pickup truck emerge from the fog.

I sped up to forty-five and desperately tried to recall the pattern of twists and turns I knew were ahead.

My Jeep lurched forward as the truck rammed my rear bumper.

"He's trying to wreck us," yelled Taylor. The panic in his voice told me he was as scared as I was.

We raced on. I pulled my left arm away from my body, ignoring the shoulder pain and gripping the steering wheel as tightly as I could. The truck bumped us again, and then swerved into the other lane.

"Oh, God, his passenger window's down," said Taylor. "He's gonna shoot us!"

I pushed the Jeep to sixty-five. A sign blurred past. One-lane bridge ahead. I moved to the center, crowding the pickup over. I knew the road bottomed out at the creek and then ascended again. The bridge was upon us. The truck swung against the side of my vehicle, but the Jeep held the road. We shot through the single lane bridge as one, missing either railing by inches.

If the pickup didn't wreck us, the speed would. I knew I could never make it through the hairpin climb ahead. I had to get the truck off my tail or be rammed into the mountain. That meant risking a few seconds with it alongside. I eased up on the gas and braced myself, ready to brake as soon as the rear was clear. Then I would be on his tail. "Hold on," I shouted to Taylor.

The truck came up beside us. I expected the driver to try and run me off the road. I risked a quick glance and saw the shadowy profile of Leroy Jackson illuminated by the dashboard lights. He turned toward me and lifted a shotgun with his right hand. I slammed on the brakes a split-second before the muzzle flashed. The Jeep's windshield exploded.

Jackson's pickup rocketed ahead as the Jeep's tires squealed against the pavement. I was thrown against the steering wheel. Rain and wind blasted in, snatching my breath away. The Jeep fishtailed off the edge of the road, and careened out of control. I saw the bent and broken shapes of dead corn stalks fly up in front of us as we tore across a muddy field. A grass embankment caught the left front wheel, catapulting us into the air in a spiraling roll that flipped heaven and earth and sent us crashing upside down in a mix of mud and weeds. My head smashed against the door beam and my left knee jammed against the steering column. I nearly passed out from the pain.

I managed to undo the seatbelt and tumble down to the crumpled roof. Taylor was either dead or unconscious, hanging from his seatbelt beside me. I had to get out. Leroy Jackson would be turning around and heading back. I had only a moment at best. I felt for my pistol but it was gone. Everything inside was scattered. I reached out farther and my hand touched a string. Josh's bow had been hurled from the back to the dashboard. The quiver was attached and a few arrows were still clipped in place.

I struggled through the hole in the windshield, dragging the bow and arrows with me. Crawling through the mud under the Jeep's hood, I avoided the headlights. I wished I had turned them off, but it was too late now. The twin beams angled into the sky, and through the sheets of rain, I could see a cross on a steeple. We had crashed beside Hickory Nut Falls Methodist Church. Maybe a phone was inside and a place to hide.

I got to my feet and my left leg buckled under me. The knee throbbed. The bow became a crutch as I limped up the hill toward the rear of the church, staying clear of the Jeep's lights. I kept wiping my eyes, not from the rain but from the warm blood that trickled down my forehead. I didn't know how deep the gash was. It was the least of my worries.

The congregational cemetery lay between me and the building. I tried to find a row of headstones to use as a guide for an aisle of open ground. Stumbling across a grave marker in the dark would not only be painful, it would also be fatal if I couldn't get back up. I had about fifty feet to go when I saw the single headlight come down the road. Jackson drove past the entrance to the church, stopped, and backed up. I dropped behind a double-grave monument as his headlight raked across the parking lot and swept the tombstones. The chill of the falling rain did not compare to the cold fear welling up inside my stomach. Fate had dealt a cruel hand. I was back in a cemetery facing a shotgun.

Leroy Jackson parked his truck at the edge of the lot where there were no grave plots between him and the wrecked Jeep. I watched lights and shadows flicker through the rain as he used a flashlight to maneuver down the short slope. I started crawling from stone to stone away from him, peering back as I dared to see whether he was coming after me.

I heard him call to Taylor a few times. Then he banged on the side of the upside-down door. There was no answer. He turned his light into the dead cornfield behind the Jeep. I saw the shadowy blur of something moving along the ground. Jackson saw it too. It must have been a possum scurrying for the safety of Hickory Nut Creek at the other side of the field.

Jackson yelled out, "Clayton. Come here. We got to get Odell to the hospital. He's bad hurt. I got no quarrel with you, Clayton." He took a few more steps toward the creek. "I never meant to sic Dallas Willard on you. That was his own doings. Come on, boy. Use your head."

Again, there was movement in the corn. He raised the shotgun and fired. Then he charged forward, firing again. The dead stalks burst apart as if an invisible thresher cut a swath of destruction.

With the blasts still echoing in my ears, I struggled through the graves to the church. I found a back door and turned the knob. Locked. I ran my hand along the edge. There was no deadbolt. I threw myself against it and the old wood jamb splintered so easily I fell inside. I hoped Leroy Jackson was too busy shooting shadows to hear me.

The room was dark and narrow. I closed the damaged door behind me and hoped to find another room where I could lock myself in. If I could just hide for a little while, surely someone would drive by, see the accident, and call for help. Jackson would have to flee.

I felt a rack of robes hanging along one wall. That was probably where the choir changed. I found a second door and opened it. The machinegun sound of rain on the tin roof increased as I stepped into the sanctuary. Dim shapes of pews were in front of me. The main chancel was beside me, bordered by the wall of the choir room. Perhaps there was another room framing the other side, one that had no outside rear entrance and could be locked. The pain in my left leg made walking excruciating. I found a door on the other side of the chancel but it was locked. Dead bolted. The solid oak panels wouldn't yield to my feeble efforts.

A light flashed in the windows of the twin front doors. I heard the latch rattle as Jackson tried to force them open. "Please, God," I prayed. "Let them hold." The sound stopped. He would be going around to the back now. I could only hope to get out the front while Jackson followed my trail to the rear. I made it to the last row of pews when he fired at the front doors. Wood and glass erupted into the sanctuary. I fell to the floor along the side of the center aisle. I clutched the bow in my left hand and drew the string. The pain in my shoulder caused my arm to collapse.

The shattered doors rattled again. The latch still held. I dragged myself halfway under the pew and pressed my right foot against the bow grip. I nocked an arrow. I would aim for his chest. One chance.

The shotgun roared again. Debris rained down on me. Jackson kicked in the doors, and stood on the threshold. He held the flashlight in one hand and a shotgun in the other. "Clayton! Are you in here? Let's make this easy."

Lying on my back with the bow horizontal to the floor, I clutched the string and stretched out my right leg, pushing the bow away from me. The initial pull of the draw was almost more than I could bear, but then I reached the break point and the bow pulleys kicked in, reducing the strain. I silhouetted my foot against the figure in the doorway.

"Come on out. I found your gun in the Jeep. You don't think I'd shoot an unarmed man, do you?" He gave a heartless, soulless laugh that echoed through the sanctuary.

Spine. I remembered Josh talking about spine and the arrow's flight. His bow matched his arrow, a simple target arrow without the razor-sharp broadhead blades that could penetrate the tough hide of a deer. With one arm, one leg, and a blunt arrow, I faced a killer.

Leroy Jackson took two steps inside. I arced my leg a few degrees, keeping my toe lined with his chest. I furiously tried to blink the blood from my eyes. He swept the light around the sanctuary, expecting to find me near the altar, the spot farthest away from him. Suddenly, the beam dropped full on me. I saw the light glint off the shotgun, and I let go.

For one sickening instant, I felt the bow twist against the bottom of my shoe, throwing the arrow higher. I flinched but there was no flash from the gun. Instead, a shower of sparks burst from the wall in a blue blaze that exploded like a Roman candle. The flashlight tumbled from Jackson's hand, flipping backwards to rest with its beam turned squarely upon his face. The eyes were wide and his cheeks and jaw twitched wildly as his whole body jumped and jerked like some electrified marionette. I saw the feathers on the arrow melting. It had struck under his shoulder blade and impaled him like a beetle against the main power cable running along the church's wall. The current, intercepted by the aluminum conductor, diverted through his rain-soaked body.

The smell of burning hair and flesh grew suffocating; then with a loud pop, it was finished. I had just witnessed an execution by electrocution.

Leroy Jackson hung from the wall, well beyond society's retribution. I crawled toward the flashlight, grasped it, and passed out.

Chapter 21

"Jesus, man. What are you going for? The Congressional Medal of Honor?"

As the throbbing in my head lessened, I realized I was back in the same hospital room I'd occupied a few weeks before. Tommy Lee Wadkins was leaning over me. His eye was studying me carefully.

I tried to move and found my left arm again strapped to my side. My left knee was elevated and a bandage encased the top of my head.

"You know what happened?" I asked, my voice cracking.

"Got a pretty good idea. You turned Leroy Jackson into a shish-kabob. Odell Taylor filled in some details."

"I was scared to death, Tommy Lee."

"No, you were scared to die. So, you kept thinking and you took action. I just never would have figured you for Robin Hood. Given the condition you were in, I'm not quite sure how you pulled it off."

"Neither am I. Is Taylor all right?"

"Yes, concussion and multiple bruises. You tossed him around like socks in a dryer. He's in the next room under guard and under arrest. By the way, do you get a discount for booking this same room?" He held a cup of water to my lips and let me take a few swallows. Then he pulled up the chair, turned it backwards and sat down like the day his investigation started.

I looked around. My head was still spinning. The clock read ten-thirty. "What day is it?"

"Only Thursday morning," he said. "Last night a passing car saw the Jeep wrecked in the field by the church. Reece relayed the call and I got there a few minutes after the ambulance. Taylor was conscious but still cuffed and hung up in the seatbelt. He was scared to death Jackson was coming back for him. Didn't calm down till he heard his brother was dead."

"Is he talking?"

"Oh, yeah. He wants to deal except there's nobody left to sell out. Only thing he'll admit to is dumping the waste. He knows he's liable for Jimmy Coleman's death but insists Leroy Jackson pressured all of them and he's no more guilty than the parents."

"What about Dallas Willard?"

"Like we figured, it was all about the land. Pryor was afraid the Willards would sell to Waylon Hestor. He told Taylor to speak to Dallas. He figured a local man was a better approach than some slick Charlotte lawyer. Leroy Jackson was in it the whole time too. He told Dallas he spoke for God's will. Jackson mixed truth and fiction to fuel Dallas' paranoia about the migrants overrunning the land if it were sold to the wrong people."

"But Dallas couldn't stop his brother and sister from doing whatever they wanted."

"Pryor didn't learn about the voting control of the estate until Taylor approached Lee and Norma Jean right after Martha died. They preferred to sell to Waylon Hestor, which meant Pryor and New Shores would have been out on a financial limb. That started the chain of events, and Leroy Jackson pushed Dallas over the edge. Taylor said part of the time between Martha's death and the funeral, Dallas stayed with Jackson. Luke Coleman has confirmed he saw them together. God knows what the bastard told Dallas to keep him in a frenzy."

There was a knock at the door and a nurse stuck her head in. "Time for his pain medicine," she said.

I waved her off. "Give us a few minutes," I said. I ached all over, but I wanted to understand everything Tommy Lee was telling me. "Go on," I told him.

"So, in a way, even the graveyard shooting started with Jackson. Then he hid Dallas with him. Dallas' truck had been parked in a ravine near the compound where it wouldn't be visible from the air. When Pryor learned about it, he told Jackson that Dallas was too much of a liability. He could bring them all down. So, Jackson decided to get rid of Dallas the same night they dumped the chemical waste. Luke Coleman drove Jackson's pickup to Broad Creek, and Jackson rode with Dallas to the spot by the rail bed where we found the truck. Taylor said when his brother flagged them down on the tracks that Thursday night, he had already killed Dallas. Taylor swears he never knew Pryor and Jackson planned to murder him."

"Of course, what else is he going to say if he wants to save his skin?"

"Yeah," agreed Tommy Lee. "Jackson kept Dallas' gun and long coat as souvenirs. I found the shotgun by Jackson's body. Dallas' initials are carved on the stock. Jackson was wearing the long coat, but the arrow hole and burn marks will hurt the resale value."

"You're too much," I croaked. "How about selling me some more water?"

Tommy Lee got up and gave me a second drink.

When my throat cleared, I asked, "And Fats?"

"Leroy Jackson thought Fats had figured out the phony snake story. Barry, I think he just enjoyed killing. A self-proclaimed man of God who played God. Perfect cover for a psychopath. Didn't need much excuse, just opportunity. The Colemans said he got to Kentucky several hours behind them. Enough time to have murdered Fats, and using Dallas' gun gave him the perfect fall guy for the crime. I suspect he saw your name and the word weather written on that note and took it. He might have been watching you for any sign you could cause trouble."

"What about Pryor and New Shores?"

"Kyle Murphy discovered the LLC is made up of insiders in the power company. Not Ralph Ludden but some lieutenants looking to make a killing. Like that deal at Enron where assets got placed in outside firms controlled by executives. Greed, plain and simple. The shit is going to hit the Ridgemont electric fan for sure. It will be a PR nightmare in these parts."

"The profiteers try to screw the mountaineers again," I said. "What about the money Fred Pryor withdrew?"

"Bob Cain had arranged for the crew to have free access that night to the construction site including the locomotive. Pryor paid everybody off in cash. He had made it clear he wanted Dallas taken care of but he knew nothing about Dallas being dumped in Hope Quarry along with the waste. Neither did Cain. When the body was discovered and we told Pryor, he made another cash withdrawal and paid Jackson and Taylor a bonus to make sure everyone's mouth kept shut."

"Cain is dirty then?"

"Yeah. But that's an EPA jurisdictional prosecution. I don't care about that ex-candidate."

"Ex-candidate?"

"Cain dropped out of the race this morning." Tommy Lee smiled. "Guess he's not entirely stupid."

"No loose ends then?"

"Oh, there's stuff that will be filled in. I expect the paint on the power pole will match either Odell Taylor's or Leroy Jackson's vehicle. But other than Taylor, we don't have many culprits left alive."

"You know, it's funny about Fred Pryor."

Tommy Lee looked away from me. "Why would you say that?"

"Like you told Taylor last night, it would have come down to his word versus Pryor's. The paper trail ties Pryor to the land scheme but not to the murders he caused. Jackson probably did what a judge and jury could not have done."

Tommy Lee made no comment. He simply paced the hospital room. Somewhere in the fog passing for my brain a light clicked on.

"Wait a minute," I said. "If Leroy Jackson shot Pryor, how did he get on my trail so quickly? Tommy Lee, I think he came from behind the barn where we had been earlier. He couldn't have made it from Broad Creek to there in less than five minutes. He was probably coming to Taylor's. They had to meet somewhere before they went after Talmadge. He saw the patrol car and ducked behind the barn. He saw you put Taylor in my Jeep."

"Sometimes an investigator can be too smart," said Tommy Lee.

"Leroy Jackson didn't kill Fred Pryor, did he?"

My friend stared out the window at the overcast sky. I understood he was struggling with something, and waited while he worked it out.

Finally he said, "Next Tuesday this county will re-elect me sheriff. They trust me to uphold the law, to protect law-abiding citizens. And this county is blessed with law-abiding citizens," he added. "What should a lifetime of obeying the law earn you?"

"Respect," I said. "And maybe a little grace from the powers that be."

"I can get the D.A. to accept Leroy Jackson as the murderer of Fred Pryor. Leroy Jackson had the motive to keep Pryor quiet. We have proof that Leroy Jackson was a repeat killer, and we have a fried Leroy Jackson in the morgue, unable to mount much of a defense. In fact, the D.A. is pressing me for my report so that he can sign off everything from the past two weeks. He's up for re-election too. All those murders will be buried with Leroy Jackson and no one is thinking of looking any further."

"But," I said.

"But you and I know we have some problems. Not only with the timeframe, but with other details as well. Fred Pryor was killed with double-aught buckshot and Jackson used number one. The pump shotgun always left a shell, and yet none was found at Pryor's murder scene. I went up to the Hickory Falls Methodist Church early this morning. Pace and I picked up pieces of the door, pieces embedded with number one buckshot. Number one shells were littered all over the place. Why would Jackson kill Pryor with double-aught and then revert back fifteen minutes later to number one?"

I felt the knot re-tying in my stomach. Tommy Lee's speech about law-abiding citizens was leading in a direction I didn't think I wanted to go. "And you know something else, don't you?"

"Yeah. I noticed one thing at Pryor's murder scene before the rain washed everything away."

"What's that?" I asked.

"Manure. Someone had scraped manure off on the steps to the trailer. Probably what would be caught between boot heel and sole and not come off even after walking, say, several miles into Broad Creek on a railroad track."

"Manure," I repeated.

"Yeah. I took a sample, but I haven't sent it to the lab. I'll wager Tuesday's election that it's horse manure."

In an instant, I understood why Tommy Lee was so upset. A lifelong, law-abiding citizen had seen his family destroyed by a faceless institution. No one spoke for him; no one came to a funeral; no one offered justice. Charlie Hartley had found the killer of his mare and unborn foal. He had made the connection between drums of Pisgah Paper Mill waste and Ridgemont Power and Electric's Broad Creek Project. He had put a face on the guilty institution. The face of Fred Pryor. The man who had sent him a check. I heard Pryor's sarcastic voice in my head. "How many cans of dog food?"

Tommy Lee must have read my thoughts from the expression on my face. "Yes," he said softly. "I can imagine that he politely wiped his feet before knocking on the trailer door. And Pryor came out like he did with us that first day. Wouldn't even let him in. No telling what Pryor said, but I'm sure it was insulting and cruel. The million-dollar wheeler-dealer who couldn't understand what other people value."

"How can you prove it?" I asked.

"Easy," said Tommy Lee. "And that's the damn problem. All I have to do is ask him. He'll tell me the truth."

I wanted to say then never ask. For once in your life, turn your blind eye to a crime and let an old man live out his days.

"I'm an undertaker," I said, "not a law officer anymore. And I'm certainly not a judge."

"I'm not asking you to be either."

I nodded. "However, I am your friend."

There was a knock at the door.

"Come in," said Tommy Lee.

Susan stepped into the room. "How's the patient?"

"Better, now that you're here," said Tommy Lee. He reached down and gave my right hand a firm squeeze. "Thanks for everything. Take care of yourself." On his way out, he said to Susan, "And you, remember this man is in a weakened condition. Don't take advantage of him. This hospital has rules of conduct."

She eased into the chair and took my hand. For a few seconds, we didn't say anything. Tears started flowing down her cheeks.

"Oh, Barry," she whispered. "When I heard the news last night, I thought I'd lost you."

"So, how am I doing, doctor?" I asked.

"O'Malley did the surgery. You've now got a nice set of stitches in your head that match your shoulder. There were torn ligaments in the knee that will require a couple months of physical therapy. We might let you out Saturday." She forced a smile. "O'Malley wants to know if you'd rather just keep us on retainer."

"And you? What are you going to do now that I've broken another Friday night date?"

"I've got to take care of an injured friend's guinea pig, but I'll be here tonight and tomorrow night, and I know when the nurses make their rounds." She leaned over and kissed my forehead.

I reached up and gently cupped her cheek, guiding her lips to mine.

Chapter 22

The November sky spanned the ridges, cloudless and crystal blue. The air was crisp and pure. The bright colors of the tree-covered hills had peaked and descended into muted browns. On the shadowed side of the barn, the chill of the late afternoon gathered force. I stepped with my crutch into a patch of fading sunlight and glanced back into the stalls. Ned whinnied once. I heard the voices of Tommy Lee and Charlie Hartley rise and fall on the autumn breeze, but the words were swallowed in the whispered rustling of dying leaves.

My head started throbbing and I pulled a bottle of aspirin out of my jacket pocket. I choked down two pills without water and watched the last rays of sun disappear behind Hope Quarry. Reverend Pace had been right. As beautiful as the scenery was, it was the people who mattered. The people Pace served, the people Tommy Lee protected, the people my grandfather and father consoled during life's saddest moments, the people who now looked to me to carry on the tradition my father no longer remembered. And because he could not remember, I would not forget.

"You ready?" growled Tommy Lee.

I turned around to find him only a few yards behind me. Charlie was nowhere to be seen. "Are we going to have company?" I asked.

"No. Charlie is leading Ned out to fresh feed."

"What did he say?"

"He said he misses his horse. He asked me to tell you good-bye and he'd be happy for you to drop by sometime."

"Then the case is still open?"

Tommy Lee kept walking toward the patrol car. "No, Barry. The case is closed. Fred Pryor was killed by Leroy Jackson."

I didn't say anything, just limped silently beside him. He stopped at the trunk, turned around and leaned against it.

"That's what the media is claiming," he said. "That's what everybody in the county believes. And who can say justice hasn't been served?"

To receive a free catalog of other Poisoned Pen Press titles,
please contact us in one of the following ways:

Phone: 1-800-421-3976
Facsimile: 1-480-949-1707
Email: info@poisonedpenpress.com
Website: www.poisonedpenpress.com

Poisoned Pen Press
6962 E. First Ave. Ste 103
Scottsdale, AZ 85251

COMING AUGUST 2004

SPIKED

by Mark Arsenault
ISBN: 0-7434-8706-0

In the fading manufacturing town of Lowell, Massachusetts, Eddie Bourque, a political reporter for the shoddy *Lowell Empire*, looks into the brutal murder of his newspaper beat partner and rival, Danny Nowlin. Bourque suspects the killing is tied to a story Nowlin was working on undercover, but the newspaper's owners, high up in Lowell's power structure, discourage Bourque from pursuing his investigation.

Mark Arsenault brings Lowell—with its slums, empty factories, and vying political factions—vividly alive, and he peoples his novel with quirky, memorable characters.

COMING SEPTEMBER 2004

FROSTLINE

by Justin Scott
ISBN: 0-7434-8704-4

In quaint Newbury, Connecticut, real estate broker Ben Abbott gets caught in a nasty land battle between two neighbors: cantankerous Vietnam vet Richard Butler—whose troubled, violent son, Dicky, has just been released from jail—and Harry King, a high-powered former diplomat and owner of Fox Trot estate. King wants Abbott to act as mediator in buying a sliver of Butler's property that just into Fox Trot.

But when a dam used to create an artificial lake for the estate is blown up, and a body turns up among the debris, Abbott takes it upon himself to investigate. He may not like the answers he finds....

FOUR FOR A BOY

A LORD CHAMBERLIN MYSTERY
by Mary Reed and Eric Mayer
ISBN: 0-7434-8690-0

Gang-plagued streets, politicians plotting each other's downfall, poverty and homelessness existing side-by-side with manifest wealth—no, this isn't modern-day Washington, D.C., but rather 6th-century Constantinople.

After a philanthropist is murdered in the city's Great Church—where he'd gone to visit a controversial stature of Christ—John the Eunuch, Lord Chamberlin to Byzantine Emperor Justinian the First, is assigned to ferret out the killer...and maybe also to act the role of a spy in a web of rivalries involving the current and future emperors.